A To[...]

continued . . .

Snoop to Nuts

ELIZABETH LEE

BERKLEY PRIME CRIME, NEW YORK

THE BERKLEY PUBLISHING GROUP
Published by the Penguin Group
Penguin Group (USA) LLC
375 Hudson Street, New York, New York 10014

USA • Canada • UK • Ireland • Australia • New Zealand • India • South Africa • China

penguin.com

A Penguin Random House Company

SNOOP TO NUTS

A Berkley Prime Crime Book / published by arrangement with the author

Berkley Prime Crime Books are published by The Berkley Publishing Group.
BERKLEY® PRIME CRIME and the PRIME CRIME logo are
trademarks of Penguin Group (USA) LLC.

For information, address: The Berkley Publishing Group,
a division of Penguin Group (USA) LLC,
375 Hudson Street, New York, New York 10014.

ISBN: 978-0-425-26141-5

PUBLISHING HISTORY
Berkley Prime Crime mass-market edition / January 2015

PRINTED IN THE UNITED STATES OF AMERICA

10 9 8 7 6 5 4 3 2 1

Cover illustration by Robert Crawford.
Cover design by Diana Kolsky.
Interior text design by Kristin del Rosario.

Acknowledgments

With thanks to:

Patty Sumter, for the laughter, the Southern charm, and the great recipes.

Dianna Rodabough of the L'il Country Store near Starvation Lake, Michigan, for a place to eat biscuits, tell stories, and laugh.

Kathy Botard, of Sheridan, Texas, for making me feel at home in Riverville.

Mary Ann Warner, for handing me a whole lot of pecan farming info and some wonderful characters.

Danica Peterson, for all the English foods. The Squirrel wouldn't be the same without her.

My daughters, Patti Mullin, Kathy Gibbons, and Cindy Anderson, for their constant support, encouragement, and concern.

My sons, Nino Buzzelli and David Buzzelli, for being the strong and caring men they've become.

Alex Anderson and Wychert Cath, for their cooking skills.

And, of course, for Tony.

Chapter One

I believed right from the beginning that it was the prize-winning hog scooting down the crowded midway at the annual Riverville, Texas, Agriculture Fair that started it all. With so much uproar and carnival noise and screaming and running, everybody was drawn to the doors of the tents and echoing metal Ag buildings to watch the two-hundred-fifty-pounder with a blue ribbon attached to his collar as he zigzagged through tall legs in skinny jeans, leaping legs in wide-cut jeans, bowed legs in ancient jeans, and bare legs in jean shorts, on his way to his familiar sty back at the ranch where he was born.

I figured, much later, that it was all that hollering and laughing and betting, while a calliope ground out tinny music and ladies on the Ferris wheel squealed and teenagers kept thumping each other in the dodgem cars, that covered somebody (probably the person who let the pig loose in the first place) creeping into the Culinary Arts building to add something deadly to my grandmother, Miss Amelia's, Heavenly Texas Pecan Caviar.

Not that the hog wasn't the hit of the day, with a lot of money being made as bets were placed on how long it would take Deputy Hunter Austen of the Riverville Sheriff's Department to capture him. My childhood friend, Hunter, stood tall in his well-pressed uniform practicing a couple of twirls with a rope someone from the rodeo, down near the Colorado River, tossed to him. I watched from the crowd as Hunter twirled a last time and sent the rope cutting precisely around his body and over the head of the frightened hog. He held on tight and lost some of his cool as the hog kept right on going, dragging Hunter behind him with his heels dug into the red dirt until finally the poor creature ran out of steam and stopped. Hunter took only a minute to sit on the ground and get his breath before jumping up, brushing dirt from his sharp-pleated pants, and taking a few overenthusiastic bows as bystanders clapped and whistled, with me whistling the loudest for my old friend.

The hog was led back to his pen in the hog building, which still left me with almost an hour before the judging of the Most Original Pecan Treat, the last and most important of the culinary arts contests at the fair. New this year, the Most Original Pecan Treat was thought, by the cooks of Riverville, to be the highest honor of all the honors handed out. The best of the best. "The crème de la crème, Lindy," Cecil Darling, an Englishman and owner of The Squirrel Diner, told me as if in secret. Cecil loved to rub Rivervillians' noses in our lack of "continental couth." I had smirked at him, nastily thinking how he'd better not plan on winning with his spotted dick or whatever he called it, since nobody had a chance to win with my grand-mother's Heavenly Texas Pecan Caviar in the running.

The whole Most Original Pecan Treat contest was set-ting up to be the biggest event the fair had ever put on. There'd been whispers around town that Miss Amelia was the one to beat, and local chefs were ganging up to bring her down and end her years of dominating the culinary arts of Riverville. Didn't matter. My meemaw had a leg up on the others with her cooking and baking the best of everything day after day at the Nut House, the family pecan store in town.

Ethelred Tomroy, one of Miss Amelia's oldest and crank-iest friends, even came into the Nut House one day to brag about her surprise entry and warn all who would listen to watch out. "Got me a winner," she said and leaned back in her run-down oxfords and nodded her gray head so the bun at the back was bouncing.

I hung around to congratulate Hunter on his hog-tying skills and maybe get him to take me on the Ferris wheel, as he'd promised. I couldn't be late for the judging, though. Miss Amelia was nervous as it was, with the whole world seeming to be lined up against her. I wanted to get there early to calm her down. I'd never seen my grandmother so twitchy and ill at ease over one more blue ribbon.

At home that morning Miss Amelia had me check and recheck the ice packs in her cooler, making sure the tem-perature was right for her special dishes. Since she'd already taken more ribbons than she could shake a stick at, she was mostly worried about the two bowls of her Heavenly Texas Pecan Caviar. One was for the judging and one for the Winners' Supper afterward.

"Gotta be just right," she muttered over and over as she

bustled around the ranch's large kitchen, making the caviar, then choosing the perfect bowls—finally settling on bowls
with the Blanchard crest on them: three pecans nested in
three green leaves above three wavy lines representing the
Colorado River.

She'd checked the labels on the bowls again and again,
muttering that things had to be just right. All of us around
the breakfast table assured her there was nothing to worry
about. Of course she was going to win the last, and most
important, culinary event of the year.

My mama, Emma, dressed for the fair in her green
Rancho en el Colorado shirt and jeans that were maybe a
little too snug, hugged Miss Amelia and held her away to
give her the order to "Calm down now, ya hear? You're
jumpy as spit on a hot skillet."

"You'll be there for the judging?" Miss Amelia had looked
around and smiled nervously at all of us except Justin's friend,
Jeffrey Coulter. Justin and Jeffrey were roommates during
their undergrad years at Oklahoma University. Jeffrey, who'd
been visiting a week now, was busily reading the financial
section of the *Riverville Courier* and sniffing from time to
time at how little news he could get of the New York Stock
Exchange. Jeffrey, one of those people perpetually wrapped
up in his own concerns, ignored Miss Amelia, as he usually
did, not having much patience with the worries of elderly
relatives.

"We're gonna be there to celebrate with you," my younger
sister, Bethany, said. At twenty-three, Bethany was still
young enough to be lost in her own world, but even she
looked up from the bride magazine she was engrossed in,
nodding and promising she would be there real soon to
help set up, since she was the decorator in the family and
the person running our new event pavilion, where she was

planning big weddings and political events and all kinds of celebrations. Bethany spent a lot of time thinking about free-flying doves and billows of white tulle, and cakes built up to look like the Alamo.

On the midway, I moved under the canvas overhang of a taco stand to get away from the hot sun and see if I could pick out Hunter in the crowd. People pushed everywhere around me. I waved and shared happy smiles with women from Miss Amelia's church, old school buddies, and other ranchers. Texans do know how to have a good time, and Ag Fair was a time for a big celebration in our community of many pecan farms.

No Hunter. Either some police business had come up or he was still laughing about his hog-tying adventure with friends and forgot about taking me on the Ferris wheel, which made me a little mad because Hunter and I were old friends, maybe even a little more than friends and I didn't like being stood up.

I checked my watch. If he didn't show up soon, there wouldn't be time to do anything. Bethany was probably there already, tending to what she called "staging" Meemaw's entry, fussing over whether the green and white bowl looked better against a backdrop of green plastic pecan leaves or whether the cut-out family crests should be sprinkled indiscriminately or made to form a border around the bowl of caviar—all things that bored me to tears.

Maybe, I thought, as I spotted Freda Cromwell, Riverville's worst gossip, and looked around for the fastest escape route, I should have been paying more attention to Miss Amelia lately. She'd been looking concerned about something, not smiling as much as usual. Summer days in this part of Texas could be long and hot. Meemaw did a lot of baking and cooking, what with the tourist buses coming to town, stopping at the Nut House, and buying up all her baked goods and pecan candies and barbecue sauces. Maybe fatigue was normal for a woman in her seventies. But with Miss Amelia, any crack in that strong façade made me worry.

Anyway, no matter what was causing it, I'd decided to lend a hand in the store whenever I could though my work out in the greenhouses took up most of my time.

Now where was Hunter? He could be maddening. So straight and serious about his job, being one of Riverville's three deputies, and so goofy and kid-like when off duty and ready to have fun.

But this was the last day of the fair. The Ferris wheel would be grinding to a halt soon and the roadies would begin to tear it down.

Feeling a little disappointed, I turned to walk back down the midway. I was thinking that maybe I'd stop in the Pecan Culture Building to take a last look at my own pecan cultivars, each with a blue ribbon attached. First in every horticulture category. First in new varietals. Best of Show for my strain of pecan tree that was a cross between the Carya *illinoinensis* and Carya *ovata*—the first drought resistant and the second an early budder. Of course, I'm a trained botanist but other ranchers hired botanists, too, and nobody, as yet, had come up with a strain of pecan trees that came close to what I was producing.

I decided to treat myself to a deep-fried ice cream, then stood licking fast and watching the crowd. Many walking by yelled out support for Meemaw in the contest. They waved and punched thumbs in the air. Others congratulated me on sweeping the new varietal judging.

I licked my ice cream as I settled in the shade of the overhead canvas and took in the sounds and sights and people all around me. I thought about how me and Meemaw sure made a pair. Meemaw with blue ribbons for her Very Special Pecan Pie, her Classy Tassies, Pecan Round-em-up Grilling Glaze, and still to come, for her Heavenly Texas Pecan Caviar.

I envied her pure Texas charm in the face of beating out all the other cooks in town. Never a wicked gleam in her eye and not once did she lord it over Ethelred Tomroy, her cranky friend, who took second place in just about everything year after year after year. And she graciously put up with Ethelred's grousing over the bad judging, the need for new contest rules, and her complaining that the contests were "Nothing but popularity contests anyway. They just like you better than they like me." Which was true since Ethelred Tomroy rarely had a good word for anybody. Still, the contest judges were usually drawn from the clergy or were officers in the Pecan Co-op or members of the Agricultural Fair committee and therefore above reproach.

I straightened my jeans and pulled my ranch T-shirt away from my sticky skin. I took a moment, stepping out into the straight-up boiling sunshine, to pull my hair out of the ponytail I usually wore and brush it out around my face with my fingers. I figured, at twenty-nine, I still had a responsibility to look as good as I could look. Maybe I wasn't in the marriage market—too busy working with my pecan trees to have time for flirting and dating, but still there was no reason I had to look like I'd just stepped out of a greenhouse, with dirt under my fingernails, hair slicked back out of my eyes, and streaks of honest Texas sweat running down my face.

I made my way past the pink, blue, and white umbrellas shielding fair food booths. I stopped to talk to kids I knew from high school, who were no longer kids and now pushed baby strollers. That took time since I had to bend over each baby and coo and carry on, and sometimes remark on the lovely hands because the baby was so . . . well, not ugly but . . . "different looking."

Soon all that was left were a few minutes to maybe visit a game booth, win myself a giant panda or a Texas flag. But there was Ethelred Tomroy steaming toward me with a fixed look on her face. With only a few seconds before impact, I took evasive action, ducking behind a couple of old cowboys wearing white hats wide enough to shade a barrel of beer.

I skirted the big hats and lolling cowboys then stepped behind a Coca-Cola stand. I thought I'd outsmarted her until she came barreling around the front of the stand to corner me.

"Well, Lindy Blanchard, just the girl I was lookin' for." Ethelred, sturdy and solid in a flowered housedress with perfect sweat circles under her arms, blocked my escape. She held her clasped hands in front of her, stopped to pant a little, and leaned back on her oxfords. "You coming over for the judging? Think I got your grandmother beat this time. You gotta have some of my Pecan Surprise Tomato Puff. Never taste the beat of it."

"Good luck to you, Miss Ethelred." I pasted on my best phony smile. "I'm sure all you ladies have an equal chance to take the prize."

"Well, maybe this time things will be fair. We got that new pastor from Rushing to Calvary leading the judging. I've been waiting for somebody with a little more sophistication than the usual around here."

"Didn't he come from Tupelo?"

"Sure did." She nodded hard, sending stray steel gray hairs waving around her head. "Elvis Presley's hometown. Mississippi people know good food when they taste it.

None of that business about flavors having to go together and things like that. Nope, I'm sure today will be a new day in Riverville, Texas. You just wait and see."

She smirked but looked pale behind the sweat beads on her face. "Saw you took Best of Show with those tiny pecan trees of yours. All I can say about that is you better not go messing with Texas nuts. Fancy education or no fancy education, we're happy with the nuts we got and don't cotton to change."

I checked my watch. "I think the judging's about to begin, Ethelred." I held the watch up for the woman to see. "Shouldn't you be getting on over there?"

Ethelred's protruding eyes bulged. "Goodness, don't want to be late for this one. No sir, don't want to be late."

And she was off as I watched her bent back move away from me. I was fuming and running things I should have said through my head when an arm slid around my waist and a familiar voice was at my ear.

"You see me get that hog, Lindy?" Hunter, red-faced and still extremely proud of himself, stood beside me. "Rope landed just where I sent it. Couldn't have been a better throw, don't you think?"

His straight and firm mouth bowed up into a huge grin. He still wore his uniform because he was supposed to be on duty, walking around, nodding to people, representing the Sheriff's Department and Sheriff Higsby, who had an election coming up in the fall.

"My favorite part was when you fell on your behind." I brushed off his arm.

"Kind of felt like rodeoing there for a while." He laughed at himself the way he often did.

"Where've you been?" I pushed at his chest. "Now there's no time for the Ferris wheel."

"Sure there is. They didn't pull it down. Won't for a couple of hours."

"I've gotta be over to the Culinary Arts Building for Meemaw's last contest."

"Oh, that's right." He struck his forehead with his hand. "Forgot."

He grinned again. "So how about I buy you some fried butter instead? Hear that's going over real good this year." He pointed to a stand with cutouts of sticks of butter flying around the selling window.

"Yeah, and a Roto-Rooter man to clear out my arteries."

"You're no fun. How about Kool-Aid Pickles, or fried cheesecake."

"I've got to go."

He smiled the kind of smile I'd warned him about. The kind that made me loose in the stomach. We'd agreed not to get serious or anything "yucky," way back when we were twelve and fourteen. The agreement still held, though once in a while wide open cracks threatened to tear down all old agreements. Like now. With that smile of his.

"I'll see you for the judging," he said. "I gotta walk around the beer tent one more time. Just to let the boys know I'm still on duty." He gave me a wave and was gone, lost in the throng of happy Texans.

Chapter Two

The familiar smells in the huge, echoing Culinary Arts Building were of sugars and roasted pecans and every spice I ever imagined existed. Standing in the wide-open doors, I took in all the women dressed in their Sunday best, and all the men, old and young, in new and old cowboy hats and worn-down boots and plaid shirts and fringed shirts. All of this was a part of a world I knew so well, with everybody smiling and gossiping and excited to be there. This was my home—Riverville and all its people. This was the place I loved most. Even while I'd been away at Texas A&M, I'd missed my town. I'd missed the pecan farm and the whispers of the tall, old trees, the smell of the Colorado River running through our property, the sweetness of the Nut House, the hot afternoons out on the porch waving to passing neighbors.

It still felt good, being a part of the farming scene again, with the November harvest and packing, the excitement of spring rains, the budding of the stately trees, my meemaw introducing a new delicacy at the Nut House. Now I had my own place in it, with an apartment over the Nut House, where I looked down on Carya Street and watched the citizens of Riverville going about their slow, hot days, and slower, warm evenings, finding time to stop and talk, ask about a sick person here, a person in need there.

I worked hard, hoping to make life easier for all of us ranchers with a strain of pecans that could withstand deep Texas drought, could fight off scab and funguses, and hold the blossoms better. All of this to take some of the misery out of the lives of the farmers and ranchers at the mercy of Mother Nature, the way my daddy, Jake Blanchard, had been at the mercy of the rains and winds and heat.

I was stopped on my way to the center of the room, where the judging tables were set up, to be congratulated by Hawley Harvey, investment banker in town and a trustee on the board of the Rushing to Calvary Independent Church. Hawley was one of those jolly, round guys who shouldn't ever wear anything with fringe on it, like the vest he was wearing today. And, of course, the way-too-wide cowboy hat and new boots that screamed "I never saw a horse in my life." He makes me think of Santa Claus, with his happy "ho, ho, ho"-ing. The only thing that puts me off about Hawley is that he likes to hug young women and kiss them on the cheek—big wet kisses. He leaned in for that hug— okay—but I leaned out so the kiss didn't quite make it to my cheek, just hung in the air between us.

"Congratulations, Lindy. Heard about your big win. You ever think about investing any of those big bucks you're going to be making, come on over to the Dallas Building any day. I'll take good care of you. Making some serious money for folks around here, you know." He nodded hard, though I hadn't challenged him. "You go ask Simon George and Elder Perkins. Turn you into a millionaire, too, like I'm doin' for the church. Yes siree. Hope you're coming to the ground breaking for our spectacular addition." The short man smiled ear to ear. His bright new boots almost brought him eye to eye with me, but not quite.

I assured him that Ben Fordyce, the family attorney, saw to all of our investments. But Hawley Harvey, never a man to be overshadowed, shook his head and gave a chiding tongue cluck. "Man knows his law. But I know how to protect yer nest egg. Turn it over and over until it grows like one of those weeds you botany people study."

I politely elbowed my way past him to Miss Amelia's table, where her Heavenly Texas Pecan Caviar was set out in the large bowl still covered with a sparkling white cloth. Small paper dishes and napkins and plastic spoons were arrayed on the paper-covered table on top of Bethany's leaves and family crests.

Miss Amelia's steel gray hair had been carved tall by Sally Witbeck over at the New York Salon of Beauty. Meemaw had even rubbed a little color into her cheeks and had a dusty line of shadow on her eyelids. She nervously rearranged her plates and napkins, then stopped to look around the huge room as if searching for someone. Her face lit up with pleasure when she spotted me.

"Lindy, I'm so glad you're here." Meemaw kissed my cheek and looked deep into my eyes. "What do you think?"

She waved toward her space on the table. "You think it's too much? Bethany wanted to bring over silver spoons but I told her it's a rule; the judges have to use those white plastic things the fair committee provides. But you know Bethany. Doesn't listen, like all Blanchard women. So I just said, *'Go ahead.'* But I took 'em off."

"I like it, Meemaw. Looks pretty."

"I was thinking it should have been like a Nut House logo, if I had one different from the ranch. Would've been a little classier, which is only right for my Heavenly Texas Pecan Caviar. But you know Bethany. Gonna do what she wants to do."

"Don't you worry. It's not the decoration that'll knock the judges' socks off."

Miss Amelia snapped her mouth shut and looked deep into my eyes. She looked tired, which wasn't usual for my high-speed grandmother. "Don't you go gettin' your hopes up, Lindy. There's more important things in this world than winning another blue ribbon, you know."

I grinned at her. "I don't buy the humble act, Meemaw."

Meemaw would normally have laughed along with me, but not today. She frowned, twisted her hands together, and gave me a look that signaled how tightly she was wound.

Ethelred Tomroy, sitting on a folding chair at the place next to Miss Amelia's, turned her body around to face us. Ethelred looked worn out, too, maybe from all the lobbying she'd been doing for herself. "I hear tell people think Cecil Darling's gonna take it today," she called over. "Got something down there called spotted dick. Some kind of English pudding with pecans and a cream sauce . . ." She quieted as Mrs. Vernon Williams, Superintendent of the Culinary Arts Building and a member of the Riverville Chamber of Commerce, took her place at one end of the long judging table and raised her hands for quiet.

"As if an Englishman could make anything better than a good Texas woman," Ethelred hissed as the festivities got under way.

Mrs. Williams, in her stylish red suit, red high heels, and helmet hair, called for the contestants to uncover their dishes.

There was a general oohing and aahing as the treats were revealed. People hurried to check out what Miss Amelia had prepared since she was always the odds-on favorite.

"Why, goodness' sakes, what's that called?" little Dora Jenkins, wife of the new pastor at the Rushing to Calvary Independent Church, one of today's judges, asked, admiring the mélange of jalapeños, bell peppers, black-eyed peas, chopped pecans, and diced tomatoes, all tossed with herbs and spices.

"Heavenly Pecan Texas Caviar." Miss Amelia smiled at the thin woman in a blue straw hat that matched her blue straw purse.

Dora looked up, wide-eyed. "Well, for goodness' sakes. Won't Millroy like that one, though?"

Miss Amelia looked over at Dora's sister, Selma, standing behind her. Selma's nervous eyes blinked and moved back and forth, from Dora to Miss Amelia, as if finding the whole business of an Agricultural Fair beyond her comprehension. The woman was dressed neatly in a pale blue summer dress that went almost to the floor, covering the one built-up shoe she wore.

"Morning, Selma," Miss Amelia greeted Dora's older sister. "Hope you're well."

"I certainly am, Miss Amelia."

"And how's that lovely garden of yours doing?"

"Just fine, thanks to all the nice people of the church and the help y'all been giving me."

"We're happy to do it, Selma. I'll be over your way next Tuesday. My weeding day, if I remember right."

"I hate to ask it of you, Miss Amelia. I mean, with the Nut House and all, I just don't see how you have the energy."

"Don't you worry about me, Selma. I'm doing fine. Long as I got my health, nothing's going to stop me."

The women moved on to take a look at Ethelred's Pecan Surprise Tomato Puff. Selma, with her one high shoe on her one short leg, dragging just a little behind the other.

Mama rushed in, a little late as usual, and a little out of breath. "Didn't start yet, did they?" Emma asked.

"Glad you made it."

I turned into a big hug from Bethany, who'd come up behind us with Jeffrey Coulter, our houseguest. He stood away, looking off into the distance then turning to Justin, saying something he found funny as Justin walked up with Martin Sanchez, foreman out at our ranch.

I nodded to Jeffrey. Enough of a greeting. To tell the truth, I couldn't wait until Jeffrey Coulter went back to New York City. When Justin was in college, studying business, Jeffrey had come home with him once, for a weekend. That had been enough for me—all that snobbery and condescension, but even then Bethany had acted silly and smitten with the good-looking guy.

Watching as Bethany turned back to Jeffrey now, and directed a very coy, Southern lady wave at him, I was afraid the same thing was happening. Although I hadn't said a word to Justin about his friend, I was getting the feeling even he was sick and tired of having the man around. Two weeks more. The guy was supposedly looking at properties for his father, a New York City investor who wanted to build a mall between Riverville and Austin. For all the properties he was inspecting, it seemed to me he was mostly underfoot, and mostly half sneering at our country ways.

"You take a look at the other entries?" Emma, her short, tousled hair held back with a green headband, leaned in to whisper. I shook my head.

"Where are the silver spoons?" Bethany's eyes flew wide

as she hunted around the table. "Somebody took my silver spoons!"

"Shh . . ." I cautioned. "Can't have 'em out. Committee rules."

"Oh, pooh on the committee's rules. I know what's tasteful and what isn't. Plastic spoons aren't." She turned to smile up at Jeffrey, giving me a twist in my stomach. I hadn't witnessed such blatant flirting since Angela Hornbeck had a crush on Hunter in seventh grade. I'd practiced raising one eyebrow for hours in the mirror, hoping to outdo Angela, who knew how to bat her eyelashes, raise her eyebrows, and flick her blond hair around—all at the same time. Good thing Angela Hornbeck moved to England after high school and married a lord or a duke or something like that and lost interest in Hunter.

Still in a huff, Bethany stepped forward to straighten a few of the family crests she'd laid out, then back to take Jeffrey by the arm and squeeze it a little, anticipating the arrival of the judges.

Suzy Queen, wife of Morton Grover, who owned the Barking Coyote Saloon, hurried over to throw her arms around Miss Amelia and give her a big smack on the cheek.

Dressed to kill in a fuchsia Spandex dress that barely covered the essentials, Suzy Q's black hair was puffed out a foot around her head. She wore makeup enough to decorate a clutch of clowns and smiled from ear to ear at all of us. Suzy latched on to my elbow and pulled me around into a big, perfume-laden bear hug.

"Most of us are only hoping to take a white ribbon, Lindy. It'll be a life-changing moment fer yer meemaw to win this one. Winningest woman at the fair. I'd say everybody but Ethelred's pulling for her."

She hurried off on high heels tall enough to tip her over at the first dip in the cement floor.

The girls stepped up next. Meemaw's very special friends. Miranda and Melody Chauncey had been a part of Riverville since the day they were born. That was over eighty years ago now and still the twins, or "girls" as they were called, were a big part of town life. The thing was, the girls were kind of rough. At least Miranda was. She was always armed, a sidepiece at her hip and a shotgun out in their ancient truck. "Rattlers," Miss Miranda would say and tap her gun with one of her arthritic hands while Miss Melody, more dainty and worried what people thought about them, would cluck, shake her head, and roll her eyes at us.

"Big day for you, Amelia." Miranda nodded hard, sniffed, and looked around the large open room. Her museum-quality cowboy hat hung down her back on a string that wasn't long for this world. She wore what she always wore—old denim pants and jacket with a plain man's shirt under it.

Melody smiled and nodded to folks around us, then leaned back to preen a little in what was obviously a brand-new outfit with a pretty fringed skirt. She'd had her hair done, too, and flipped it up around her head with one manicured hand. She was dolled up the most I'd ever seen her, and I admired her spunk in the face of her sister's indifference.

Ethelred, who'd been listening to all the good wishes sent Miss Amelia's way, was on her feet now, leaning heavily against the table. "I just might have you beat, Amelia."

She gestured toward her red dish.

"Why, bless yer heart, Ethelred." Miss Amelia turned a sweet, almost fluttery, smile on her old friend. "I really do hope you get yourself a ribbon."

"I'm not talkin' just any ribbon. I'm talkin' blue. That's

what people been sayin' to me. Blue, 'Melia. You know what that means."

She was interrupted by the sound of shushing as it traveled from one end of the large building to the other. The judges, clipboards in hand, stepped through the large, roll-up door at the far end, freezing everyone in place.

The girls scattered. Ethelred shuffled fast to stand at her own table, and the rest of us formed a half circle in front of Meemaw, waiting for the good news.

Chapter Three

Millroy Jenkins, pastor at the Rushing to Calvary Independent Church, out almost to Highway 10 on the way to Houston, led the procession into the room, making a point of smiling kindly and diplomatically at each and every cook as he made his way to the far end of the long judging table to begin tasting the pecan entries.

Dressed casually in gray slacks, an open blue jacket, and a white shirt not buttoned at the collar, the pastor wasn't as dour and serious as the other two judges, who followed closely behind.

Eloise Dorrance, with the Riverville Chamber of Commerce, had been a judge many times and knew to keep her well-coiffed head turned away from the eager contestants.

The last judge was Mike Longway, the dapper, middle-aged president of the Riverville Pecan Co-op. Mike, true to his nature, always added a flourish and an eye roll to his tastings. Mike did relish a rapt audience. After he tasted, he'd move on to write on his clipboard with his hands cupped around his marks, adding a bounce of his eyebrows, and then a grin toward all of the hand-wringing women watching.

As the tasting began, Millroy Jenkins put a plastic spoon to his mouth, smacked his lips, and threw dish and napkin away. He smiled at the contestant as he walked off to make notes on his judging form. Eloise followed close behind. She tasted, sniffed a time or two, wrote, and moved on. Mike Conway tasted, mugged as was expected of him, and attacked the next dish.

Miss Amelia stood tall, her pale eyes following the slow procession of the judges. Her hands were clutched in front of her, one wringing the other. From time to time, she turned to look around at the crowd, as if expecting to see someone, then she would turn back to smile nervously at me and Bethany and Mama, then back to the judges as they made their way toward her.

Next to where Miss Amelia and the rest of the Blanchards waited, the Reverend Jenkins tasted Ethelred's Pecan Surprise Tomato Puff and smacked his lips. He smiled at the pale, almost fainting, woman, perspiration standing out on her high forehead, hands clutched at her breast. She tried to smile but ended by giving the man an unattractive grimace.

The pastor reached out to rest a hand on her shoulder for reassurance then moved on, throwing his plastic spoon and napkin in the small garbage can under the tasting station.

"Miss Amelia." The Reverend Millroy Jenkins nodded at Meemaw. "Hear you're the one to beat here."

The pastor stuck a plastic spoon into Miss Amelia's bowl then stuck the spoon in his mouth so that his lips closed right up to the spoon handle. He hesitated a minute, standing with the spoon sticking from between his lips, then pulled the spoon back out, still half loaded with the caviar.

He wiped his mouth with his paper napkin, cleared his throat, and gave Miss Amelia a halfhearted smile. He dipped his head toward the rest of the family, wadded the paper napkin in his hand, ran it slowly across his mouth again, then threw spoon and napkin away.

As the pastor walked on to Suzy Queen's Blessed Pecan Dip, the other two judges stepped up. Eloise Dorrance dipped her spoon into Meemaw's glass bowl and put it directly into her mouth.

For a moment her head came up and her eyes grew wide. I took the woman's reaction for wonderment but soon saw she was grasping for a napkin, sending a shower of paper to the floor. She brought the napkin to her mouth and spit out the caviar.

I could feel my family stiffen around me.

Miss Amelia said nothing.

When Eloise had passed, Miss Emma, outraged, whispered, "What the heck's wrong with Eloise?"

There was no time to answer before Mike Longway got to Miss Amelia's bowl. Maybe picking up signals from the other judges, Mike seemed wary as he dipped his spoon in and drew it out with only a tiny taste of caviar on it. He dipped his tongue cautiously in the caviar, then drew it quickly away.

The spoon went into the garbage can and Mike moved on to Suzy Queen.

"What's going on?" Justin, in his best overalls and plaid shirt, stepped up to ask in as low a voice as Justin ever used.

Miss Amelia shrugged and stood staring at the backs of the judges as they made their way to the far end of the table then moved to stand away from everyone, heads together, making their decisions.

Ten minutes went by. Twenty. There seemed to be a heated debate going on as Eloise shook her head again and again and Mike Longway looked up at the ceiling for help.

A half an hour passed and still no decision from the judges. The crowd grew restless.

Finally, Mrs. Williams went to the three to see if she could help.

I could see she was pressing the judges to get on with it so they could set up the Winners' Supper before everybody left. Volunteer servers waited at the back of the building for the tables to be free. There were new tablecloths to be spread, flowers to be set, and stacks of dishes and cutlery to be put out. Volunteer cooks waited impatiently outside the building for the signal to snatch the barbecue off the grills.

Any one of the volunteers could have told these slow judges that a good supper was a matter of timing. Too long on the grill and the chicken and ribs could end up tasting like burned toast. Winning salads and side dishes couldn't be taken out of coolers too soon or they'd be warm and gummy by the time people actually got to enjoy them.

I watched as Mrs. Williams, aware of all the preparation yet to be made, insisted on results. Finally she turned and bustled officiously to the center of the room, a wide smile on her face.

"Can I have everybody's attention?" she called over the screech of the microphone, then tapped the microphone a few times, leaned into it, and asked for quiet.

"Our judges have made their decisions in this new event added just this year, Most Original Pecan Treat. The Chamber of Commerce, along with the Riverville Pecan

Co-op, and the entire fair committee want to thank every-body who entered not only this event but all the others. You've made it an amazing year for Riverville and the Agricultural Fair, bringing all these wonderful dishes to be judged. In my mind everybody's a winner, don't you think?" She waited for the "Yes sirs" and "You betchas" and the applause to quiet. "So I'm gonna ask the Reverend Jenkins to come up here now and read off these final winners."

The Reverend Jenkins moved to the microphone, bow-ing to Mrs. Williams and then to the large crowd of people looking up eagerly as they surged toward the stage.

The pastor cleared his throat. He looked uncomfortable. His eyes shifted from one face to the other, then down to the card he clutched in his hand.

Meemaw was wringing her hands, then forcing herself to hold still.

"Er . . . ah . . ." he began. For a reverend used to preach-ing hellfire, he was surprisingly uncomfortable. He ran a hand over his perspiring red face. "Like Miz Williams said, I think everybody who entered here's a winner. I tasted things I never tasted before in my life."

"And still standing . . ." a man near the back of the crowd called out. There was the requisite laughter. The parson chuckled and went on. "I'm new to Riverville, as y'all know, and never imagined there was this much bak-ing and cooking talent here."

He smiled from one side of the room to the other, set-tling into himself, commanding attention, shedding his light around like a beacon. "Very tough choices here."

I appreciated the man's kind of "aw shucks" humble-ness but couldn't help wishing he'd get on with it. I was already thinking of home and checking the new irrigation setup out in my test garden. The day had been a hot one. That meant hot for my trees, too.

"I'm gonna start with the honorable mentions, if that's okay will y'all." The pastor beamed another smile around the room. "If I call yer name, would you make your way over to Mrs. Williams to get yer certificate?"

He nodded to where the woman stood at the foot of the stage steps waving honorable mention certificates in the air.

There was disappointment and murmurs of disagreement as five names were called, including Cecil Darling's, and those five people made their embarrassed way through the crowd to get their loser's certificate.

"Now, on to the white, red, and last but not least, the blue ribbon." He glanced a last time around the crowd.

"Third place, in our Most Original Pecan Treat event, the last event in this year's Riverville Agricultural Fair, along with a gift certificate for a free facial at the Stony River School of Beauty goes to . . ." He looked at his card as if he couldn't quite make out the name and then called out, "Suzy Queen Grover for her Hot and Spicy Pecan Dip."

Men from the Barking Coyote and the other waitresses hooted and hollered. There was whistling and stamping of feet, and people barked various howls as Suzy Queen, pulling down on the hem of her fuchsia dress, hurried over to pick up her white ribbon and gift card from Mrs. Williams.

Anticipation grew as Reverend Jenkins leaned back into the microphone.

"Now, for second place. The red ribbon, and a fifty-dollar gift certificate to Morley Brothers Hardware"—he gave the expected pregnant pause—"goes to Mildred Firney for her Pecan Crescent and Apple Butter Rolls. Mildred?" He looked out at the crowd where a tiny woman in blue shorts and dotted green shirt held on to her startled face with both hands, so completely bowled over it took two of her friends to lead her across the room to claim her prizes. Mildred came to herself quick enough to hold the red ribbon high over her head as she made her way back through the appreciative crowd, talking to first one person and then another, luxuriating in her win.

The crowd grew quiet. This was the big one, the blue ribbon and a one-hundred-dollar gift certificate from Carya Street Movie Rentals.

I took Miss Amelia's elbow and squeezed. Miss Emma turned her tired face to her mother and smiled. Bethany pulled Jeffrey over to stand by her.

"First place in the Most Original Pecan Treat goes to . . ." The pastor paused for effect.

He seemed to be looking straight at Miss Amelia, who was looking hard back at him. "Goes to . . ."

When he said, "Ethelred Tomroy, for her Pecan Surprise Tomato Puff," the crowd gasped.

Angry words were shouted out. The name "Miss Amelia" went from woman to woman and man to man. The applause, when it came, was tepid as Ethelred Tomroy pushed her way to the front, telling folks to get out of her way, smiling wide and looking very pleased with herself as she assured everybody they'd heard right. She was the big winner at this year's Ag Fair and unlikely to let anybody forget it for the whole next year to come.

Chapter Four

The Winners' Supper got under way with all the pomp and circumstance of any important supper. Ladies and men from Riverville's churches and business community, all volunteers, pushed the long tables around into rows. Tablecloths were spread, and a bowl of Selma's flowers sat at the center of each table. The buffet was put into place. Coffeepots were plugged in, and sweet tea containers set up. In ten minutes the cooks had the barbecue snatched from the grills, plated, and headed for the meat end of the buffet.

A funereal line formed in front of where Miss Amelia and I stood in the kitchen doorway after stowing dishes and dishtowels and Bethany's decorations. One after another, women came up to hug Miss Amelia and say how shocked they were at the winning choice. "How on earth could those numbskull judges have passed over your wonderful Texas Caviar?" more than one asked. Person after person whispered what a shame it was. Nothing at all for Miss Amelia, the best cook in all of Riverville. All sentiments I angrily echoed.

"Seems something crooked is going on here," Treenie Menendez, Miss Amelia's right-hand woman back at the Nut House, stood on tiptoe near Miss Amelia's ear to whisper. "That Ethelred Tomroy can't hold a candle to you and everybody knows it."

"What were they thinking?" Finula Prentiss, a waitress at the Barking Coyote who'd never been a particular friend to the Blanchards, came up to say while pushing a silky strap from her stretchy top back up her shoulder. Her tough little face was outraged. Something about Finula—you had to hand it to her, she got over being mad about nothing at all whenever it suited her. Maybe it was memory loss from too many bourbons at the Coyote, but then, maybe I'm just being mean because I don't have men panting along behind me like a pack of thirsty dogs.

Other women from the Barking Coyote leaned around to nod and assure Miss Amelia that nobody else's recipes but hers would be served up at the Barking Coyote on their special Saturday nights.

"Morton's coming by for pecan pies later. Hope you've got a whole slew of 'em there at the Nut House," Suzy Q stepped up to add.

One after another, people expressed their disgust, their outright shock, and leaned close to suggest a payoff or some other low and scurrilous plot.

Miss Amelia waved them all away, saying how it was time for her to get her comeuppance; give somebody else a chance. "Did you see how happy Ethelred was? I've got too many ribbons as it is. No more place in the store to hang 'em."

The complaints fell to a dull murmur when Ethelred Tomroy walked in with the big blue ribbon stuck to the bodice of her dress. She made a show of taking a fresh second version of her winning dish from a cooler, forcing her way through to the microwave, then out to set her winner in the place of honor on the buffet table.

Miss Amelia and I set a winning Very Special Pecan Pie down among the desserts, along with a plate of her Luscious Pecan Sandies—both blue ribbon winners in other contests. We headed to the food table to post a note and ribbon near the ribs, saying they'd been made with her blue ribbon Pecan Round-em-up Grilling Glaze. Hawley Harvey's wife, Eula, came over to put in her two cents about the judges, wondering how they could pass over anything Miss Amelia made. "Don't see how that pastor can be so blind. That's what Hawley just said to me. You ask me, I'd take that extra batch and make him taste it. Show the man what he's missing. That's what I'd do." She shook her long blond hair—like nature never gave her—and flounced off, the ties on her sundress twitching behind her.

"Eula's right," I said. "Shame you can't put your caviar out anyway. Best thing I ever tried in my life, no matter what that clergyman says."

Meemaw leaned low to whisper so only I could hear her. "Not this batch, Lindy. I tasted it. The pastor was right. Terrible. Won't kill anybody but sure turn them off Texas Caviar for a while."

My mouth fell open. "Do you think it was sabotage? Why . . . who'd do a thing like that?"

We both turned to where Ethelred was sticking out her chest for a fellow churchgoer to admire her ribbon.

Miss Amelia made a face. "Can't win all the time,

Lindy. I sure hope the pastor gets to try my real recipe sometime. Poor man, what must he think about me if I didn't even get an honorable mention? And no wonder. Tasted like old shoes, you ask me."

"Hmmp," was all I said, thinking the pastor wasn't worth the effort to impress. My bigger concern was who would want to hurt Meemaw? Why, that was downright playing dirty.

Mama came back from closing up the Nut House booth and was ready to get on home. Bethany stopped by to let everybody know she and Jeffrey were going over to The Squirrel for dinner. "Jeffrey knows fine continental dining, you know. He's been to Europe and Canada."

"I'm very sorry your . . . eh . . . whatever that dish was . . . didn't win," Jeffrey leaned in to say, then smirked and threw an arm possessively across Bethany's shoulders.

Miss Amelia opened her mouth to snap off an answer, but as I watched, she looked down at her pretty, smiling granddaughter, and shut her mouth.

"You don't need to stay, you know." Meemaw turned, red-faced, to me. "I can still hold my head up by myself."

She pointed to her purse standing on a counter, stuffed with silky blue ribbons embossed with first place. "I'd like to help out here awhile then get over to the Nut House and hang up the ribbons so people don't forget how many I won. You want to help?"

What I really wanted was to get home to my trees, but I nodded anyway, figuring this wasn't the time to leave Meemaw alone.

With a new look going over her face, Miss Amelia went to one of our coolers and pulled out a fairly large bowl.

"You know what? I'm giving that pastor one more try at my caviar."

"Hey, you're not supposed to do that . . ."

"I'll be right back," she said, holding her head high out of pure Texas courage, carrying that new bowl of caviar, and pushing her way through the crowd toward the pastor.

I leaned out, watching as Miss Amelia sidled up to the Reverend Millroy Jenkins and proffered her bowl. She leaned down, whispering something in the pastor's ear. He skewed his neck around to look up at her, a huge smile on his pleasant face. He nodded.

Miss Amelia handed him a spoonful of her caviar. I would have said he put that spoon in his mouth a little tentatively, but soon he was spooning more on to his plate. Miss Amelia said something that made the pastor laugh, then walked back to the kitchen, covered her bowl, and put it down into the ranch cooler.

"There." Miss Amelia nodded at me and took a deep breath. "That takes care of that."

"You didn't offer any to Dora or Selma. They're sitting right beside him. Seems kind of rude."

Miss Amelia wrapped a big white apron around her middle. "You let me run my own life, missy, and I'll do the same for you. Now, while the others are eating, why don't you and me start clearing up some of this mess?"

She pointed to the dirty pans and bowls and serving pieces that would keep us busy for the next hour. I groaned. Not my idea of the way to spend a hot Texas evening. If only I had the courage to bid Meemaw adios and leave her to handle her own commitments.

When the kitchen was as clean as we could get it, before the next onslaught of dishes came through the swinging doors, I removed my apron and was about to pull off my rubber gloves when noise erupted in the outer room where the supper was going on.

It wasn't the sound of loud congratulations or the expected speeches getting under way. The noise was of voices yelling, chairs scraping over cement, a call for help, and then an echoing thunk as a body hit the floor.

Chapter Five

Miss Amelia and I ran out into the big room where people were yelling orders at each other while someone knelt on the floor beside a person who had fallen.

People crowded around, demanding to know what was happening. Who was it? Some speculated somebody had a heart attack. "We need a doctor," a man kneeling on the floor shouted. Word was passed. Soon the crowd parted and a doctor stepped up to lean over a prone body.

I slid around people standing in front of me, trying to see who was in trouble. Miss Amelia followed behind me, holding tight to the back of my shirt.

The head table was empty; only jumbled dishes were left on a cloth that had been pulled almost off at one end. The judges and fair committee folks were on their feet, staring down at the floor behind the table.

"Seizure!" Mike Longway passed the doctor's words

over his shoulder. "Somebody get something to hold down his tongue."

Miss Amelia, behind me now, gasped. "Is that Pastor Jenkins on the floor?"

I got in as close as I could. I saw a flash of a blue jacket and gray pants. Arms were thrashing. Nothing about what was happening in front of me looked good.

"I think it is. He's shaking all over."

"Whatever happened?" Miss Amelia, hands to her cheeks, demanded over the growing noise in the room.

"I hear the ambulance," I assured her. "They'll get him right over to the hospital. He'll be fine."

The noise in the room quieted as men rushed in with a gurney, made space around them, and huddled over Pastor Jenkins. Soon they had him bundled in white sheets and lifted on to the stretcher.

Dora Jenkins, her face stricken, ran out beside the men. Next to her, Selma hurried as fast as her bad leg would let her.

When the ambulance, with one wild blast of its siren, was off to Riverville Hospital, there was a collective sigh of relief in the room. We looked guiltily around at each other, as if we'd been caught not doing enough for the poor man, or being too enthralled, watching him writhe on the floor. People spoke to each other in low voices as they picked up their things to leave, glancing over their shoulders in bewilderment.

With the fair closed and nowhere else to go with their shock at what happened to Pastor Jenkins, Rivervillians, thunderstruck over the events at the Winners' Supper, headed, one after the other, to the Nut House, which Miss Amelia insisted on opening, over my strenuous objections.

"People won't know where else to go," she explained to me as she pushed the big door wide and hurried inside to set up a container of sweet tea and a stack of paper cups for anybody who needed a nice drink to soothe their nerves.

As the store filled, a fine mist of worry hung in the air around us, along with a lot of speculation. False medical information and a lot of cookie crunching went on as people ate pecan sandies and waited to hear news coming from the hospital. They turned to me pretty quick, knowing of my long friendship with Hunter. I guess they figured I gave them an edge on the news.

"Heart attack. Know one when I see one," Ethelred Tomroy, blue ribbon still pinned to the front of her dress, announced as she made her way through the crowd to fall heavily into the rocking chair set near the front counter.

"Well, now," Miranda Chauncey, one of the twins, said. "Looked like something bad. Don't care what they call it."

Melody stood beside her sister, hands crossed in front of her. Melody sniffed a loud sniff at her sister's remarks. Her eyes, surrounded by deep wrinkles, could still stretch wide at some of Miranda's more outlandish outbursts.

"You ask me"—Miranda leaned back on the counter, arms crossed over her chest—"I'd say it looked like some kind of gastric attack. All that pukin' and shakin'."

"Fer the Lord's sakes, Miranda," Melody, standing off to one side, chastised. "Will you have a little respect here? The reverend's over there in that hospital fightin' for his life, fer all we know. Just keep yer trap shut."

"Just 'cause you can't call a spade a spade, Melody, don't mean I have to pretend everything's nice as pie right along with you."

Before the twins really laid into each other, Miss Amelia took the bag of pecan candy from Miranda's hand, rang it up, then took a rumpled dollar bill from the woman's wrinkled fist.

"What do you think happened, Lindy?" Jessie Sanchez, town librarian, our foreman's daughter, and longtime friend, joined me off to one side, eyeing the chattering neighbors. "Have you talked to Hunter?"

I shook my head.

"I hope it's nothing serious. I feel so bad for Dora. She's new here and that's almost enough trouble for anybody, let alone having this happen to her husband right there in front of the whole town." Jessie's pretty, dark-skinned face was drawn tight with worry.

People around us murmured sympathy for the reverend's sweet wife but were soon back to speculation.

"Could be food allergies." Ethelred, with the rocker going at a fine pace, stuck another of her theories out there. "The man was eatin' up a storm all afternoon. Nothing in my prize-winning tomato puff to hurt him. Know that for certain. But something else did."

"Wouldn't it be awful if it turns out he's allergic to pecans?" Someone sent a shock wave through the crowd.

Jessie, still beside me, shrugged. "I don't expect we'll hear anything too soon. Might not be until tomorrow . . ."

I was grateful when Mama came in to take Miss Amelia home. Meemaw closed the cash register with a final slam, and rolled her eyes at me, letting me know she was on her last nerve and couldn't take any more.

"Think you might call Hunter?" she asked before she went out the front door. "See if he knows how the pastor's doing?"

"I was thinking the same thing, Meemaw." I leaned in to kiss my grandmother on the cheek. Even in her seventies, Miss Amelia usually had more stamina than women half her age. Tonight she looked as if she'd finally met a day that was almost beyond her fine-tuned ability to cope.

I stepped to a quiet corner of the room to call. His private cell rang a long time. I left a message to call me whenever he could.

I'd barely hung up when my phone rang.

Hunter, calling me back.

"It's bad, Lindy," was the first thing he said.

I frowned as the worried faces of Miss Amelia and the few stragglers still in the store turned my way.

"What do you mean 'bad'?"

"I mean the pastor just died."

"What!"

Miss Amelia tugged at my arm. People gasped and whispered urgently around me. I shook Meemaw off and stuck a finger in my ear so I could hear.

"Dead, Lindy," Hunter said.

"Heart attack?" I demanded, then looked into Meemaw's shocked face.

"Afraid not, Lindy. The doctor just came out to talk to the sheriff . . ."

His voice dropped. "Don't say a word but he's telling us it could be poison."

Chapter Six

I wasn't about to add to the shock of the people in the Nut House. I never mentioned the word "poison." I didn't hint at anything beyond a sad, natural death. I let them commiserate and decide between them who would stay at the parsonage with Dora and Selma first and who would go over later. They were talking flowers and the eulogy—some opting for a few fellows on the board, one saying Hawley Harvey delivered a good eulogy . . .

When the shocked people were all gone and the store empty, I gratefully made my way up the stairs to my apartment and shut the door behind me.

I walked through my tiny living room, filled with ranch house castoffs, to my alcove kitchen, where I got myself a Coke from the fridge, then made a stop at the bathroom, so tiny it was one step from the toilet to the shower. Drinking from the Coke can instead of getting a glass dirty, I went into my bedroom with its twin bed, small dresser, and wall of bookcases. I kicked off my shoes, dug out an old pair of pajama bottoms and a faded T-shirt, and went back to the living room to sit down at the desk and flip the computer on, hoping to keep my mind busy until Hunter called back as promised.

I looked for a magazine article I'd copied. About a new strain of nut trees a lab in California was developing. Better, they claimed, than anything in existence. Almost totally drought resistant because the trees hoarded water in a wide network of deep roots.

It was the very thing I was after, except I was going for scab and other diseases as well. I leaned back to stretch, then rub at my tired eyes. How important all of that seemed a couple of hours ago. Now there was a dead man, and death sure eclipsed ordinary living.

I was too tired to concentrate and snapped off the desk light. For the next hour I paced back and forth, trying late-night TV then giving up and sitting down to stare at my phone.

When it rang, Hunter's voice was serious, but hesitant "Lindy? Did I wake you?"

"I couldn't sleep . . ."

"I'm home now. What do you think about this poison stuff? The parson ate what everybody else was eating, didn't he?"

"As far as I know. They're not expecting some mass poisoning, are they? Any others been brought in sick?"

"Nobody. And I have to tell you, the doctor listed the death as suspicious. They've already taken the body for autopsy. Sheriff Higsby says they'll have to run a full toxicology panel. First thing we want to know is what kind of poison we're talking here."

"Autopsy! Good Lord! Is that necessary? It will about kill Dora. Why, just the thought . . ."

"Got to tell you, Lindy, Sheriff Higsby's already talking to people who were there. He's asking questions. We can't wait on this."

"What does 'suspicious' mean exactly?"

"Murder, Lindy. Sheriff says it looks like murder, unless the pastor chose the middle of the fair supper to kill himself."

I fell still, unable to quite grasp what he was talking about. Somebody murdered the parson? The man had been in town for only eight months. How'd he make that kind of enemy in so short a time?

"Looking close at his wife and sister-in-law, too."

"Dora? Selma? Are you crazy? Those women wouldn't hurt a fly."

"You ever hear of Lucretia Borgia?"

"That was a few years ago, Hunter. And why would his wife or sister-in-law poison him in a public place when they could take weeks or months to do it slowly at home?"

"That's another thing. The sheriff thought it might be something that's been coming on for a long time. Like a little bit of poison here and there. But the doctor says he doesn't think so. A quick-acting poison from the symptoms."

"What symptoms?"

"You know, throwing up and spasms and losing his ability to stand and then even to hear."

"Terrible."

"He thinks it's something that works fast, and that brings me to another thing the sheriff was wondering about . . ."

I had a feeling I knew what was coming.

"Thought you should be warned. Sheriff Higsby says . . . well . . . because of the way the judging went . . . geez, I mean . . . he wants to talk to Miss Amelia in the morning."

"Meemaw?"

"She lost, Lindy. Lost bad. Miss Amelia's not used to losing."

"And she killed one of the judges to get even?" My voice went an octave higher as the preposterous suggestion hit me. "You think she keeps a pocketful of poison for losing occasions?"

"She's one of many people we have to talk to. Knew she had a hard day and didn't want to push things tonight. I thought maybe you'd warn her and bring her in yourself, about ten."

"For heaven's sakes, Hunter. My grandmother? Poison a man over one more blue ribbon?"

"Had to tell you. We're friends and all. Don't worry, though, we'll get it cleared up right away."

"Friends! Suspecting Meemaw! You buzzard. You, you . . ." I took a deep breath.

"Just wanted to warn you, is all," he was saying as I hung up.

I drove out to the ranch at 6 a.m. Nobody was up when I let myself in the front door. I wasn't about to bother anybody. They'd know soon enough that Miss Amelia was under suspicion because of losing a contest to Ethelred Tomroy.

In the kitchen I put a pot of coffee on the stove and sat at the table with the newspaper I'd picked up in the drive. Story about the pastor being hospitalized after the fair was in there, but nothing about his death, and nothing about poison being the cause.

Soon enough everything would be out there for the whole town to wonder at: *Local pastor dead from eating local woman's losing caviar* . . .

I snapped my head back, closed my eyes, and groaned just as Mama walked, bleary-eyed, into the kitchen.

"Thought you were a dumb, noisy burglar, Lindy," Emma said as she stretched and yawned. "What are you doing here so early?"

"Oh, Mama . . ." I felt my bottom lip start to tremble as it always did around my mother. "Somebody poisoned Pastor Jenkins."

At first her mouth dropped open. She stared hard at me. "You sure?"

I nodded.

"That's terrible, baby girl. Hunter tell you that? No wonder you came home." Emma leaned down to kiss the top of my head, undoing me completely.

"Oh, Mama," I blubbered. "The sheriff thinks maybe Meemaw did it because she lost the contest. They want her down to the station in the morning. I was so mad at Hunter for daring to hint that . . ."

"Hint at what, Lindy?" The weary voice came from the other side of the room.

Miss Amelia stood in the open kitchen door in her blue flowered robe and blue slip-ons. "What's that boy saying to get you mad now? Seems we got enough to think about, what with poor Pastor Jenkins dying."

Mama and I turned to watch the woman hurry over to turn off the coffeepot, spilling coffee all over the stove. She noticed us watching and got an odd look on her face. "What's going on? You two know it's only a little after six o'clock, don't you? Who needs coffee this early? Justin's probably gone out with the trees already and Bethany won't be up for a couple of hours. If you're thinking that Jeffrey will be needing coffee anytime soon, don't bother. That slugabed won't be out here until after lunch." She yawned and shook her head.

"What's going on?" She looked straight at Mama and then at me. "Something's up. You two can't hide a mouse, let alone an elephant, between you. You hear from Hunter again?"

I nodded.

Mama got up to put a hand on Meemaw's shoulder. "Hunter told Lindy they think it was murder."

"Murder? That's crazy. I didn't hear a gunshot—everybody in that whole place would've been screaming their heads off. Nobody coulda stuck a knife in his back—"

"Poison."

Miss Amelia set the coffeepot on a hot pad then sat down hard in a chair.

"Poison? Why . . . All I've got flashing through my head are those men whose wives do them in. That's sure not Dora."

She thought harder. "Or a steer that eats the wrong plant and turns up his heels. That kind of poison?"

"Kind of like that," I admitted.

"Never get me to believe it of Dora or Selma. Those are two fine ladies."

"The sheriff thinks it happened right there at the Winners' Supper."

Now Miss Amelia was frowning hard. "Then half the people at the supper should be lying dead in the street."

Miss Amelia thought hard for a long time. "Bet the sheriff wants to talk to me, right? Only thing the parson ate different from everybody else was my caviar, 'cause I wanted him to taste how good it really is. Sheriff want me down there this morning? That what you're all upset about?"

I nodded. Miss Amelia got up and took the coffeepot to the sink, where she poured the contents down the drain and went about making a fresh pot. More than a subtle hint about my awful coffee, I imagined she just wasn't thinking straight.

She turned back to Mama and me after leaving the coffeepot on the sink, where she'd set it. "Think I'll go grab a little more sleep. I'll be ready at nine o'clock."

She headed for the kitchen door, then stopped and turned. "Any idea what a woman wears to get interrogated?"

She was gone and I was left alone with Mama to pass the next couple of hours. I called Ben Fordyce's office at her suggestion. Ben was the family attorney. His office didn't open until ten so I left a message there and at his home, saying how important it was we speak to him.

Bethany came down looking for breakfast at eight o'clock. I got an even bigger surprise when Jeffrey Coulter, all dressed up and in the kitchen by eight thirty, said he wasn't hungry and took right off to look at a piece of property up toward Houston.

Bethany pouted when he left without asking her to go with him, which made Mama get her back up and tell her to stop acting like an idiot. "Get that boy right oughtta yer mind," Mama warned in her best scary voice. "I don't like him and I'm having a talk with Justin soon as I can. I think it's time that one moved on."

I got out of there before I joined the fight for no good reason. Almost nine. Time to hurry Meemaw along to her interrogation and time to get away before the whole family was mad and fighting though nobody knew exactly what they were fighting about. I imagined having your grandmother suspected of being a poisoner would get on just about anybody's nerves.

Chapter Seven

It looked like a jamboree in progress when we pulled up to the Riverville Sheriff's Department. People were lined down the front steps and hanging on to the brass handrail. Some were on the cement pad, backs pressed against the double glass doors leading into the station. Miss Amelia made her way in front of me, greeting everyone and making a path, like a cruise liner, for me to follow.

Inside the building, the crush was as thick as outside. I spotted Hunter behind the high front counter and made my way toward him.

"What's going on?" I flipped a thumb over my shoulder at the crowd.

Hunter, as neat and put together as always, looked around at the crowd. "Everybody from the fair. And I mean about everybody. They all want to help. Guess you could say the whole town's in shock over the pastor's death. Trouble is, with so many wanting to be interviewed, we don't have time to talk to the people we should be looking at."

"I brought Miss Amelia in. You don't expect her to wait behind all these others, do you? Woman's as stressed out as a person can get. Not herself at all. I'm worried about her, Hunter."

"'Course she's not waiting. Let me go see if the sheriff's ready for you ladies."

When he was back, nodding for us to follow him and holding the swinging gate open, I asked, "Anything new?"

Hunter eyed people nearby and lowered his head, dropping his voice to just above a whisper. "The medical examiner was up all night working on this."

Hunter walked between us, a hand on our back, leading down a long hall. "Didn't get stomach contents 'til a while ago, but from what he's seen already, he thinks what did it was what he called 'a volatile organic poison.'"

I knew what he was talking about from my plant studies. "Alcohol, formaldehyde, ether, nicotine. Things like that."

Miss Amelia made a dismissive sound. "Nobody drinks or smokes that much at a fair dinner." She turned eyes with dark circles around at Hunter. "ME find anything besides my Texas caviar in him?"

"Afraid that's all, Miss Amelia. Bits of those contest dishes but too small to do the damage that was done."

"There are all kinds of poisons in that group," I told Hunter. "Maybe you can trace the killer that way."

"Hope so. The ME's called in a toxicologist to help. They'll be doing tests. Tissues and such. Should know later today or tomorrow what we're looking for. One thing he did say. Kind of smelled like parsnips—you know, mousy. At least that's what he says."

I made a face. "Is he sure? I mean—no heart attack or organ failure? Nothing like that?"

"The man's ninety-nine percent sure it's poison."

Sheriff Higsby stood and doffed his wide cowboy hat when we walked in.

"Miss Amelia." He nodded in her direction, and then to me. "Thought you might bring Ben Fordyce with you."

"Talked to him on the way in to town," I said. "He didn't think it was necessary. Said he'd come right over if we needed him, but he couldn't believe you were serious about suspecting Miss Amelia of anything, let alone poisoning people."

We took seats and waited nervously as the sheriff mumbled into a tape recorder then pushed a small microphone toward us across his desk. He leaned back, pulled a pad of paper from the top drawer, and lined up three pens beside it.

He looked up reluctantly.

"Seems we've got ourselves a tragedy here, ladies. You know the parson died."

Miss Amelia tsked and shook her head. "Terrible thing. Poor man. Seems too . . . oh, I don't know . . . not like something that would happen in Riverville."

"Know what you mean. A bullet or two over at the Barking Coyote, well, expect that. Happens. Whenever people want somebody to die, they figure a way to do it."

He adjusted his body in his chair, as if he couldn't get comfortable.

"I understand you gave the pastor some of that Texas Caviar of yours. That right? That what it's called?"

"Heavenly Texas Pecan Caviar. If you mean at the Winners' Supper? Why, yes I did."

"But that particular entry wasn't a winner, was it?"

"You're right there, Sheriff. Not even an honorable

mention. I tasted that first one the judges got to taste. Awful. Something happened to it. Nothing in there to spoil. Still, maybe standing out on the table, the way it did. I don't really know what happened. First time ever in my life. I was ashamed the poor man had to put something that bad in his mouth. But I had another dish so I decided at the last minute to give him another chance. I pulled that second one out of my cooler—it was labeled and all. I took it up to him and he tasted it then took a good-sized helping, saying how good it was. Figured that would take care of it. At least I could hold my head up again."

Sheriff Higsby almost smiled. "What I'm figuring is that if any of those other dishes had poison in 'em, people would've been fallin' like flies by now. But that didn't happen . . ."

Miss Amelia nodded quickly at the man. "I see what you're getting at. If my caviar was the only thing poor Pastor Jenkins ate that nobody else ate, why, I'd have to be the poisoner."

"Meemaw!" I sat forward, shocked at what the woman was saying. "Don't go saying things like that or I'm getting Ben over here."

"Well, Lindy . . . that's why we brought the cooler with us."

She turned to Sheriff Higsby. "Got the contest bowl and the Winners' Supper bowl in it."

Tears fogged her eyes. She took a swipe at one eye with her clenched fist.

"Thanks, Miss Amelia," the sheriff said. "I know you're not the kind to have switched out the caviar. Glad you brought 'em in without me having to ask."

He got a sad smile out of her as she slowly got on her feet. Meemaw was showing her age. Her shoulders were bent more than I'd ever seen them bent. Even her usually neat gray hair looked messy.

"You don't think, for even a second, Meemaw had any-thing to do with this." I stood, too, turning from Hunter to the sheriff.

Hunter looked so pained. "We don't think that for a sec-ond, Lindy. The thing is, since we all know it wasn't Miss Amelia, *who was it*?"

I glanced over at Meemaw. Her fingers were making dents in the leather of her handbag, she was holding on so tight. She'd stopped pretending to smile.

"You're talking murder," I whispered at Hunter.

"We know that. And not just a spur of the moment, heat of anger, kind of thing like what happens over to the Bark-ing Coyote. This was planned. Pretty awful. A harsh and cruel death. Nothing to do with Miss Amelia. Still, we've got to look at everything."

"If you ask me," I said, "you gotta look back to where the parson came from. Why he'd want to move to Texas from Tupelo."

Hunter nodded, like he knew there was a lot more on the line here than an investigation. "Already in the works. I contacted the sheriff's office there in Tupelo. Should hear back pretty soon."

"I got one more thing." The sheriff put up his hand. "Why'd you take that caviar out to the reverend and not taste it first? Could have been bad, too?"

"Spur of the moment. Some folks were saying I should let the parson taste the real thing. Never thought for a min-ute anything was wrong with it. Been in the cooler all day."

"How many people in the kitchen when you took the bowl out? Anybody mention maybe you shouldn't take it to the big room? Anybody try to stop you?"

"Every woman in town was in that kitchen, getting their bowls ready for the tables if they were winners, or washing

up and putting bowls and pans away if they didn't win anything. Nobody was saying much to anybody. Too busy. Just
a few, I remember, said it was a shame the pastor couldn't
taste the real thing."

"I hear you had dishes at the supper anyway, 'cause you
won in other categories."

She nodded and groused a little. "Sure did. Plenty of blue
ribbons. Didn't need one more."

The sheriff's face was just a little sad. "None of those
others woulda meant as much as taking a blue in that last
contest, now would it, Miss Amelia? You gotta be honest
with me here."

She scrunched up her pretty, lined face and looked over
at me as if asking for help. I nodded for her to go ahead,
tell the man the truth.

"Guess you're right, Sheriff. I did want that blue ribbon.
Would've made me the winningest cook in Riverville history. I suppose I was disappointed. But I'll tell you something, I've lost important events and people before, lost my
husband early, but I don't go flinging poison into my dishes
to get even. I didn't poison the pastor. I wasn't out to poison
all of Riverville. You can accuse me of putting cheap bourbon in my recipes when I'm out of Garrison's, but I'm no
killer and you all damn well know it."

She was out of there faster than I could keep up—
through the crowded front office and out the door. Hunter
was a few steps behind.

At the truck, he held the door for her, asking, "Where
would you look for a killer, Miss Amelia?"

Mad now, she took a long minute to cool down, then said,
"Find out what kind of poison it is and follow that. Maybe
somebody buying a lot of ant poison in town or sending

away on the Internet for things they shouldn't have been ordering. I'd start there."

She turned to Hunter. "I'll tell you what I'm going to do." She settled her bag in her lap and straightened her shoulders. "I'm going to talk to Dora and Selma, soon as I can. That is, if they're up to it. We've got to start figuring things out.

"I'm not saying those fine women had anything to do with it, but they were sitting next to the parson the whole time. Maybe somebody got the poison in after he took that helping out of my bowl."

"We'll know right away. Soon as I get your cooler to the medical examiner."

I looked over at Hunter and rolled my eyes. I felt like running around the truck and twisting the end of his nose as hard as I could—the way I did when we were kids. I knew he was walking a fine line, but if he had to fall off in one direction or the other—it had better be in ours.

On the way back to the Nut House, where Meemaw wanted to go, I almost had to laugh. "Hunter and the sheriff were about accusing you of murder," I told her. "Then you turned it around so they're asking your help with things. I don't know how you do it. Wish I'd gotten a dose of your spell casting."

"Humph," she said. "I wish so, too. The way you treat that boy . . ." Meemaw shook her head.

"What boy?"

"Why, poor Hunter. I see how you treat him. How long do you expect a man to take your smart mouth and not start looking someplace else? You're not getting any younger, Lindy."

"Meemaw!" I was shocked; she'd never interfered in my love life before. I figured maybe she was still mad at everybody and swinging the tail end of that anger at me.

"Poor man turns red every time you start in on him. Falls all over his own feet around you."

"Let's see how *you'd* act if somebody accused *me* of murder. You think I'm gonna be nice about it?"

"I wouldn't act one way or the other." She gave a distinct snort. "I'd find me a gun and put 'im out of your misery. I know who we Blanchards are. Still, you don't have to treat poor Hunter the way you do."

"Okay," I said, a little huffy myself by then. "Then we better get busy finding out who's after you, Meemaw. 'Cause I'm not shooting any cops. Especially one that could be the father of all those babies I could be birthin' in the future."

Chapter Eight

The front part of the parsonage was a historic, restored Sunday House, one of the two-room frame buildings built by early German ranchers whose places were far out of town, too far to make it in and back in one day. Those old families came to Riverville on Saturday, took care of their shopping and doctoring and visiting, stayed overnight in their two-room house, and went back to their ranch after church the next day.

The building was on the register of historic places in Colorado County, but it had been added to and updated over the years though the front was never changed, still low and stone with plain, four-paned windows under a long over-hang. A sturdy piece of Texas history. I'd always loved the old house, remembering it happily decorated for a Christmas tour a time or two.

The drive leading up to the house was lined with cars along either side. Parishioners were there already with their casseroles and platters of tacos and jugs of sweet tea. I parked next door, in the Rushing to Calvary Independent Church parking lot. This, too, was almost full of cars.

We got out, me with one of Miss Amelia's pecan breads in my hands, and Miss Amelia carrying one of her not-too-special pecan pies, meaning no bourbon in this one. We picked our way delicately across the side lawn and up a dirt path that led through Selma's garden to the house. The garden surprised me since I hadn't been there in a very long time. As far as I could see, the garden moved up a slope and then down toward the Colorado River, borders and beds all neatly trimmed. Beds of salvia, coneflowers, echinacea, and one bed filled with different sizes and shades of sunflowers. There was hibiscus, and vines—morning glories folded into tight little blue and white and pink funnels. Purple passion vines climbed a lattice fence.

"Look at this garden," I said. "How on earth does she do it?"

"I'm glad Selma's got something that makes her happy. Came out of a bad marriage, from what I understand. Guess she started in digging soon as they got settled and the next thing every gardener in the church was giving a day or so a week to help her out. You know, with that bad leg of hers, people thought it was their duty," Miss Amelia said.

I leaned close to whisper to my imposing grandmother, "Would I look heartless if I came back out to walk around?"

"I'll bet you anything Selma would be happy to show it to you, if you asked. Can't imagine the woman loves anything more."

On the low, wood-floored front porch, I rang the doorbell. Hawley Harvey, dressed in all his Sunday finery, opened the door and invited us in with a sweep of his arm.

The voices inside the house were subdued, but still a steady murmur rising and falling as groups in the living room shifted and wandered out to the kitchen, then back.

"Food goes in the kitchen, Miss Amelia," Hawley directed, more somber and quieter than I'd ever seen him, no Santa Claus "ho, ho, ho"-ing here. "Whole passel of women out there now dishing things up. Rest of the food might go over to the church for after the funeral."

"Who's leading the service?" Miss Amelia bent to ask in his ear.

"Guess I'll be doing it—a celebration of the pastor's life." He stopped to sigh and lean back, hands twined together at his chest. "Have to fill in until we get a new parson. Such a shame. Can't believe the man ate some bad food and died . . ." He whisked his hands together. "Just like that."

"More than bad food," Miss Amelia, affronted by the words "bad food," said back at him. "From what I hear."

Hawley rocked on his heels, looking disturbed, like an upset cherub. "Now, Miss Amelia, you and I know for a fact nobody in this town's running around poisoning people. There'll be some other explanation for it. You watch and see. The man was a pastor of the church, for heaven's sakes. I wouldn't go around tellin' people he was poisoned." He shook his head hard. "No sir, I wouldn't go spreadin' that story."

Miss Amelia snapped her lips together and said nothing more. I, sticking close behind my grandmother, figured if Hawley Harvey wanted to deny the truth, there wasn't much we could do about it. Truth did have a way of popping out—no matter how uncomfortable it made people like the deacon feel.

"You go on out to the kitchen," I urged my grandmother.

"I'll go say a few words to Dora and Selma. I feel so bad for them. It's good to see everybody here for support."

At first I waited to talk to the sisters, but they had a solid wall of women around them. I didn't go to church often, other than dropping Meemaw off for services, so I didn't know Dora and Selma that well, but it was what I felt I had to do—one human being for another.

I waited for a crack in the wall and slithered up close to where the two were sitting. Little Dora, a brown kind of woman with brown hair and brown eyes and a brown cast to her skin, was dressed in blue, not black, as I'd expected.

Dora sat in a rocker and Selma in a similar rocker next to her. Dora's face was red with perspiration and exertion. She had the vacant, faraway look of someone in deep shock, blinking hard when she looked up at me.

"You're Miss Amelia's granddaughter, aren't you?" Her voice quivered.

I bent forward and took Dora's hand to express my sorrow, but Dora pulled her hand away and buried it in her lap. She looked wildly over to Selma, who leaned in and patted her sister's hand, then smiled wanly up at me, saying something about me having to understand; these were stressful times.

"I just wanted to say how sorry I am . . ."

"Oh, please . . ." Dora waved a hand in my direction. She put a lace-edged handkerchief to her nose. I figured she wasn't being unkind, just unable to talk about it to one more person.

Selma hesitated and looked around me to where Miss Amelia had come from the kitchen to stand. "This is such an awful thing . . ."

"Dora and I want you to know we don't believe your

grandmother had anything to do with this. Not for a minute." Selma leaned stiffly toward me. "It's just all too much for Dora. A terrible shock."

I turned to the crying woman. "I know you haven't been in Riverville long, Dora, but . . . everybody knows Miss Amelia. Why . . ."

As my voice dried in my throat, Miss Amelia stepped up beside me. From the look on her face, she'd heard every word.

"I never did anything to hurt your husband, Dora . . ." Miss Amelia started, only to be waved away by Dora. "I never would."

Selma leaned toward her sister to quiet her. "Now, Dora, we don't know anything yet."

She bent to listen when her sister grabbed on to her sleeve and motioned her close. Selma looked up at me and Miss Amelia, her eyes almost begging us to move on.

"I'm so very sorry and Dora says she's sorry, too, but she can't help but wonder why you gave poor Millroy more of that dish of yours, when he already passed over it for any kind of award." She stopped, bending low to listen as Dora whispered to her again. "She says it just doesn't seem right. And . . . what?"

She listened as her sister whispered behind her hand.

"She says she's so sorry and she hopes we can all sit down and have a heart-to-heart someday, but not now."

Selma let out a deep breath. She seemed to wither down into her brown chair. When she finally looked up at us, her words were weak, almost more than she could get out. "It would be best . . ." she said. "Oh my, I hate this, but it would be best for Dora if you . . . came back at a later time. Oh dear, I hope you understand . . ."

Miss Amelia said nothing more. She straightened her back, looked around at the clusters of women pretending not to listen, nodded to the room in general, and taking me by the arm, marched to the front door with her head held high.

Chapter Nine

The air in the garden had a current of chill buried beneath layers of heat and pure, hard sunshine. August. In one corner a sprinkler shot water in a large circle, bending flowers and leaving incomplete rainbows behind it.

I was in no mood now to look at flowers, but I needed to let Miss Amelia walk awhile, to get her breath back. I chose a path that led through beds of tall butterfly weed, purplish smudges of muhly grass, yellow bells, and pink gaura.

"Goodness," Miss Amelia said after a time of letting out deep sighs. "Can you believe Dora and Selma, and probably most of the others in there, thinking I would do something like that to the good pastor?"

"They don't really—"

"Don't play with me, Lindy. I know what I heard and saw."

"Everybody's confused, Meemaw." I steered her down the red dirt path toward the river. Since I was a little girl, I'd found that the peace and coolness along the Colorado's banks calmed me when I was upset. Just watching the water flow on—sometimes swiftly, most times slow and easy—could make bad stuff go away. It was a place I associated with something much bigger than I was, something much older, something much more spiritual than I felt in places like the church, where good people gathered but just their presence deadened something I valued, and their perfumes made me sneeze.

That never happened to me on the tumbled shores of the Colorado River, where, from time to time, the wild hogs ran and scared me half to death.

"We'd better get going, Lindy," Miss Amelia protested. "I don't want to come up against any of the people in that house for a while."

We were almost to the water. I could smell it, along with the sprinkler in the garden. The path sloped fast where the cultivated flowerbeds stopped and a tangle of weeds and tough wildflowers began. With my botanist's eye, I swept the banks of the river—taking in huge plants with enormous leaves. I identified the tall plant: *Cicuta maculata,* with a purplish tinge at the base of the leaves. And another *apiaceae*, short-leaved, bipinnately divided. No flower umbrels but still I recognized it as Queen Anne's lace.

"Watch yourself." Miss Amelia pointed to a couple of deep holes in the earth. "Break a leg down here."

I turned to climb the path, back among Selma's manicured flowerbeds.

"I still don't see how she does it," I marveled despite myself.

Miss Amelia, too distracted to pay much attention to the garden around her, muttered, "Now don't go giving yourself a major case of garden envy. The Riverville Garden Club does a lot, to tell the truth. I'm here every Tuesday. But maybe not this week. One of the deacons paid a landscape designer to work all this up. Now, can you get me home?"

She sniffed and turned away from the flowers as a group of ladies made their way ahead of us, out of the house and over to the parking lot. Miss Amelia put a hand out, holding me back. She slowed to let the ladies get in their cars and drive off before urging me to walk faster.

The road toward town was almost empty. I was heading for the Nut House when Miss Amelia leaned over to whisper in her best peremptory voice, "If you don't mind, Lindy, I'm going home. I'm feeling . . . well, I don't know how to say it, but I've got the feeling I should get back to the ranch and stay there."

"Meemaw!" I frowned over at the woman. "You can't do that. I'm taking you to the store. Treenie needs help . . ."

"You realize that Sheriff Higsby must've gone out of his way to tell Dora about me? I never woulda thought it. Not in a million years."

"That's his job. Dora was there. She's just putting two and two together and getting nine."

"What I'm sayin' is . . ." The tired-looking woman took a deep breath and closed her eyes. "It looks like people around here want to believe the worst—and there's not much we can do to stop them."

"Yes, there is. I'm calling Hunter soon as I take you back to the Nut House. See what poison it was and if they ruled out your caviar yet."

"Sure would help to know what that means: 'volatile organic.' "

"Comes from burning fuels like gasoline or even natural gas. Diesel exhaust. Paints, glues—things like that. Formaldehyde. Dry-cleaning fluids."

I thought awhile. "A lot of dyes, I think. Poisonous plants. Chloroform. Some ethers and alcohols. Lots of things, Grandma."

She slouched in her seat and muttered, "You know we're in this alone, Lindy. Just you and me. Thought the sheriff was with us, but it looks like maybe he's thinking of playing one against the other."

"Well, I'm with you, Meemaw. Just don't cave on me. I need you. That brain of yours . . ."

Miss Amelia chuckled. "Your grandfather used to say I had a head like a criminal. Could always figure what they were thinking. Helped him when he was in the Texas State Senate, I'll tell you."

She said nothing more until I pulled in front of the store. "I meant it, Lindy. I want to go home. You and Emma and Bethany can work out a schedule here between the three of you. Bethany's spending too much time with that Jeffrey anyway. I'm just tired now. For the first time in my life, I'm feeling old and kind of . . . well . . . maybe I just need to rest."

Against my better judgment, I pulled out and headed home.

Chapter Ten

Ethelred Tomroy was the first one in after I opened the store. Miss Emma had been up to her ears in bookwork, and Bethany was off somewhere with Jeffrey Coulter, who'd come back from his property search and suggested a day in Columbus. Since Miss Amelia declared she wasn't showing her face at the Nut House until things were a lot clearer, that left me, which seemed bad enough, and then here comes Ethelred.

"Where's Miss Amelia?" Ethelred demanded, out of breath from climbing the three front steps. "I gotta talk to her. I don't believe a word people are sayin'."

Ethelred's face turned an ugly shade of purple. "I hope to heaven you Blanchards got your wits about you and called Ben Fordyce. Ask me, these gossips got to be made to shut up. I'd threaten to sue the whole passel of 'em, it was me . . ."

"Why, Miss Ethelred." I was filling one of the open

counters with pecan gift boxes. I leaned back to eye the woman. "Thought you and Miss Amelia were enemies."

Her wide mouth dropped open. "Enemies! Me an' Amelia Hastings? You out of your ever-lovin' mind, girl? Me and Amelia been friends since she came here, after your grandfather died over there in Dallas. I think I was the first one to welcome her to Riverville, comin' from one of the oldest families, the way I do."

"Well, all that competition . . ."

"That's nothing but two friends trying to outdo each other. Amelia's always winning those ribbons and I don't, personally, think she's that much better than me. Popularity contest is all it is."

"Doesn't seem that way right now." I looked around the empty store. "Not like they were waiting on the porch to get in this morning."

Ethelred frowned, eyes searching the usually bustling aisles. "Don't go looking for trouble, Lindy. Everybody's got other things to do."

She stopped to straighten packs of candied pecans on the front counter. When she looked up, she squinted at me with one eye, like people do who are trying to get something out of you. "I've really got to talk to her. Think I'll go on out to the ranch."

"She's resting right now."

"I understand that well enough, but I gotta talk to her. About going with me somewhere tomorrow."

"Sorry. It's not a good time right now."

She drew in her nostrils tight and fixed me with a mean look. "I'm going out there, Lindy. Don't care what you say. She promised and, well, there's no way around it."

I threw my hands up, figuring Miss Amelia could tend

to herself. Ethelred always did run right over me. It was all that stuff about respecting your elders no matter what bull-heads they could be.

She was gone and I was thinking about closing up when the bell over the front door jingled again. I felt a shiver of dread. *Who next with questions about Miss Amelia?* That's probably all I'd get today, I figured. People not so much inter-ested in the Special Pecan Pies or cookies or boxes of nuts, but people looking for a tidbit of gossip to share with their neighbors: *You think she coulda done it? Musta lost her mind when Ethelred beat her out for that blue ribbon* . . .

It was a relief to see Jessie Sanchez coming up the aisle at me. Her shirt was bright red, her wide skirt many colors. Her long black hair swung at her shoulders. My friend. Colorful. Sympathetic. Easy to be with. I truly hugged her and gave her the warmest smile I could muster. She smelled good. Like warm soap and books and just somebody who didn't argue for nothing, didn't gossip, and would make me laugh even when I was as far down as I was right then.

Jessie sank into the rocker with the red chair pads while I pulled a stool from behind the counter.

"Saw you in here when I was driving by. Miss Amelia all right?"

"She doesn't want to come in anymore. Thinks every-body in town's talking—and I suppose they are. More upset than I've ever seen her."

"Can you blame her?" Jessie answered. "Library was buzzing with it. That's really why I thought I'd run over and see how she was doing. I can't imagine anybody think-ing your grandmother would hurt a fly. Told a few what I thought today. Gossiping right there among the books. You know how much my family owes her. Even that first day we got here from Mexico—your grandmother greeted us like we were old friends. Helped us move into the house."

Such a pretty, earnest face. She hadn't always been treated well by Blanchards, despite what she said. It was my uncle Amos who proposed and then dumped her. The man had a lot going against him, including a taste for booze. Then I found him dead in my greenhouse. Made it even worse for Jessie, him coming home to do some good for once, and being murdered.

"Would you stop by and talk to her when you get home?" I asked. "Ethelred's on her way out there. She might need a brighter face to look at."

Jessie reached over and squeezed my hand, then stood. "I'll stop by later. My mother's waiting for the chilies I said I'd bring."

"I'll be out in my greenhouse later. I gotta catch up on my records. But if you want to come on out and talk? I feel like I'm going in circles on this. Maybe if the two of us tried to figure things out . . . Will you have time?"

"For you, my friend, I'd come anytime."

"Let's make it eight."

She left with a Very Special Pecan Pie in her hands.

When the front door of the shop closed behind Jessie, it opened again immediately, Rivervillians coming in to buy a pie or some pecan candy or a box of pecans: one after another: *"Need a pie for supper, Lindy." "Gotta pick up a jar of that Texas Caviar of Miss Amelia's." "Kids want some of the sandies."*

Another hour of one local after another. All, I suspected, there to show support, which made me feel good. And all telling me to give Miss Amelia their greetings. Nobody mentioned murder. These folks didn't need to.

I was closing out the cash register as the bell jingled again, making me want to groan. I'd just said good-bye to Eula Hawley and was feeling drained of my last bit of strength.

Hunter Austen, still in uniform, made his way hesitantly up the aisle as if he wasn't sure my greeting was going to be a warm one, or icy. He knew both moods well.

I chose a place between a pleased *"Happy to see ya"* and a frigid *"Yes? Can I help you?"*

"Hi, Hunter."

He nodded. "See they got you working here. All that college just to end up pushing nuts?"

His tone was light, but I wasn't in the mood to be teased by anyone, let alone by a cop investigating my grandmother.

"What's going on?" I finished with the register and slipped the folded moneybag in my purse for deposit later.

"Wanted to see how you were holding up."

I nodded. "Fine. Just fine. People been coming in all day to say how shocked they are that Sheriff Higsby suspects my meemaw of poisoning the parson."

Hunter took off his stiff deputy's hat that left a hat ring around his closely shaven head. He gave me an exasperated look. "You know darned well the sheriff's saying no such thing. If anybody's putting stuff like that around, it's somebody else. Sounds like an Ethelred Tomroy thing, you ask me."

"Ethelred was here this afternoon. Demanded to talk to Meemaw. Something about promising to go somewhere with her. Tried to head her off but there's no stopping Ethelred under full sail. She went right on out to the house. Meant to call and warn Meemaw, but I forgot. Anyway, Meemaw will get rid of her fast enough. But I'll tell you, Hunter, she *is* in a state. All this uproar about her poisoning the parson. Terrible."

"Then what we've got to do is get her busy finding what

happened there at the supper. She sure was a help when your uncle died. I'd like to get that mind of hers going again, sifting through things, coming up with what really happened at the fair. And to tell the truth—the way this one is going, we need all the help we can get."

He watched as I thought over what he was saying.

"She was going a mile a minute over at the sheriff's office," he said, coaxing.

"That's when she fell apart. Think it all sank in, that people could suspect she'd do a thing like that."

"What we've got is maybe one hundred and fifty people who were there in the Culinary Arts Building at the supper or during the judging. What we don't have is anybody who doesn't have high praise for the pastor. Got no motive . . ."

"Except a disgruntled old lady mad at losing a blue ribbon."

He went right on. "Got no way the poison was administered . . ."

"Except in a disgruntled old lady's Texas Caviar."

Now he sighed. "He could've eaten something right before coming to the judging. And then there's the possibility we've got a crazy person on our hands. Somebody who really wanted to kill a whole lot of people and just got the parson."

I thought awhile. "Did you find anybody in town buying ant poison? Or no—have to be ether or alcohol . . ."

"Don't need to look. We know what killed him. ME called a while ago. Spotted water hemlock. The root ground up and put into whatever it was the parson ate."

I leaned against the counter. "Hemlock? Like Socrates?"

Hunter spread his hands. "The homegrown kind."

"Spotted water hemlock, eh? Grows right here in the swamps along the Colorado. Plain old *Cicuta maculate*.

Cicutoxin—the stuff even wild hogs know to stay away from. Where the heck would the parson have gotten ahold of such a thing?"

I saw Hunter's face and felt a chill run up my back. He wasn't looking anything like normal.

"You've got something else to tell me, don't you?" I demanded. "They tested Meemaw's dishes. Is that it?"

He nodded slowly, pain—like lightning—written across his eyes.

"Well?"

"That first dish? The one the judges tasted? Traces of alum. Nothing else. No poison but somebody was out to sabotage her, for sure. Gotta take a look at that. The other one. The one Miss Amelia gave to the parson . . ."

"Oh, no," I moaned and waited for the worst.

Hunter nodded. "Loaded with ground spotted water hemlock root. Just enough to kill the man."

He kicked hard at the old wooden floor with one of his boots. "I'll be out to the ranch in the morning."

"Can't I do it? I mean, bring her in. Be easier on all of us."

"Sheriff said it would look like we're going easy . . ." Hunter looked sick to his stomach.

No sicker than I was feeling.

"I'm gonna warn her," I said.

"Wouldn't expect you to do any less." He turned to leave.

"And Hunter," I called after him. "You know I'm never going to forget this. What you're doing to my family. Anybody who goes after them is no friend of mine."

His face was blank, as if he didn't dare show a single emotion. I felt a little like that, too, wanting to hold everything in, and then wanting to scream at him not to ruin what we've got going between us—this new thing that felt a lot like . . . I don't know . . .

When he turned and walked away, it was like a part of me was with him, a part being ripped out of my body as the door closed.

Chapter Eleven

Jessie stuck her head in the door of my office just a little after eight. She had two bottles of beer in one hand and rattled them at me as she walked in and pulled a metal chair over to my desk, where I had been sitting for about an hour with record books open and unseen in front of me.

We hugged, as usual, with me holding on to my friend a little longer than was usual. I was feeling sorry for myself. I didn't usually indulge in self-pity, but tonight I was up to my ears in it with my work behind schedule; my grandma headed for prison—or worse, maybe to Huntsville, where they put bad folks to sleep; my love life over before it got a running start. All that and a few old and new complaints about me—too damned bullheaded; out to save the world when I couldn't even protect my grandmother; too dumb to see the guy right in front of my nose. I would have come up with a much longer list if Jessie hadn't shown up when she did.

"I stopped by your house but Miss Emma said Miss Amelia was in bed."

"She's been there since Ethelred left. I asked that woman not to come out but you know Ethelred. Takes a cannon-ball to stop her if she's on a mission."

"Been looking peaked lately. Ethelred, I mean. You notice? Maybe age catching up with her."

I shrugged, thinking I had a lot more important things to mull over. I took a long swig of beer, then settled back to enjoy a few minutes with my friend.

"Kind of sad, when you think about it," Jessie said. "For all that swagger of hers, she's got nobody but your meemaw. The rest of the people here in town don't care about her. All that 'old family' stuff, like it means a hill of beans when it comes down to getting through the day."

"So she came out and dropped her troubles on Meemaw's shoulders, like she always does. That woman doesn't have one thought about anybody but herself."

I pushed papers into their file folders, set them at the front edge of my desk, and finished off my beer in one long drink.

"What's up?" Jessie asked. "See you've got a lot on your mind. Not that the family troubles wouldn't be enough."

"I guess I dumped Hunter." I look up and felt the pain behind my eyes that comes before tears.

"Oh, no." She leaned across the desk and put her hand on mine. "What happened?"

"Hunter's coming in the morning to take Meemaw to the sheriff's."

Her dark eyes grew large. "Is he arresting her?"

"No. Just taking her in for questioning—again."

"You took her last time. Why the formality?"

"Sheriff said it wouldn't look good if they didn't follow

procedure and I guess his procedure is to send a deputy to bring in a suspect."

"She's a suspect?"

I nodded. "They found spotted water hemlock in the dish she brought out for the parson to taste."

Jessie couldn't find words for that bit of news.

"I know," I said. "Me, too. I've been practically speechless since Hunter told me."

"What was wrong with the first bowl? The judging bowl? If that one was poisoned, how come the judges didn't all fall over right then?"

"First bowl had alum in it. That only makes you pucker up. But what the hell, Jessie? Both of the bowls were tampered with. Sure looks like Meemaw's got an enemy."

She raised her eyebrows at me. "What do you figure's going on?"

"Maybe it's all of us—the Blanchards—they're after."

"Are you working with Hunter on this like you did before?"

I shook my head a little too hard. "Not anymore. That's for sure."

"What'd he do?"

I sniffed and nodded and swallowed—all the while trying to hide a misery attack coming on me.

"What kind of a friend is he? He's treating Meemaw like a criminal. For all I know, they'll be throwing her in jail. I just can't . . . I can't forgive him for turning on us like this."

"Not turning on you, Lindy. He's doing his job."

"But his job will destroy my family. I can't have anything to do with him. Not anymore." I took a swipe at my nose with the side of my hand.

Jessie leaned back in her chair and made a face at me.

"Why don't you just wait and see what happens before you go dumping him? He needs your help—you and Miss Amelia. And you need his."

"Meemaw is not doing a single thing to help herself. All she's doing is lying in bed. I'm getting mad at her, too. I can't do anything all by myself."

"All three of you need to find a way to get moving. You sure need Miss Amelia. That woman can figure out the answer to all this before the rest of you get your brains in gear. This is no time for her to be lying down on the job. And no time, either, for you to be dumping the man who's been your friend for twenty-eight years."

"I don't know what to believe anymore. I look one way—an old friend is trying to prove my grandmother's a killer. I look the other way—people who've known the Blanchards for years are snubbing us and talking behind our backs. It makes me mad. It makes me sad."

"Don't you think Hunter understands what you're going through? These aren't normal times. You two will go back the way you were when this is over."

"I don't know. Like mountains growing up between us. You know, things get said and then something else happens and the things said get worse."

"You want me to have a talk with Hunter?"

I gave her an exasperated look and shook my head. "It's not like explaining me skipping school to Miss Archwood in the eighth grade, Jessie. You just can't step in and make things right this time."

"Why not? Hunter knows me. He knows I wouldn't say a word about your business unless it was important. Lindy, you can't just kiss trees for the rest of your life."

I picked up a paper clip and flipped it at her.

"Okay, if I can't play cupid with Hunter, how about helping out at the Nut House this weekend?"

"Bethany's going to be there—like it or not. Too much time with Justin's friend and none of us like him. I think even Justin's getting tired of having him here. Justin's getting quiet and you know what happens when he gets quiet like he is."

She drained the last of her beer and stood up. "I've got to get on home but I'll keep my ears open. All this gossip, maybe somebody will say something that helps."

She came over and kissed me on the top of the head before leaving. "You let me know if I can do anything."

She put a hand under my chin and forced my head up. "And you stop this moping and get going. You say Miss Amelia's not trying to help herself, well, neither are you. Just think about what's happened. Somebody tried to ruin Miss Amelia's chances of winning that important blue ribbon. Well, I'd say nobody else would have put alum in her dish but Ethelred Tomroy. Better go have a heart-to-heart with her. Then think of this second dish—full of lethal poison. Could kill in . . . what? Half an hour? Nobody but the parson got it because it wasn't put on the main table where the winning dishes went. That was because it wasn't a winner—and who the heck could have predicted Miss Amelia's dish wouldn't win? Maybe the person who put the alum in the contest entry—so, Ethelred, but I don't have her pegged as a mass poisoner, do you?"

I shook my head—a little reluctantly since I'd like to blame Ethelred for everything.

"So, maybe whoever put the poison in her dish for the Winners' Supper had no idea she'd lose. Maybe they didn't care who they poisoned. Or—as long as I've been going to these fair events—it's always been a clergyman honored to be first in line at the buffet. Back to Reverend Jenkins as the target."

She was telling me things I already knew but hadn't put together due to my enormous case of feeling sorry for myself.

"Now get on back to the house. You've got a lot to do tomorrow. You ask me, Sheriff Higsby would be a lot better off setting Miss Amelia after the killer than taking up her time answering questions."

Jessie, like any good friend would, was giving me a verbal slap on the head while opening a solid path for me to follow. I was more grateful to Jessie than I could ever tell her. But we'd known each other so long, I figured she already knew.

Chapter Twelve

She wasn't sleeping when I tiptoed into Meemaw's prettily flowered, blue-and-white bedroom the next morning. I tapped her lightly on the shoulder and watched as a single tear crept from her tightly shut eyes, over the edge of her nose, to make a wet spot on her pillow.

"Meemaw." I tapped her again.

She sighed and finally opened her blurred eyes, brought her legs over the side of the bed, and sat up to look straight at me.

"Hunter here to get me?" she asked in a deadened voice.

"He's downstairs."

"I figured he'd be coming for me. Poison in my caviar, right? Only thing Millroy ate different from everybody else. Hunter arresting me?"

"No! Just wants to talk to you again."

She sighed and made a slow move to get up, searching over the side of the bed for her slippers and then waving me from the room. "Let me get dressed. Tell him I'll be right out. Oh, and call Ben. Say I need him there this time."

I headed for the door but she stopped me.

"Hunter tell you what kind of poison it was? You know I never bought a poison in my life. Not to kill ants or fleas or anything. So they sure can't blame me if it was arsenic or anything like that."

"Spotted water hemlock," I said.

"You mean that stuff we've got along the river? Well . . ."

I closed the door behind me.

When Miss Amelia came from her apartment into the kitchen, she was straightening the collar of her flowered blouse. She'd put on blue slacks and white huaraches. Her hair was neatly combed back from her face and her signature pink lipstick was drawn precisely over her lips. As pretty as she looked, her face was pale, her eyes sunken. I thought I'd never seen a woman quite so ready to walk her last mile.

Hunter got up quietly from his seat at the long table, stiff hat turning in his hands. He bowed his head as he wished her "Good morning."

Justin was leaning back against one of the tile counters, both hands behind him holding on tight. He glowered at Hunter. I knew my usually calm brother was having a hard time with this. Hunter was his lifelong friend, but none of this was about friendship anymore. It was about Blanchards fighting for Blanchards. I knew too well, in this kind of fight, we won or died like my uncle Amos did.

Bethany and Mama sat on the edge of their chairs. Their faces were stiff with worry. It looked and felt like the morning of a hanging.

Jeffrey Coulter stood off to one side, watching. When I glanced at him, wishing he'd go away, he gave me an unpleasant smile.

"Are you really going to pull my grandmother back into the station, Hunter?" Justin's voice was strained. He pulled away from the sink to stand as tall as his five feet ten would let him.

Mama piped up. "I called Ben, Mama. He'll meet you there. He said to promise you won't be there long. Said if the sheriff's not charging you, you're not staying."

"Why in hell are you doing this to her, Hunter?" Justin took a step toward his old friend. "You know this woman here never hurt a soul in her life."

"Wouldn't if I didn't have to, Justin." Hunter looked a little like the one in danger of being hung.

"Swear to God, Hunter. I never thought I'd want to kill you like I do right now." Justin made a move that died quickly, just fizzled out as his hands fell to his sides.

Jeffrey Coulter made a noise and shook his head.

"Please, Jeffrey," my soft-spoken sister said, her round blue eyes wide. "Don't you get involved."

Coulter shrugged his shoulders and stepped way back from the rest of us.

"Hunter's doing his job," Miss Amelia said. "You let him be."

She might have been sticking up for him, but when she turned, her eyes were defiant. "I know I'm the one with means and motive, Hunter. That's what people always say. Even my good friends will start to wonder: *Miss Amelia got mad over losing out to Ethelred Tomroy. Went ahead and diced up a good dose of hemlock and gave it to the parson 'cause he passed up her dish*. That's what they'll all be thinking after a while. Doesn't make it true."

She turned to me. "You coming with us, Lindy? No use keeping Ben and the sheriff waiting."

After hugging Justin and Bethany and Mama, and ignoring Jeffrey Coulter, we got out of the house.

None of what was happening seemed real, not Hunter's hand on top of Miss Amelia's head as she got into the back of his patrol car, and not joining her on the other side of the tight backseat with a metal grate between us and Hunter.

He sat in the front, not looking back. It was like one of those dreams where things are going wrong but your brain warns you how much worse it could still get.

At the sheriff's office, I wasn't allowed in the back with Meemaw. All I could do was sit in the outer room and wait for Ben, who came rushing in about ten minutes after we got there. "She in back?" he asked hurriedly.

I nodded.

"Hope she's not answering any questions. I'm getting her right out of here."

The hurried man in his rumpled tan suit, overstuffed briefcase at his side, went through the swinging gate and around to the back.

Ben was an old friend of Daddy's from the time when Ben first came to town. That was a few years before Daddy was murdered out in the pecan grove. Now Ben seemed like one of the family.

Within fifteen minutes they were all back out in the lobby.

"You through grilling Miss Amelia, Sheriff?" I shot an angry look at the man standing behind her.

"Not 'grilling' anybody, Lindy. You been watching too many cop shows."

"I'm just glad she didn't come out in stripes," I, still fuming at the sheriff and at Hunter, said between clenched lips.

Sheriff Higsby ignored my snit. "Need to talk to you,

too, Lindy. Want to hear if you've got any ideas about all of this. All I'm doing is looking for help here. You got anything . . ."

I looked around the nearly empty room and thought fast. Was there any way I could swing suspicion away from Meemaw? The kick in the butt I got from Jessie had already started my brain.

"What about that prize hog?" I asked. "Find out who let him loose to send everybody running out to watch him go."

He frowned at me, thinking hard.

"And there's talking to the deacons at the church. What about any problems the parson was having with anybody? You do that yet?"

He shook his head, beginning to look sheepish.

"I'd say it's somebody local—because of the spotted water hemlock—except it grows straight across the South."

The sheriff listened and I felt good. It was like doing something positive at last. The feeling even got to Miss Amelia, who put a finger in the air at one point, but I was on a roll.

"All the ladies brought in two bowls of their entries. One for judging. One for the Winners' Supper—in case they won a ribbon. So how would anyone know which one was going to the judges and which one was for later, for the supper?" I asked everyone in general.

"I can answer that one," Miss Amelia perked up.

"You're not supposed to say a word, Meemaw," I cautioned her.

"You be quiet, young lady. I'll take care of myself." She turned to the sheriff. "The judging dish was already out on the table by the time the hog got loose. The other one was all that was left in the cooler."

The sheriff thought awhile. "Then tell me this, how'd

he know you weren't going to win and be serving that other bowl to everybody?"

Miss Amelia snapped her mouth shut. We all knew what he was saying but it was too awful to think about: Maybe the killer didn't care.

The sheriff turned to Ben. "I talked to Dora. Asked if she knew what happened when Miss Amelia heaped that caviar on to her husband's plate and she said she doubted he even wanted any more since he didn't like it to begin with. Seemed odd to her, and Selma, too. That's what they told me. Figured I should tell you."

At that bit of treachery, I fell silent, until a new thought struck me.

"What about them? They were sitting on either side of the parson, only ones close enough to dose his plate. Why don't you change your questions, Sheriff? Ask them if they killed Millroy, then ask them what they've got against my grandmother."

The sheriff took too long to think. Miss Amelia lifted her head toward the door. She wanted out of there.

To our backs, the sheriff called out, "And about the Nut House, Miss Amelia. You'd better stay away from there for a while. Not that I'm scared you'd do something, mind you. Just that we don't know what's going on around here yet. I been kind of thinkin', maybe you're the target. Somebody doing this to scare folks away from your store and your baked goods. Seen worse things done when people got to be rivals."

She turned slowly, at her most regal now. "Just who do you imagine has got a store to rival the Nut House? I, for one, can't think of a single place." Miss Amelia moved out through the door. "You think of one, Sheriff?" she asked over her shoulder. "How about you, Hunter?"

Hunter, framed in the doorway behind us, shook his head.

"You're not thinking of Ethelred, are you? Woman's not as bad as people think. Just wanting a little glory. That's all." Out on the porch, she put a hand up, shielding her eyes from the sun.

"Hunter, you call Lindy you got any news, you hear me? Sooner rather than later. I get the feeling you two aren't talking much and that's just plain stupid at a time like this."

"Yes, ma'am," was all he said.

Since I was mad at her for interfering, I got a rough grip on Meemaw's arm, then let up as I felt a tremor go through her body. She promised Ben she'd be home that night if he wanted to come over and talk. I led her carefully down to the truck parked at the curb, and said nothing more until we were on our way out of town.

Chapter Thirteen

"Call that boy back," Miss Amelia said after a long and very quiet five minutes on the road.

"Which boy?" I had my eye on a white car traveling too close behind me. I tapped my brakes, warning him off my rear end. I took another look but couldn't see who was behind the wheel.

"Hunter."

"Huh? What do you mean 'Hunter'?"

"Just what I said. I want you to call him."

"And tell him what?"

"Tell him we're not going home yet. I want to see him over at The Squirrel. We've gotta talk. I'm starting to get the feeling he's the only one's able to help."

"I'm taking you home, Meemaw. Mama said to get you back to the ranch as soon as possible."

She sighed. "First we're going to The Squirrel. I didn't get any breakfast and I'm hungry. Then I'll go home. I'm going to Columbus with Ethelred this afternoon. Ben's coming over tonight. Got a full day ahead of me."

"For heaven's sakes, why are you going to Columbus with Ethelred?"

"Because I said I would."

"What? You going shopping at this particular moment in your life? Wait 'til I tell Mama."

She sat back and drew in one long, angry breath. "I guess you and Emma see me as nothing but a sad old lady who doesn't know what she's doing. I've been kind of feelin' like that lately. But not anymore. Looks to me like somebody set me up to take the blame for the man's death all along. I take that personally, Lindy. Very, very personally. Now, you call that boy. Tell him to meet us at The Squirrel soon as he can get there."

I sputtered for only a minute before swallowing my pride and calling Hunter.

The white car stayed behind me right up until I made my turn on to Carya Street. It hung back, even let a couple of cars pass, then it disappeared. No use saying anything to Meemaw. She would only turn around, gawk at him, and embarrass me.

What I was worrying about was the press. They'd be flooding into town soon enough, I figured. A poisoned pastor was great fodder for sales. Add to that a seventy-seven-year-old grandmother as the major suspect, and before we knew it, a wind of words would be blowing straight across Texas.

I pulled into The Squirrel's dirt lot and parked among a dozen or so other pickups. I checked behind me but the white car was nowhere to be seen.

"Hunter said he'd be along in half an hour or so," I reminded Meemaw as I checked my purse to see if I'd brought my wallet along. "Had some report to get in."

"Guess he was surprised to hear from you, the trouble you two seem to be having."

"Leastwise he's coming," I said, giving nothing else away.

"You know that boy would never turn on a Blanchard, if that's what's bothering you."

"Don't count on it." I blew away the idea and pushed my door open.

Hot morning. One of those days when the sun felt like it was sitting on top of my head. When the air felt like melting wax on my skin. Not that I didn't like it—better than cold winter days. Still, I hadn't had a shower that morning. I felt my clothes were molded to me by sweat. Not a good way to feel if I was going to see Hunter so soon—up close and personal.

Meemaw slid off the front seat on her side. "That boy's loyal and you know it." She raised her voice at me as I came around the back of the truck. "That boy's been crazy about you since he was running around with his diaper hanging half off."

"That was puppy love."

"You call it whatever you like, young lady. I know that special gleam in a man's eye when I see it. Think it's about time you started gleaming back a little."

I stopped just outside the door to the restaurant, pulled my jeans out of my backside, and thought over what she was saying. "Let me see if I'm getting this right. What you're saying is you want me to shamelessly use his feelings for me to get what we want out of him. That it?"

Her mouth flew open. Her eyes flew wide. "You think that about me, Lindy? Well, shame on you."

The restaurant was half empty. Ten of the people at the tables kept their faces turned away when we walked in. The other half waved and gave Meemaw a thumbs-up.

We settled down in a back booth with no one around us. Miss Amelia opened her purse and fiddled inside, taking out a piece of paper and a pen. "Think I'm gonna mark down a few names, Lindy," she said loud enough for all to hear. "Got a 'no pie' list going for folks turning on me like those you just saw."

She made a few notes but I could see they had nothing to do with a list of names.

"Meemaw." I leaned across, shaking my head at her, but liking that the old spirit was back. "You are turning into a vengeful person."

"Least I won't be a 'sittin' on death row' person." She sat back and smiled at one of the snubbers, who looked away fast.

Cecil Darling made his way toward us, hands thrown above his head, eyes rolled to heaven, a spout of specious pity about to pour from his flaccid lips.

"Whatever do you know? The mass murderer of Riverville here, gracing my fine dining establishment." There was a wicked gleam in Cecil's eye. "Whatever can I do for you ladies? Arsenic pudding? A little strychnine clotted cream? Or better yet . . ." He clapped his hands together and rolled his eyes heavenward. "The pièce de résistance, the dish to end all dishes . . . oh, excuse me . . . not end, but the equal of all other dishes. My very special cassoulet de cyanide."

He turned to bow to the appalled patrons, who looked furiously down at whatever they were eating.

"There." He leaned toward Miss Amelia, a happy gleam in his eye. "That will take care of them for you."

Miss Amelia looked up, surprised by the pompous little man. "You are a truly brave Englishman, Cecil. Churchill could have used you in the dark days of World War Two."

He beamed, smile spreading from ear to ear. We ordered the special of the day: bubble and squeak, though ordinarily we would never have ordered one of his fussy English dishes. Today was different. This was a day of firm liaisons and choosing up sides. Of eating scrambled-together leftovers while smiling and making polite conversation. Though the smiling did stop for a minute when Miss Amelia pulled something she thought was part of a turnip from her dish.

"Humph. If you call this fine dining, hot dogs and beans must be food for the gods," she whispered across the table at me.

Cecil, his movable face stretched into wonder, came back after the food was served to lounge beside our table again. "So the sheriff let you go, did he? What's this world coming to, I'd like to know? Dangerous characters let loose on the streets."

"Said he was coming for you, Cecil," I said, not able to stop myself. "People saying you've been poisoning them for years. And, you know, you're not from Texas. Everybody knows a foreigner's got to be the culprit."

Cecil gave us both a forced smile. "And how do you like my bubble and squeak?" He nodded toward our plates.

Miss Amelia pretended to taste a bit of it again. "Reminiscent of my own shepherd's pie. With the addition of bits of rubber."

He pretended to great hurt. "Next time try the bangers and mash. You'll love it. Just your kind of thing, I'd say. A cluster of dead sausages buried in a funeral pyre of potatoes."

"How did England ever let you go, Cecil?" Miss Amelia relaxed back in the booth and smiled at the fussy little man.

"And wasn't there something we could have done to stop it?" I added.

Before he could come up with a witty quip, waitresses from the Barking Coyote Saloon, probably soon heading into work, walked in with a few loud "look at me" laughs. They hurried over in a tumble of long legs, short skirts, and tall hair, to hug us and mew their sympathies.

"Not one person in this town thinks you had anything to do with this parson business," Suzy Queen huffed then leaned down close so that her bouncy breasts hung uncomfortably in front of Miss Amelia's face.

"Anybody give you trouble," she whispered near Miss Amelia's reddening ear, "we'll take care of 'em over to the Barking Coyote. Won't know what in the heck they're drinkin'."

Finula Prentiss grinned behind her, a kind of wolfish look I'd seen on her face before. Suzy Q was a fine person, but Finula Prentiss had never been a favorite of either one of us. Finula was in the business of what Meemaw called "kissing cowboys" or what I called "horizontal entertaining."

"That woman would turn on you fast as look at you," Meemaw always said.

I watched as Meemaw gave Finula one of her tight head nods, pulling back from the thick scent of musk.

Before sashaying away, Finula smiled wide down at me. "Think the two of you should come on in for some line dancing again. People still talkin' about that last time."

I agreed we should. I hadn't forgotten that last time either.

Miss Amelia, as stiff and tall as a pecan tree, gracefully holding the hand of Jefferson Foster, a grizzled old cowboy who never said a word to anyone and was never known to take to the dance floor before that night.

And me sitting there like a wallflower, praying to be asked to dance—something I usually detested—and not left there alone to sit out the "*Waltz Across Texas*."

The women toddled off to a table, passing Hunter as he made his way toward us.

"Glad I ate," Hunter said as he set his hat on the table then leaned down close looking over the remnants of food on my plate. "Grabbed a sandwich after you all left."

He smelled good. And looked good. And smiled good. And gave off heat that might have made me think of taking long naked swims in a Greek pool if I wasn't so self-conscious about what I was or wasn't feeling about him. I pushed over so he could move in beside me, well aware of the big gun on his hip. He clasped his hands together on the table and leaned his wide, blue back toward Meemaw.

I didn't want my grandmother noticing how red my face was so I frowned hard and leaned back with my arms crossed.

Hunter turned to look over at me. "We gonna be friends again?" He smiled wickedly and flashed those blue eyes at me.

At my still sour face, he asked, "Find a worm in your lunch?"

Sufficiently cooled off and scrubbing Greek pools from my head, I looked to Meemaw, who sat with one eyebrow lifted in my direction. I could hear words like "sad excuse for a female" going through her head.

"I guess I know well enough why you wanted to see me, Miss Amelia," Hunter started right in. "Trouble is, I might not be able to help, not without giving away information the sheriff wouldn't want me to hand out."

I made a small sound of disgust. Miss Amelia stopped me with a look. "Of course, Hunter, can't go givin' away the sheriff's case." She smiled big at Hunter. I could swear she was flirting.

"Hunter's been our friend for longer than he's been a deputy," I said as if he wasn't there next to me. "You'd think that would be more important—"

"Whoa, there." Hunter reared back. "You got something to ask, ask it. I said I'll do what I can. I think the two of you know that by now. What I can't do, I'll work my way around. Now, what's goin' on and where are you two thinking of heading with this? I know you well enough to know you're cooking up something."

"We all know I didn't poison the parson." Miss Amelia started in, fingers tapping lightly on the paper in front of her. "Let's start right there. The man is dead, so that means somebody else killed him. I've been goin' over everything in my head, and I think there're places we've got to start looking and places we don't know about that we have to uncover. You with me on this so far?"

Miss Amelia looked from me to Hunter.

"Here's what I'm thinking." Meemaw settled down into herself. "We know the poison, thanks to the sheriff and Hunter here. Easy to get spotted water hemlock just about anywhere in Texas. Thing is, first, you've got to know what it looks like, second, how much it would take to kill a man, and third, how to get it into the victim."

"All of that's pretty easy. Not a single family in Texas hasn't heard of a steer or horse or even a dog dead from chewing on hemlock," Hunter said.

"Okay, so we've got that nailed down. Could be anybody in Riverville . . ."

"Or outside Riverville," I put in. "The Jenkinses have only been here about eight months. Who knows what they left behind in Tupelo? Parsons have been kicked out of churches for a lot of reasons and those reasons not reported to their next parish. Boards just glad to pass problems on to somebody else. I think that's what you've got to look into, Hunter."

"Already been in touch with the police there in Tupelo," Hunter said. "They're checking on it for me. The officer I spoke to said he'd never heard a bad word against the pastor. But we'll see what he comes up with."

"Never struck me as the kind of man to leave grudge holders behind him." Miss Amelia frowned. "Still, somebody's got to talk to Dora and Selma. Maybe after the funeral. I hate to even think about it—the two of them in mourning, and mad at me. But this can't wait."

"You going to the funeral in the morning?" Hunter asked.

"I'm going," I said, all set and determined.

"Don't think I should," Miss Amelia said. "Sad . . . but."

"Yes, you're going. With me. Nobody in this family's done anything to be ashamed of. We're going. And that's that."

"I'll be glad to be there with you, too, Miss Amelia," Hunter offered. "I don't think there's any reason in the world you shouldn't go."

She looked across the table at him and seemed pleased.

"In fact, I think all the Blanchards should be there," I said. "Been through worse."

Miss Amelia nodded. "Still, I can't be the one to go talking to Selma. And sure not to Dora. Poor thing."

"Why don't you leave that to me and Lindy?" Hunter put in. "The sheriff's been thinking the same thing since you mentioned it. Just holding off out of respect. Talked to 'em both once but they weren't in any shape to say much beyond how you forced the parson to eat a whole lot of your caviar. Just mad at everything and everybody, I'd say. Looking for somebody to blame. Maybe, with a few days past, they'll think different."

"That takes care of the past and the present." Miss Amelia ticked off an item she'd scribbled on her paper. "Now, let's talk about the recent past. What's been going on in the church? How the pastor's been acting—anything different? Probably talk to a few church members to begin with. Maybe even the whole church board. Start with Hawley Harvey and move on to Elder Perkins. Those two think they're the movers and the shakers around here, let them come up with something."

"Hunter and I can talk to both of them," I offered. "Anything else?"

"What am I missing here, Hunter?" Miss Amelia asked. "I know you don't want to say what the sheriff's doing that's different, but if you've got any ideas, or any information that can help us, why, I just hope you'll trust me enough to share."

Hunter put one of his large hands on top of Miss Amelia's. He nodded stiffly a time or two. "Nobody's after you, Miss Amelia. The sheriff—everybody—knows you didn't have anything to do with this. I'll have a talk with him but I don't think he'd be unhappy in the least to know I'm working with you. What I said before, that was just in case there was something he wanted kept secret. You understand—it's my job."

"I thank you for your confidence," Miss Amelia said in return, the two of them into a kind of friendly formality that made the hair on the back of my neck stand on end.

"One more thing. That hog. Who was around his pen about that time? And who was in the kitchen around then?"

He nodded. "Talked to people in charge of the kitchen. Nobody could say who was around, or when. Everybody ran when the yelling started, is what people told me. I'll get right on that hog pen, see who was watching the pens and if anybody remembers somebody there who shouldn't have been."

We all hushed when Cecil Darling came back holding out a dessert tray filled with dishes of a colorless pudding studded with tired raisins and drizzled with a bland-looking sauce.

"My prizewinning spotted dick," he crowed, pushing his tray under our noses.

As one, we threw up our hands, warding off the lethal-looking dessert.

On the way out, Meemaw leaned toward me to whisper in a smug voice, "Only honorable mention."

Chapter Fourteen

When all us Blanchards filed in through the wide-open doors of the Rushing to Calvary Independent Church, the entire congregation turned to stare. Miss Amelia led the way, head high, eyes pinned straight up to where Hawley Harvey stood in front of the white, cloth-covered casket, waiting to deliver the eulogy after Elder Perkins led the congregation in scripture and prayer and a short sermon. That Hawley Harvey's face paled when he saw us and drew up into a look of disdain or even scorn didn't make my heart slow down any. There were evidently people here who'd already judged Miss Amelia, or maybe the whole family, and we would have to meet them head-on.

Behind Miss Amelia came Mama, cheeks burning but ready to fight anybody saying one nasty word to Meemaw. Bethany followed Mama, a butterfly barrette holding back one side of her bright hair, making it curl around her cheek.

I wore my best mauve, go-to-meeting summer dress—no

black in this church because Rushing to Calvary celebrated
death as the beginning of a trip to live with God. Nothing to
be sad about. Behind me came Justin, looking like Justin
always looked only his jeans were pressed. Jeffrey was last,
dressed to kill in a white summer suit with pale blue shirt
and tie. Everyone, including Justin, had tried to talk Jeffrey
out of attending since he never met the man and knew few
people in Riverville, but he'd insisted that our fight was his
fight, and as a guest of the family, he must be there to support us.

We sat next to each other, one long row of Blanchards in
a pew near the back. Not one of us bowed our head, only
looked straight forward, meeting every shocked stare from
a judgmental congregant who thought we had no business
being there. We gave back smiles to those who smiled, and
nodded. Though we were a row of impenitent penitents, I
had the awful feeling of being a stranger in my hometown.

Back at the ranch we'd all agreed that though Miss
Amelia might be gossiped about, we were going to show
faith and solidarity by staying at her side throughout the
whole thing. No going off to talk to friends, which made
Jeffrey throw back his head and laugh. "Since I have no
friends in your quaint little town, I'll be the first to pledge
my allegiance to your poor grandmother."

We hadn't exactly cringed, but there'd been strained
smiles and, later, whispered wishes he'd go back to New
York.

Justin still had his cowboy hat clamped to his head so I
nudged him with my elbow. He was out in the groves with
other men so much of the time I couldn't help but wonder if
Justin was going wild, like one of the hogs down by the river.

"Sorry," he muttered, just then realizing he was sitting
in a church. He snatched the hat from his head.

I looked at the backs of people's heads—all people I knew. I didn't go to church here, hadn't gone anywhere in a while, but I'd brought Miss Amelia to services many Sundays and picked her up afterward for a dinner at the Ninnie Baird Hotel, where Mrs. Baird's breads and pies were still served at tables lined along the wide front porch. It was one of our rituals, like our Friday nights at The Squirrel.

I did like Pastor Albertson, the old pastor, who left the year before with not even a going-away party thrown for him. One day there. The next just gone. People wondered, I remembered. Some, I heard, were a little hurt and a bit angry with the man.

And I had liked Pastor Jenkins when Miss Amelia introduced us on the front steps of the church. He was one of those earnest men who mostly took a single, straight-arrow path through life, the kind of good man who could make me start examining the way I lived, looking for deficiencies, which was another good reason to stay away from church.

And I liked what Miss Amelia told me about the new man's preaching style—no wildly stomping around with a mike stuck in his ear, thundering fire and brimstone out over the people. "Good man," Miss Amelia said often from the moment the pastor and his wife and sister-in-law came to town. "Knows his Bible and doesn't act like the rest of us don't know a damn thing."

The service began as soon as we were settled. Elder Perkins, a tall man with a large belly, adjusted his lapel mike and looked out over the crowd. Tyler Perkins had eyes buried in folds, like an old cowboy, except he'd never ridden the range, that I knew of, nor ever rode a horse. Above a collar straining at the top button, his face was going bright pink. On his head a shock of surprising and unruly bright red hair rose straight up.

Elder Perkins smiled down at his wife, Joslyn, president of the Women's Church Committee, then out at the congregation.

First we sang a doleful hymn, then we prayed, then came a resounding sermon about the evils rampant upon the earth—which I tuned out on—and then a couple more songs from the choir with Finula Prentiss in good voice, especially on her deep and rolling "Ah—mens."

When Deacon Hawley Harvey got up to give the eulogy, the congregation, as one, settled way back in our seats, knowing the way to the cemetery was going to be a long and tortuous one.

Hawley Harvey was known as a talker, someone of many words and many roads to where he wanted to go. President of the church board, he could drive meetings way into the night, with most of the board members coming out without a clue what he'd been talking about to begin with.

But Rivervillians are mostly kind people. We all sat quietly while Hawley, in his brown seersucker suit with sweat rings under his arms, shoe black hair brushed tight to his round head and sprayed in place, rambled on about the pastor, about the church, and about God's strange messages delivered in strange ways.

I looked at my watch. Half an hour the man had been at it. Going over and over the pastor's kind ways, how he'd folded his arms around the congregation the moment he came to town, and how there'd been no dissention among them since the Reverend Jenkins had pulled the reins of leadership into his strong and capable hands.

From time to time there was a muffled sob from down front, where Dora and Selma sat. Mostly there were sighs, as Hawley droned on and on.

The church was hot. Too many warm bodies in too

close a space. I could feel my head lighten, and feared I might topple over.

Another reason I didn't go to church anymore: The church ladies of Riverville saved their heaviest and most flowery perfumes for Sunday services and funerals. And the men—a good slap or two of cologne before heading out. Then the ushers shut the doors to the church and let them all stew in one thick potpourri until, more than once, back when I was a kid, I'd gotten light-headed and stumbled out into the fresh air and sunshine, falling to the grass to get my equilibrium back.

I looked behind me when I heard the door open. All I saw was that it wasn't Hunter, who hadn't showed as he'd promised. I felt a slight shiver of anger then pushed it out of my mind.

Hawley was going into the second half hour of his eulogy, beginning to rock back and forth on his high-heeled boots. I didn't think I could take much more. He'd gone way beyond listing the qualities of Pastor Millroy Jenkins, all the way into upcoming plans for the new addition to the church and how the church was prospering. Forgetting where he was and what he was doing there, he even laughed out loud a time or two—thanking God for a bull market that was bringing them all such great prosperity.

He went on to talk about the upcoming ground breaking, inviting everyone—"If you invested in the church or not"—to come and be a part of the glorious celebration.

I was about to nudge Justin to move his knees aside and let me out, when Morton Grover, saloon owner and also on the church board, rose from his seat in a front pew, where he'd been sitting next to Dora and Selma, to go up and stand quietly beside Hawley, his head down, hands folded in front of him. I figured the poor guy had to get back to

the Barking Coyote and was out of patience with the gar-
rulous Hawley.

Hawley glanced at the man now standing next to him
and looked perplexed, as if he didn't have a clue what he
wanted. He kept right on talking and carrying on until he
finally pulled in a long breath and Morton stepped right
into the momentary quiet to invite everybody out to the
cemetery for the interment, then back to the church for a
luncheon afterward, provided by the church ladies. Hawley's mouth dropped open, obviously having more to say
on the subject of church improvements and their burgeoning coffers. The pallbearers were out of their seats as if a
gun had gone off. The people followed, standing at attention as the casket was rolled out the doors and into the
hearse, which then drove the pastor around to the back of
the church acreage, where tombstones lined over two acres
of flat and sandy ground.

My family linked arms and walked, instead of drove,
out to where the casket was set over a yawning hole in the
earth. There were more words said, this time only by Elder
Perkins. Everyone was directed to file by the casket for
their last good-bye, and then back to the church for the
delicious repast the ladies had been working on since the
pastor died.

Chapter Fifteen

After the ceremonies, the family stood outside the church as Miss Amelia and Miss Emma argued over going in for the luncheon.

"Now Mama." Miss Emma leaned close to murmur. "I've got a lot of work to get to. Orders coming in from everywhere. That Giacomo, in Italy, is threatening to take his business to another farm if I don't lower my price. You know how it is this time of year, everybody wanting to lock in prices and all the wrangling that goes on. I don't have another hour to stand around talking and eating."

Miss Amelia narrowed her eyes at her daughter, who had the good grace to look away.

"I know. I know, Mama. I won't be showing respect . . . but hell's bells, I've been here all morning—with Hawley going on and on the way he did. I've truly got to get back to the ranch. Not like anybody else is going to do my job for me."

"Me, too, Meemaw." Justin, big dark cowboy hat clamped firmly back in place, stepped up. "Got the men cutting brush down by the river. I've gotta get back." He wandered off as if already making his way home.

"And I've got a couple from Sheridan comin' out this afternoon to look us over before they book their wedding." Bethany stuck her head into the center of the group and added her two cents. "I have to get home. And anyway . . ." She stopped to glance around to where people were giving the family a wide berth, and then to where Jeffrey stood off to one side, talking earnestly with Hawley Harvey. "Poor Jeffrey would like to get going. He doesn't know a soul here."

"Seems he's met Hawley Harvey," I pointed out as the two men stood engrossed in deep conversation. "Probably trying to talk Hawley out of church property for that mall his daddy wants to build."

Bethany blew off my meanness and waved a hand in Jeffrey's direction as if it was some cute trick he was doing, meeting the locals.

"What Jeffrey wants doesn't mean a hill of beans, Bethany," Mama hissed at the back of Bethany's head. "I don't like you hanging around that boy the way you do. I'm about ready to show him the door. Last thing we need right now is somebody staying at the house while all this is going on. Tell you the truth, young lady, I'm getting the feeling even Justin is ready for his old college buddy to say adios."

Bethany turned and clenched her jaw. "I'm old enough to know who I want to be with and who I don't want to be with, Mama. There's nothing wrong with Jeffrey but being from New York City. You chase him away and I'll just go visit him there. See if you like that any better."

Mama pulled in a long breath and held it as if she was going to blow Bethany clear back to the ranch. Looking around, as people turned our way, she let out that breath, nodded to a few of the folks, and left. The way she held herself as she hurried along the path, I knew somebody was going to catch hell back at home.

Out of the corner of my eye, I caught sight of Freda Cromwell, town gossip, scuttling by without as much as a "Morning." I had to laugh. One good thing to come out of all of this: Freda Cromwell was snubbing the murdering, battling Blanchards.

So it was just me and Meemaw at the lunch. Surrounded by the Chaunceys. Miranda wore a slightly newer version of her old pants, shirt, jacket, and boots. Melody was dressed in a fancy dress complete with fringe. Her hair had been curled by what looked to be a very hot iron—it lay in tight sausages around her head. Ethelred had attached herself to Meemaw and sat craning her neck around to see who was looking.

For me, the only other good thing about being there for the platters of cold cuts and cheeses and the rows of creamy casseroles and baked beans and pot after pot of chili was when Hunter finally came in. He walked right up to where Miss Amelia and the rest of us sat at one of the tables. He tipped his hat, nodded, then took a place beside me.

"Sorry," he leaned in to whisper close to my ear, warm breath moving my hair, tickling my face. "I took a chance, going over there to the fairgrounds. I wanted to take a look around again. Hog pens still up. Talked to Milo Froymann, superintendent there, and a couple of other men."

"Anything?"

"One told me those pens were all the same. Had to be either left open without thinking, you know how occupied people get during Ag Fair. Or, they said, the latch could've been pulled back on purpose and left for the hog to find his way out."

"So anybody could've done it."

He nodded, then whispered, "They said lots of people were back there. Open to the public. Judging was all over. Nothing but folks coming through to talk to the ranchers or groups of kids coming through with 4H and summer school groups. Said there was a big group from the parson's church came through just before the hog got out but he didn't remember anybody hanging around or looking suspicious."

"You talk to Selma yet?" I asked, thinking of the woman and not wanting much to disturb her. "I can see there's no way I'm going to get to talk to her today, let alone poor Dora."

I looked around for Miss Amelia and found her surrounded by neighbors and town folk. Evidently people were very seriously choosing up sides. More than half of them came over to hug Miss Amelia and say how sorry they were she got caught in the middle of all this. The other half stood around with their plates of beans and made muttered comments, mouths too full to make much noise.

Somebody's Chanel No. 5 was making my eyes tear up. I took Hunter by the hand and led him back outside.

"I've been thinking, too," I said when we were halfway up the path toward Selma's garden. "Whoever hired Pastor Jenkins might just know a little bit more about him. Would that be Hawley? Maybe the board? Meemaw said sometimes a pastor comes to a new church with a little bit of baggage. Could be the case here."

"What I heard," he said, "is Selma was always saying how happy he was where they used to be, over there in Tupelo."

"Heard her say that, too. Right when I first met them. Heard her say how good Dora and Millroy are to her. She owes them a lot so you've got to remember, she might be one to color the truth a little out of gratitude."

I thought awhile. "But that's another thing we have to look into. What happened to Selma? I think somebody was saying she used to teach. What went wrong, she's so dependent now? When did she hurt her leg? We can't overlook a single thing, can we, Hunter? I mean, I'm not planning on packing Meemaw's bag for Huntsville anytime soon." I smiled but I meant every word I said. Nobody. Nothing would stand in the way of getting the truth about what happened at the fair.

"I'll drop Meemaw over at the Nut House and meet you back here. Don't you think we better talk to some of the elders?"

"Sheriff did already. But it won't hurt to ask a few more questions. I'll be here when you get back. They should be around when this is over. We'll figure out what to do about Dora and Selma later."

I agreed because nothing else was coming to me at the moment.

Chapter Sixteen

With everyone gone, the church was empty but still stuffy. Old colognes hung in the air like ghosts of dead flowers, still tickling my nose. Dust motes swam in long rays of sun coming through the narrow side windows. Hunter and I shut the big door quietly behind us. Churches always seemed strange to me when they were empty of people, as if they weren't really churches except on Sundays. I thought it was like a funeral home without a funeral going on. Or a department store at closing time, when everything changed and silence reigned.

We walked quietly up the aisle and across to the door leading back to the offices.

Neither of us had been able to reach Deacon Harvey or Tyler Perkins, president of the church board. All we'd gotten was their voicemail or a long ringing at the church. It was taking a chance, coming without an appointment with either man, but one we had to take.

The business of running the church fell to the board and a host of deacons and trustees. Hawley Harvey and Tyler Perkins, who owned the Perkins Pharmacy in town, were both known to spend a lot of time in their church offices.

In a long, carpeted hall, with closed doors running down each side, we ran into Tyler Perkins coming out of the bathroom, red hair slicked down, comb rows and gel making perfect lines up and over his head. The look he gave us was startled. He was deep in thought when he stepped into the hall, zipping up, and almost running into Hunter.

"Well, you two sure know how to surprise a man," was his first, terse remark.

"Tried to call you, Mr. Perkins," Hunter began.

"Tyler. Call me like everybody else, boy."

"Well, what I was trying to say was that me and Lindy here called and couldn't get you. We need to sit down and have a talk about Pastor Jenkins. Lindy's here representing her grandmother—since the woman's been dragged into all of this. I'm here officially, I'm sorry to say. Could we go back to your office, do you think?"

"Told all I know to the sheriff." Tyler Perkins frowned heavily at Hunter and then at me. "But I suppose so. I'll give you another few minutes." He was giving us that "got work to do—I'm very aggrieved" look self-important men love to give.

"Really busy." There was a little laugh with it. "Got more work than ever, what with the ground breaking coming up. No pastor. Now we got to find us a new one. Takes a lot of work, checking them out. I'm supposed to be over to the pharmacy right this minute. Quite a call on a man's time, you know. Taking care of the people of Riverville. Bodies and souls, you might say. But if the two of you have

to talk right now, then let's go on back and get it over with."
All this was followed by the big sigh I was expecting.

Hunter and I perched at the edges of the plush chairs
Tyler directed us to. He sat behind his wide, polished desk,
hands folded, back straight, eyebrows up.

"Well now, how can I help the pair of you?"

"What we need to know is if there was, or still is, any
ongoing problem here at the church. Anything the pastor
was worried about? Any clashes he had with parishioners?"

He thought awhile, then leaned his head back to exam-
ine the ceiling.

"Nothing I was aware of. 'Course, the board sometimes
didn't see eye to eye with the pastor. Boards don't, you see.
That's what a board is for. The pastor was big on handing
out money to people in need, and the board's big on protecting our resources. Especially now, with the ground
breaking and the money going to increase the size of the
church. We're doing very well. Investments paying off in a
big way, but still you can't foresee what we'll run into. You
gotta plan." He smiled at Hunter. "You gotta plan or be left
behind."

He grinned over at me. "Sometimes you ladies, well,
you get to thinking more about curtains and dishes than
bricks and mortar. That causes problems, time to time."

His chuckle made prickles of anger run up and down
my back. I kept my lips tightly sealed. My thoughts about
Tyler Perkins were dark and growing darker. Words like
"condescending creep" ran through my head, but I was
used to that mentality, had dealt with it before. Even in college there'd been a couple of professors and male students
who'd looked down at me and acted as if degrees in horticulture and bioengineering had to be place holders until a
good marriage prospect came along.

"Was there anything in particular the board and Pastor Jenkins didn't see eye to eye on?"

"Nothing I know of, and I am the president of the board, you know. Nothing much gets past me. Maybe Hawley Harvey's heard something." He checked his watch. "Should be in any minute now. I'll turn you over to him soon as he gets here."

"So nobody ever had a falling-out with the pastor? Nobody angry, maybe dropping out of the church?"

Perkins took his time before shaking his head. "Couple of grumbles here and there."

"Who from?" Hunter urged. "At this point, anything could be important."

He thought awhile longer. "Tim Rogers, as I recall. That blew over. The man's getting on, ya know. Can't come up with another thing. You know the pastor'd only been here for eight months. Not long enough"—he chuckled and shook his head—"to make a lot of folks mad. Well, except your grandmother had a beef about the air-conditioning in the church on Sundays. Kept saying she was freezing."

He gave me a sheepish look.

I sat forward, prying my lips apart. "What about Pastor Albertson? Can you tell me why he was let go?"

"Retired." Tyler Perkins turned cooling eyes on me. "Are you suggesting something different, young lady?"

"Just asking," I came back at him.

"Retired, the way I said."

"And he had to get out of here so fast there was no time for the church to give him a party? People were hurt at the time, you know. They liked the man and thought he turned his back on them."

"Your grandmother complaining about that, too?" He let his eyes close and his head sink back. He pulled in a long breath. "If only these people would let us run the church and keep out of church business. We got us a very hard job here—so many people wanting to have a say without wanting to do the work. Happens everywhere. But the women especially. People like your grandmother, always coming around and asking questions . . ."

With my face warming and my spine turning to steel, I had to take a deep breath before I dared speak to the man. Hunter, maybe sensing what could be a coming explosion, turned around to give me a narrow-eyed look of warning.

"My grandmother," I began between firmly clamped teeth, "could probably run this church, the Nut House, and the whole Rancho en el Colorado, if she wanted to. I don't like you referring to her as 'these people,' Mr. Perkins." I emphasized the "these people."

Tyler looked immediately contrite. He sat up straight in his chair. "I'm just a little on edge here, Lindy. What with the awful business of the pastor dying and all. Truly sorry. Nothing meant against Miss Amelia. A fine woman. Fine woman."

"Am I disturbing anything?" Hawley Harvey stuck his round face in the door and smiled at everyone. "Anything I can help you with?"

Hunter stood to shake hands with the man, who stepped in behind our chairs.

"These two would like a word with you, Hawley. If you got a minute, that is." Tyler Perkins looked relieved to pass us on to Hawley. I remembered how he'd look at us in church and happily thought this wasn't a happy minute for him.

"Sure thing. Always got a minute for our fine neighbors." He sucked it up and smiled.

"It's about the pastor's death."

Hawley nodded and changed his face from one of greeting

to one of sorrow. He pulled back toward the door. "Still can't believe it. Can't imagine who'd do a thing like that. Probably some freak accident."

"Hunter and Lindy have got some questions to ask. I been doing the best I can about the day-to-day workings of the church. I was just telling them, maybe you heard something I didn't hear. I mean . . ." Here Tyler gave a soft chuckle. "Finances—well, you're the one bringing in the funds. Church business, I'd say that's my area."

Hawley frowned at Tyler then readjusted his face back to "welcome." "You two come on down to my office whenever you're ready. I'll do my best to help you out."

I stood, ready to go, but Hunter had a couple more questions to ask, about procedures and a list of weddings and funerals the pastor had officiated at since coming to the church. For good measure he asked for Pastor Albertson's phone number and where he was, but Tyler Perkins claimed not to know either one.

Down in his larger and more sumptuously decorated office, Hawley Harvey had little to add. No problems other than the wrangling over the size of the addition and some big plans for the church some of the board members thought were a little too much—like day care for women who worked and a plan to take in the homeless when one of our big storms was coming.

"Already wrangling over all that room in the addition. Especially the ones who were against it to begin with." He leaned back and grinned. "Then there are the others. All they were looking at was the big messes we'd have in the meeting room and who was going to clean it up? What I told the pastor was, wait a while. Let 'em get used to the idea. We're planning to make this church even bigger one day. One of those megachurches. Then we can do the

Lord's wonders, right here in Riverville. Wonders for the church and for the people in the church." He beamed a big smile at us.

As to the reasons behind Pastor Albertson's dismissal, he, too, said, "Retirement. That's all."

"Happened awfully fast," I said, sensing a small hesitation before the man answered.

He shrugged. "You've got to understand, Lindy. Down at its heart a church is like all businesses. Sometimes things are done for the good of the whole. I'll tell you this much—Pastor Albertson wasn't as progressive as Tyler, and some of the others felt that's what we needed in our main man. When he was asked whether he could go along with the changes, he only said it was time for him to retire. That's the all of it. Simple as can be."

"You were on the committee that hired Pastor Jenkins?" Hunter asked.

He nodded. "Four of us took on the job."

"Nothing in his record from back in Tupelo gave you any pause?"

He thought, then shook his head. "Nothing but glowing references."

"What about when he lived back in Atlanta before that?"

"Not a single thing."

"Anything in his wife's background or his sister-in-law's?"

"Nothing. Of course, we didn't take a look at Selma. Poor woman. Couldn't imagine her having some deep, dark secret or anything."

We shook hands on leaving. Hawley told us, sincerely, to come back anytime. He'd help out the best he could.

On the way out of the church, I decided I didn't want to go back to the Nut House or out to my greenhouse yet. I was too mad and revved up to do something, anything, to take some good news back to Miss Amelia.

"Let's go out to the fairgrounds. I want to take a look at those hog pens. I keep thinking—whoever let that hog out has to be the poisoner. If we can find somebody who saw the latch being opened on purpose . . ."

"Did that already."

"I know, but I've got a couple of ideas and I just want to keep moving right now."

"Lindy." Hunter stopped to give me a warm look. "I know you're mad because of what Tyler Perkins was saying. But the man's not thinking. Imagine—their pastor poisoned. Now the church has no leader, and they've got this big ground breaking coming up."

"He was thinking straight enough to insult my grandmother." I hurried down the walk ahead of Hunter. "Let's get out to the barns at the fairgrounds and see who's around. I need to blow off steam and maybe somebody will be there you didn't get to talk to."

"What about Dora and Selma?"

"Tomorrow. Won't be so many people at the house by then."

I kept going but Hunter put his hand on my arm, turning me to look at him. "Are we okay?" He was dead serious, almost choking on the words. He'd colored to a high red, running up into his hair. I would have felt sorry for him if I wasn't so mad at everybody about then.

I gave him a kind of nod. Said, "Same as always, Hunter." Then I moved right on, in one way kicking myself for not saying some of the things I was really feeling. In another way not wanting to complicate my life any more than it was right then.

"Think that Milo you talked to will still be there?"

"Might be. Or some others."

"Good. I want to talk to somebody who knows what went on last Sunday. Especially about the church group that went through. Seems awful neat—the church people going through and then the hog getting loose."

"Not a bad idea," he said.

And not a bad compliment, as compliments go. My brain was cooking. Me and Hunter were back to being friends. If it weren't for that business of somebody poisoning the minister, why, I'd have been really pleased with myself.

Chapter Seventeen

Milo Froymann turned out to be an old bowlegged cowboy with a big hat and a mean squint when he looked up at us, an inch of cigarette hanging out of the corner of his mouth. We found him loading the last of the steel pens on the back of his pickup.

The gigantic barn smelled of hay and manure. It echoed with metal bangs and muffled voices and, once in a while, loud laughter.

Hunter introduced me to the man, who touched the rim of his hat in greeting.

"We're here looking into what happened at the Winners' Supper," I explained.

The man screwed his craggy face into a grimace. "Terrible thing. Told the deputy here all I knew."

"What I was thinking about," I started to say, "was who was around when the hog got loose."

"Me, too. Wondering about it." Milo Froymann pulled at his bottom lip and looked at the floor to think awhile.

When he looked back up, he gave me a long stare. "So yer a Blanchard. Yer grandma's the lady from the Nut House, ain't she? Fine woman. No cook like her in the county. But I did hear, too, what some people are saying and I want you to know that Miss Amelia never put no poison in that pastor's food. I know people. I'll swear to it, you want me to come to court for you."

Hunter stepped up, explaining that he was the one who lassoed the hog and we were wondering how it got loose in the first place. "I know I asked you about this before, Milo. But you ever hear of a hog getting loose during the fair before?"

Milo took a long time thinking and scratching at the back of his head. "Well, tell ya, it don't happen often, but once in a while one of those hogs gets it in his head to take off, looking for home. Sometimes it's kids who raised these big boys and they get excited when they're here and leave the latch undone. Had it happen with a couple of sheep a few years back—but those animals was easy to herd right back into their pen."

He leaned against the truck behind him and eyed Hunter. "Kind of funny, though. Everybody yelling and that hog running like a devil with his pants on fire. Took a big guy like you, with a rope, to bring him down. Heard you gave him a good ride."

He chuckled and Hunter's chest went out.

"Anyway, only thing I can tell you is somebody got careless and left that latch up."

"But wouldn't somebody notice before the animal's out running the midway?"

Milo took even longer to think this time. "Lots of people were going through looking at the livestock that morning.

Seemed that whole church the pastor belonged to came in all at once. Place filled up with them laughing and looking and talking. Still, people around or not, somebody wants to lift a latch on purpose—and that's what I think yer gettin' at—wouldn't be hard. As superintendent, I try to keep the crowd under control, if we can work it. But sometimes . . . well, we asked those church people to come in a little later than they did and here they all come in a big crowd an hour before they was supposed to. I was going to give them a kind of grand tour, being church folks and all. Marti Floyd set it up. I was all ready but then they come in when I was busy doing something else. You know, when you got the fair going on, you're busy as a cat in a room full of rockers. I wasn't too pleased with them, I'll tell you."

"Who'd you deal with at the church?" I asked.

"Don't remember right off. Ask Marti. Surprised to have them show up so early."

"Think I could talk to Marti Floyd?"

"Have to call him at home. His job is done here for this year."

"Any strangers you see around that morning?" Hunter went on.

"Now, son, the fair's for people from the whole county. Come to that, the whole world. They want to come take a look at our livestock. I couldn't tell you if one stranger or five hundred came through that day. I had my hands full as it was, with the judging and people with their noses out of joint 'cause their hog or heifer didn't do so well."

His eyes flew open as that cigarette end burned down to his lips. He spit it out pretty fast and rubbed a gnarled finger over the place where he'd been burned.

Squint deeper than before, he told us, "Nope. One day in the year I wouldn't know a stranger if I fell over 'im."

Maybe I could have dragged the conversation out for another half hour or so, and learned something important, but my phone rang.

It was Miss Amelia, half whispering into the phone.

"You'd better get back to the Nut House, Lindy."

"You're not supposed to be there."

"Just got here. I'm not cooking or baking. You can tell the sheriff that. I'm a woman with a business and I'm gonna look after that business, no matter what anybody says."

"So why do I have to get over there?"

"Selma Rickles just called me. She's coming to talk to us. Just you and me, she said. But you can't say anything to anybody. If you ask me, something's spooked Selma. I've never heard anybody so nervous."

"I'll be there." I checked my watch. "Five o'clock okay?"

"Should be about right. Then I'll tell you what Deacon Owen Martin was saying to Ethelred this morning. Seems he's got worries of his own, with no pastor at the church and everybody trying to run things."

"Did you go to Columbus with Ethelred?"

"Yes, I did."

"Have a good time shopping while the rest of us are out hunting for a killer?"

There was one of her long pauses. "Someday your smart mouth's going to get you in big trouble, young lady. You mind your business, and I'll tend to mine."

Put in my place one more time, and an hour before I had to get over to the Nut House, I charmingly agreed to stop at McDonald's for a Coke, and then an ice cream—since Hunter was paying.

Hunter said something about, "If Muhammad won't come to the mountain, the mountain will come to . . ."

after I told him Selma wanted to see me and Meemaw. I knew I wasn't supposed to tell anybody but we were in way too deep to be hiding secrets at this point.

On our way to McDonald's, I called Marti Floyd.

"Sure I remember the church folks coming through," the man's slow voice said.

"Why were they there an hour early?"

"I have no idea. Threw us into a spin, I'll tell you. I had to take 'em through. No grand tour like Milo does it."

"Anything unusual about them? Did they all stay together? Anybody wander off?"

"Kids, as usual. People hollering at 'em. Things like that. Couple of bishops came with 'em. All friendly and interested. Nothing else."

I thanked the man and hung up.

McDonald's was empty, being halfway between dinner and supper. One girl lounged behind the counter, yawning as she handed us our drink cups and me a cup of ice cream with chocolate on top, which I ate first, followed by my soft drink, which didn't taste too good after ice cream.

"What do you imagine Selma wants to talk about?" Hunter said. "And why wouldn't she be bringing it to the sheriff?"

"Maybe she came up with some little thing that's bothering her."

"Hope it's one big thing," he countered. "We could use it."

I thought a minute. "You hear anything from Tupelo?"

"The sergeant there told me to give him a day or so to ask around, but let me call now, see if there are any messages." He shook his head as he fumbled with the radio on his shoulder. "The more I think about it, the more I think somebody followed the parson here to Riverville with murder in his heart."

"You're just wishing. Nobody could be a stranger around here and know that much about Miss Amelia and how she usually won at the fair and this time didn't, and how her other bowl was in the ranch cooler."

He nodded. "Guess you're right. I was just hoping the guy was from out of town and I wouldn't have to be locking up some neighbor for murder."

"Better than locking up my grandmother."

He called the station while I sat beside him, trying to stay cool, though the air-conditioning didn't seem to put a dent in the afternoon's heat.

When he was off his radio, he looked over at me, a puzzled expression on his face.

"What'd the sheriff have to say?" I asked.

He went on thinking until he finally gave me a look, more confusion than information. "Just that he was going through some old complaints, thinking he remembered something about the church."

"What'd he find?"

"A complaint about Pastor Albertson."

"What kind of complaint?"

"Something to do with the pastor trying to cheat him— it was Tim Rogers came in. You know him. Old guy lives down by the old train depot. Sometimes helps out at the feed store."

"Yeah. So? Tyler Perkins mentioned something about that. He didn't seem to think it was anything. Just another old guy grousing. How'd he try to cheat him?"

"Sheriff wasn't really clear. Seems there was a problem going on. Some of the church people were invited to invest in something or other and were making a lot of money. But they wouldn't tell Tim a thing about it. He went to see Pastor Albertson and didn't get any satisfaction. Got so mad he went to the sheriff. Nothing to be done about it. Church business."

"Did the sheriff talk to Pastor Albertson?"

"Seems he did. Said if he remembered right, the man was shocked that Tim was that mad about something not worth getting upset about. The pastor said he didn't know much about it but that he'd look into it. Next thing the pastor was gone, replaced by the Reverend Jenkins. Sheriff told me—but he said this is confidential—that maybe the church board found out something or other the pastor was doing and asked him to leave before anything came out. Sheriff went out this morning and talked to Tim but the man didn't even remember filing the complaint."

"Won't do us any good to go talk to him then. Got to be in here somewhere—who did this. Like a mystery buried in a cave. Could be this one's secret. Could be that one's. We've just got to find out what the secrets are and trace them to their core."

"I'm hoping for Selma right now," Hunter said. "Something's got to be bothering her—all this hush-hush stuff."

"I'll let you know."

"Want to meet for supper later?"

I shook my head. "My trees need me. Martin's doing a good job, what I saw, but those trees . . . well . . ."

He nodded at me. "Like your babies. I sure know that. But call me after you see Selma. I'm going back to the station. I'll call Tupelo again. Just a hunch but I'm getting tired of sitting around, waiting for something to break."

Chapter Eighteen

Selma Rickles was nowhere to be seen when I ran up the steps and into the store. There were a few shoppers grazing up and down the aisles. One woman was having a loud discussion with her friend over whether to buy the pecan barbecue sauce or the pecan ice cream sauce.

Miss Amelia strode around the big room as usual, despite being warned away. She was filling half-empty tables with bags and gift boxes stuffed with pecans or pecan sandies and bourbon pecan balls and Outhouse Moons. The bigger boxes held Classy Tassies, along with a half-dozen turtles, angel cookies, and pecan date bars. Sometimes she put in pecan pralines. Sometimes oatmeal pecan cookies. Miss Amelia changed up the boxes from time to time, depending on what she felt like baking that month. Every box was tagged with the Blanchard family crest and tied with a big green bow.

"Selma upstairs?" I asked, stopping beside my busy grandmother.

Miss Amelia frowned hard when she looked up. She put a finger to her lips then rolled her eyes toward Ethelred Tomroy sitting in the rocking chair near the front counter. She shook her head. "She called."

"When's she coming?"

"That's the thing. She's not."

"What happened? I thought she had something to tell us."

Miss Amelia looked around then nodded toward the kitchen doors.

"I'd like to show you something I've been working on, Lindy," she said in a loud voice. "Really proud of it. Come on out and tell me what you think." She headed toward the back of the store. I figured this was the way to impart whatever the message from Selma was without Ethelred's perked-up ears overhearing.

Miss Amelia leaned in close to whisper. "That woman's determined to be my protector. She's making note of who doesn't come in anymore for their pie and who is really supporting me by buying bags full of pecan boxes. Can't get rid of her." She rolled her eyes at me.

I smiled as I tried to get past Ethelred, but the woman had placed the chair strategically so people coming to the counter or to the kitchen had to go around her.

"Now, stop a minute, Lindy." Ethelred grabbed my arm. "I want you to tell me what you think of this automobile I'm thinking of buying to replace my old Buick."

"In a minute, Miss Ethelred, okay? I've got to—"

"No. I need your advice. Now look here, it's called a SLK Class—whatever that means? They don't have nice names like some—you know the Mustang and such. Just this SLK Class."

"A Mercedes?" That stopped me cold.

"Yeah." The woman looked up at me as she waved a sleek brochure in my face. "That's it: Mercedes-Benz."

"You thinking of buying one?"

"Wouldn't be looking, young lady, if I didn't plan on buying."

I bit my tongue. "Any of them would be fine, Ethelred. Good cars. Now, I've got to—"

"Okay, go ahead. Think I'll take a look at those Porsche cars first anyway."

"Ethelred, why the heck would you be spending money like that?"

"Might as well spend it while you're still here," the woman said and set to rocking hard in her chair, slapping her brochure closed in her lap.

"But . . ." I had a few more things to add but Miss Amelia called me from out in the kitchen.

Once through the door and huddled with Miss Amelia back by the coolers, I asked, "What in the heck's going on with Ethelred? She's thinking of buying a Porsche or Mercedes to replace that 1991 Buick of hers?"

Miss Amelia waved a hand in the air. "Pay no attention. She gets like that from time to time. I'm sure she's not cashing in all her bonds to buy a car.

"Anyway," she went on, looking over to where Treenie was pulling a batch of cookies from the large oven. "Selma asked us to come over there to the parsonage. She said she wants to show us something she just found."

"Found? She give you a clue what it is?"

"Not another word, but I'll tell you something, Lindy. The woman is awfully nervous. Hard for her to get the words out. I told her we'd be there as soon as you got back from wherever you and Hunter got to. You learn anything, the two of you?"

"Nothing but a bunch of folks from the church were

touring the building around that time. Milo Froymann—
you know him?"

Miss Amelia nodded. "Two special pecan pies a week.
I'd worry about him eating so much sugar but he's out rid-
ing every day. Got quite a few head of cattle to take care
of." She shrugged. "Maybe he feeds the pies to his hogs,
for all I know."

"Not much help there. Whole group from the church
came that day. He was a little put out because they showed
up an hour before they were supposed to. Milo was going
to give them a tour of the exhibits, some kind of talk, I
guess. Not too happy about it. Seems Marti Floyd acts as
some kind of director during the fair and he set it up."

Miss Amelia nodded as she took off her apron and hung
it up on a peg beside the back door. "I know Marti. I'll call
him myself, see who he dealt with at the church and if he
ever found out why they came early."

She grabbed her handbag from under one of the stainless steel tables and we went out the back way, with Miss
Amelia giving Treenie a warning to keep an eye on Ethelred
since she liked to help herself to the spiced nuts and leave
without paying.

"One box, okay," Miss Amelia called out over her
shoulder. "But if she starts loading her purse for relatives,
distract her."

We parked in the parsonage drive since there were no
other cars blocking the way this time. The front door
opened before we got up on the porch. Selma Rickles
stepped out and closed the door quietly behind her. She
motioned for us to follow her off to the side of the house,

then stopped, waiting for us to catch up. "Sorry about this but something . . . well . . . I'm not sure. Maybe I'm making a mountain out of a molehill."

She walked on ahead, limping down the garden path with me behind her, half admiring the beautifully tended beds all over again and half confused about where we were going.

Miss Amelia trailed behind me, saying nothing, probably feeling the way I was feeling—that maybe this wasn't the time to be making over a special bloom or two.

Selma didn't stop at any of the beds. She walked until we could hear the river, a mellow flow of water, then small rushes of sound from whirlpools trapping leaves and branches. I knew the sounds of the Colorado like a separate current running through my life and felt better just for being close.

Where the graveled walkway ended, Selma took a step beyond, off to where the rushes and tall weeds grew.

When she turned to look at us, she bit at her lip, then pointed down beside where she stood, to a wild stand of plants over six feet tall. The tall stems of the thick-growing plants were covered with purple spots. The flower heads were flat and wide, made up of many separate small white flowers. I didn't need to be told what I was looking at: spotted water hemlock. Responsible for killing animals and men. And one man in particular, Parson Millroy Jenkins.

"Do you know what this is?" Selma asked, her eyes wide, voice breathless.

"Spotted water hemlock," Miss Amelia said quickly. "Grows all over Texas, Selma, if that's what's worrying you. Not just down here near your garden, but out at the Rancho en el Colorado, too. Just about everywhere, wouldn't you say, Lindy?"

I nodded. "I hope you weren't thinking, because it's found here, that anybody would think you'd be the one who—"

Selma was shaking her head. "No, no. That's not it. Look down there."

She pointed to the ground, to where the tall stems were pushing out of the damp earth. "You see those holes?"

Miss Amelia and I moved in close, with me getting down on my haunches to look.

"I never noticed them before today," Selma said.

"Probably wild hogs. Lots of them around here." I found it was necessary to soothe the distraught woman.

"I'll bet anything hogs are smart enough not to dig up poisonous roots. Otherwise you wouldn't have a wild hog problem in Texas."

"Well, I have to agree with you there," Miss Amelia put in. "It's said the most toxic part is the root so I don't imagine they spend much time digging down around them like that."

"And if you look close . . ." Now Selma bent to point at where the earth had been disturbed. "You can see where the flat side of a shovel, or a small spade, dug right down and pulled the roots away from the plant. See that? See how you can see some of that yellowish root, where it's been hacked off?"

We had to agree with her, not just a breaking away, but a distinct cut.

Miss Amelia stood back to look at the ground around where Selma was pointing.

"I don't see any footprints," she said. "Nothing to show somebody was down here."

Selma only sighed. "If it happened last Sunday—that was only a few days ago but the ground's damp down here. See how some of the earth is already sinking in around the hole where the roots were?"

"What are trying to tell us, Selma?" I came right out and asked.

"That's the plant that killed Millroy. I'm sure of it. Somebody came here after that root. What I'm saying, Lindy, is that it was done on purpose—the digging, sneaking down here, taking the root home, grinding it up, and putting it into that Texas caviar Millroy ate at the Winners' Supper."

"You don't think I did all that, do you?" Miss Amelia stood as straight as her back would let her and looked fiercely at Selma, who shrank under the look.

"No, ma'am. Sorry, but at your age . . . well . . . I just don't see you sneaking over here like that. And anyway, you just said yourself, you've got plenty of hemlock on the Rancho en el Colorado."

"I can still dig a root or two, if I have to," Miss Amelia groused while barely listening and not taking kindly to references to her age and any diminished capacity.

"Well." She finally got over being put out and folded her arms as she rocked back on her heels. "This does put a different light on things. Any idea who might have done it? How'd they figure to get by you without you seeing them?"

"I can't see the garden from the house except a little bit of it out the bathroom window." Selma chewed at her lip. "I've got kind of an idea, though. That was what I was going to talk to you about before I even came down here and found this."

"You want to go up to the house and talk?"

She shook her head. "Not in front of Dora. She's been through so much. What I've got to tell you could just devastate her."

She turned terribly hurt eyes on us. "I know the very thought is just about killing me."

Chapter Nineteen

The church was the quietest and safest place to go. We turned on one overhead light against the growing dark. Miss Amelia and I settled into one pew, Selma in the pew ahead of us, sitting with her arm over the back, looking deeply into our faces before beginning whatever it was she had to tell us.

"I know you've noticed my leg," she said, surprising me since I hadn't expected her to begin this personally.

We nodded.

"Well, of course you would. I'm not bringing it up for sympathy. It's just that my leg's got a lot to do with what I'm going to tell you."

She took a deep breath then turned to look hard at the front of the church—a bare place with nothing beyond the podium. When she turned back, her chin was high. She seemed buoyed and ready to tell whatever it was that was so hard for her to say.

"It's about how I got this bad leg," she said. "My ex-husband, Shorty Temple—we lived in Tupelo—he hit me with our car."

I stifled a gasp.

Miss Amelia sat still and waited for more.

"Shorty was a drinker." Selma looked down at her hands. Her limp hair fell forward so it covered one cheek. "Until he got addicted to alcohol, he was a good man. He managed a B&D Sporting Goods store there in Tupelo. He made a good living. We were doing well. I taught school. After the drinking started, he lost his job and then lost his confidence and we lost our house. Everything went wrong. When Shorty had nobody left to blame for the way his life was going, he started blaming me. You've heard all of this before, I know. Happens to a lot of people. Thing is, when it's you, it's always different.

"Shorty began to take things out on me. At first he'd just holler. Then he started to hit me and one day he hit me so bad I had to have my jaw wired back together."

She looked down at her hands. "I can see by your faces you're thinking I should've just left. And you're right. I should've. But I didn't. I remembered the good days and kept thinking, 'This will pass. He'll stop drinking.' Millroy kept telling me I had to get out for my own safety. Dora was in a state. Every day she called to plead with me to get out of there. Well, finally I agreed. I couldn't take any more so I packed a suitcase and went to stay with Millroy and Dora. I left a note for Shorty that I was leaving him for good. I guess that was the last straw for him. One day, he came after me. I was out walking in the neighborhood and I heard a car coming up behind me pretty fast. By the time I turned around, the car hit me. I flew. I don't know how far. Straight through the air. Landed on a neighbor's steps.

The car kept on going. The sheriff was there in a couple of minutes, then the ambulance. Something said maybe I broke my back. Guess a bone was sticking out of my leg. The thing was, somebody got the license number and they picked up Shorty in half an hour. He was back, driving through Dora and Millroy's neighborhood like he was still looking for me to be lying there.

"Shorty went to prison for attempted murder."

Right then the silence in the church didn't feel like a good thing. Miss Amelia laid a hand on Selma's, over the back of the pew.

"Terrible," Miss Amelia said.

"Shorty never said he was sorry. I got letters from prison saying how he was going to get even for me sending him there. How a wife shouldn't turn on her husband the way I did. And all kinds of crazy things. Since he was locked up and I was dealing with enough, learning to walk again— I've got a steel rod in the leg instead of bone—I never answered him and just threw them away. Then he started writing to Millroy, threatening him for taking me away from our home. Millroy prayed about it for a long time and then went to the police. Shorty was back in court. He got more time. But the letters stopped."

"How long ago was this?" I asked.

"About seven years ago."

"How long was Shorty in prison for?"

"He got ten years."

"And what was the additional sentence?" Miss Amelia asked.

"That was it, all together."

"So ten years. Doesn't sound as if he's anybody to worry about."

She cleared her throat. "Thing is," she said. "He came

up for parole and the warden said he was well behaved, that he was going to church, and talking to some of the other men about religion."

I didn't say anything, suspecting what was coming.

"He got out a year ago. He came to the parsonage in Tupelo, looking for Millroy. We called the police but he left town or something. Anyway, they didn't find him."

Miss Amelia sat back and thought awhile. "If I get what you're saying, you think he followed you here to Riverville?"

She nodded.

"But Selma, the kind of man you're describing would have come after Millroy with a gun. Maybe a knife. Not poison."

She lowered her head. "When Shorty was saved in prison, his mind was already half destroyed. When he got religion, he got it all the way. What I heard was that he was a kind of fundamentalist believer. You know, the kind who tells everybody else that what they believe is the wrong thing in order to make themselves important. Poor Shorty, it was a way to feel better about himself and, I guess, feel better about what he did to me.

"He went back to writing letters to Millroy before he got out. Nothing threatening. Millroy thought it was an answered prayer at first when Millroy said he'd been saved and started quoting the Bible. Millroy even answered a couple of them. Until Shorty began saying things like Millroy had to get straight with the Lord, stop preaching some of the things he was preaching, and only use the Bible for his homilies."

I made a face. "What did he mean by that?"

"He started saying that the Lord was going to test Millroy and find him wanting." She held very still. "Millroy showed me one of the letters he got after Shorty was released. Shorty was saying that Millroy needed testing, to see if he was preaching the true word. This time he quoted Mark 16:18. You know that one?" She looked to me. I shook my head, then threw in a shrug.

"It's about the snake handling," Miss Amelia said. "Can't quote it, though."

Selma nodded. "The verse goes: *They will pick up snakes with their hands; and when they drink deadly poison, it will not hurt them at all; they will place their hands on sick people, and they will get well.*"

If a feather had fluttered to the floor at that moment, it would have made a crack in that thick silence.

"What did the pastor do after that?" Miss Amelia finally asked.

"Millroy went back to the police. Shorty was warned but the letters didn't stop until a couple of months before we left Tupelo."

"Why do you think he stopped writing?"

"Maybe because he had to stay out of trouble or face going back to jail. By then we were all spooked. Dora was frightened. She insisted Millroy look for a job someplace else, where Shorty couldn't find us. Millroy hated leaving Tupelo. He was happy there, but for Dora, and I suppose for me, he found this position here."

"Has anyone seen Shorty here in Riverville?" I asked.

"Nobody but us would know him."

"Have you seen him?"

She shook her head. "I haven't seen him, but after we moved here, Millroy got a letter one day. Shorty's return address in Tupelo was on it. Said he was going to come talk to Millroy. Millroy tried to hide it from me and Dora, but Dora found it on Millroy's desk and was in a tizzy, afraid he'd come and hurt him. Got so bad, Millroy was even thinking about moving again. But no more letters arrived."

"What did that last letter say?" Miss Amelia asked.

Selma shrugged. "Just said he was thinking of coming to Riverville. That there were things they had to talk out between them. Knowing Shorty's history, Millroy was almost ready to go see the sheriff. He was mad this time. He said Shorty'd taken up all the space in his life he was going to get. That was the week before the fair closed."

"Why didn't he talk to Sheriff Higsby?" Miss Amelia asked.

Selma shrugged. "I don't know. Something else seemed to be on his mind that last week. Something different worrying him."

"Did Dora notice?"

"We both did. She said he wouldn't talk about it. Just that he was prayin' on it and would act when the time was right. Dora didn't say anything and I didn't say anything, but I think we were both afraid it was something to do with Shorty again."

"So you divorced the man."

She nodded. "Right after he went to prison. I filed papers then took my maiden name back."

"So what you're saying is you think Shorty did this."

Selma looked down at her hands. "I can't help but think it. I've been going half crazy since it happened. I mean, I can't say anything to Dora—she's in a terrible state as it is—but I'm afraid she's thinking the same thing."

I waited a minute, then said, "Whoever did this, Selma, had to know about Meemaw pretty well. I mean her always winning. How she brought two bowls with her. What our cooler looked like. How would a stranger, like Shorty, ever get that kind of information? And know who to try to blame it on?"

She shrugged. "Only thing I can say is Miss Amelia's pretty famous here in Riverville. You know how men meet in the beer tent, always gossiping about one thing or the other—leastwise that's what I hear. I guess it wouldn't be too hard to find somebody he could put the blame on."

I wanted to cringe. Of course Meemaw was well known in Riverville. Of course she'd been winning for years. A few questions about the fair, about who was likely to win—anybody could learn anything about her. She was just Meemaw to me. To Riverville, Meemaw was famous.

Selma looked over at Miss Amelia with a lot of pity. "If it weren't for hoping you did it, Miss Amelia, I don't know how me and Dora would've gotten through the last few days. It's like, as long as maybe Miss Amelia was getting even for being judged out of the competition, then it can't be anything from the past. It can't be anybody who can hurt us even more. Dora's watched me suffer through all of this and she's my sister. She'd do anything to spare me more grief. But I don't want to be spared. I don't want you accused, Miss Amelia. I just want the truth to come out once and for all."

I felt as if my brain were going to burst. Too much. People with so many reasons for wanting to believe in lies—no matter who got hurt. I didn't know who to get angry at first. I wanted to ask if Shorty was still in Tupelo and if Selma had an address, but there was the sound of a door opening behind us, and when I turned, Hawley Harvey stood there, slick black hair sticking out from under his big hat. His mouth dropped open when he saw us all together.

Chapter Twenty

Hawley Harvey wasn't happy.

"Saw lights on in here, when they shouldn't be turned on. Wish you ladies would think about the electric bill before coming on over here to sit and gab."

He frowned and shuffled his feet as we got up to file out past him.

"This is a place of worship, ladies. Not a coffeehouse," he called after us then slammed the door to the church on us. I heard a key turn.

Since I had to drive Miss Amelia back out to the ranch, I figured I might as well spend the night there. I stopped at the darkened Nut House to run up to my apartment and get a change of clothes for the next day, as well as some files I was looking at—in case I got a chance to work. Martin Sanchez was taking care of the watering and monitoring for what could be disease or bug infestation, but I was

beginning to feel the old ache to be with my trees. I'd just
started tests on a tree with scab fungicide and desperately
wanted to keep close watch and make careful notes.

When we were on our way out to the ranch, I called
Hunter to give him the information Selma had given us
and ask about news from Tupelo.

Though it was only nine o'clock, Hunter sounded as if
he'd been sleeping—maybe in front of the TV. He wak-
ened quickly when he heard my voice.

"Sheriff there told me about Shorty Temple and the
years he was in prison. If the parson went to the sheriff's
office about those letters, they'll have a record. Probably
have something by morning. You want me to come by?"

"I'll be out at the ranch," I said. "Just call me."

It felt good to be at home, in my old room. A small,
square space I'd plastered with posters of Third Eye Blind
and U2 and Wilson Phillips. And a big poster that ran
almost to the ceiling of Elvis Presley. Not that I'd had a
crush on him or anything. It was Mama, insisting every
girl should have a poster of Elvis because she'd been to one
of his concerts in Dallas and never forgot it. There was a
little bit of a shrine feeling to the room now, Mama not
touching it, maybe thinking if she left it just the way it was,
I would move back home. The thing with Mama was she
didn't see why I had to move out in the first place. Even
though I was finished with college and just about to start
the climb up to thirty, Emma figured I should live at
home until I was whisked off to Never-Never Land with a
charming prince. I still smiled at our confrontation the day
I announced that the apartment above the Nut House would

suit me just fine. Emma'd been incensed, a daughter of hers, living in town, alone, in that big old Nut House building.

"Why, Lindy Blanchard, what would your daddy say if he was alive to see what you're doin'?" Mama had demanded, going so far as to stamp her foot.

"Daddy would be saying, *'You go, girl. Time you got on with living.'* Last thing Daddy would've wanted was me waiting around to snag some cowboy of my own."

That quieted Mama, who knew that was exactly what Jake Blanchard would have said. An independent man, he expected his children to be just as independent and all along planned for me to go to college and follow any path I wanted to follow.

I dug in a dresser drawer for a pair of pajama bottoms and a washed-out T-shirt. After a shower, teeth and hair brushed long enough, I climbed into bed and feel asleep fast, hardly aware that there were no creaking stairs or old aching walls around me.

When I awoke the next morning, the sun was already up. I heard voices coming from the living room. While I lay there stretching in the sunlight coming in the uncovered windows, there was a knock at the door.

"Lindy?" Bethany stuck her head in the door. Her voice trembled. "You gotta come downstairs. Sheriff Higsby's here talking to Meemaw. Oh, Lindy. There's more trouble."

I was out of bed and grabbing clothes from hangers. I figured I'd better take time to wash my face, brush my teeth, and comb my hair, but the jobs were done fast.

Everyone was gathered in the living room. Sheriff Higsby sat hunched forward in a chair that looked too small for him. Miss Amelia sat with her back straight, fierce, pale eyes on the sheriff. Mama and Justin and Bethany stood at different places in the room, all three with their arms crossed in front of them and all three looking mad enough to spit. Jeffrey Coulter hung out near the archway to the front hall. His arms were crossed over his spotless white T-shirt. If a man could be said to look bored in the midst of disaster, Jeffrey was looking miserably bored.

The sheriff struggled to get up when I entered the room. He was burdened with his sidearm and handcuffs and wide belt tucked under his burgeoning stomach. He had difficulty pushing off from the little chair. I waved him to stay seated.

"What's this about, Sheriff?" I walked over to stand beside my grandmother, my hand on her back.

"Complaint, Lindy," he said and slapped a clipboard he'd laid on his lap.

"What kind of complaint?"

Miss Amelia looked up at me. "Ridiculous, Lindy. Not worth any of us paying attention to—"

"I'm real sorry I had to bring this out, Miss Amelia. You know I wouldn't do it if . . . well, it's part of my job."

"I understand, Sheriff." Miss Amelia managed a weak smile.

"I'm asking again, what kind of complaint?" I demanded, feeling as if I were caught in some Alice in Wonderland scene of manners and deportment.

"A dog's dead." The sheriff looked down at his clipboard as if hiding embarrassment.

I couldn't help but laugh. "What's that got to do with my grandmother? Dogs die every day."

"Seems the owner thinks he was poisoned. She's demanding the dog be tested for hemlock."

"Hemlock? This is crazy . . . Who . . ."

"Freda Cromwell. Called it in last night. Sam had to go over and take a look at the animal."

"That dog was about nineteen years old, wasn't he?" Justin, astounded, demanded.

The sheriff nodded. "Freda's hysterical. Can't believe King Charles is dead and won't believe it's by natural causes. Made a couple of wild statements about spotted hemlock taking out Blanchard enemies. And how she's been against the Blanchards and they're turning on her, killing off her dog. She's even saying she expects to be next."

"Can't be soon enough," Justin growled just at hearing level.

Miss Amelia gave him a look all the kids in the family knew well.

"I can see why poor Freda's upset," Miss Amelia said. "That English springer spaniel's been almost blind for years. You've got to give it to Freda, she took good care of him. In a way you could say King Charles was her only close friend."

"Not just blind, but fat as a sausage," Justin groused. "How long did she think he was going to live?"

"Now, Justin. Freda's got her problems—"

"As if you don't!" Emma was incensed.

"I had to come out here, Miss Amelia." Sheriff Higsby stood and slapped his clipboard at his side so it rang against his .38. "Miz Cromwell insisted. She's having the autopsy done today. I'll call Doc Winslow later. See what he finds."

"You know what he's going to find, Sheriff." Mama stood to lead him to the door. "Unless that poor old blind dog wandered close to the river and chewed on the spotted hemlock, the veterinarian's going to find nothing but old age."

The sheriff chuckled on his way out the door. "That's what I imagine, Miss Emma. And I'll be sure that news gets around town before Freda gets a posse out after you."

With the sheriff gone and nobody hungry for breakfast,

I thought maybe I could take a couple of hours out in my greenhouse, maybe take a walk through my test gardens where the older cultivars were transplanted and some of the newer ones were being weathered off.

"You want me to call Treenie and ask her to open the store today?" Emma, pushing her cropped hair up with her fingers, asked Miss Amelia.

Meemaw frowned and stood, stretching to her full five feet nine. "Don't you dare. I'm leaving right now."

"Mama, nobody would blame you for taking time off. Never imagined people of Riverville would turn like this."

Miss Amelia made a scoffing sound. "It's not the 'people of Riverville,' Emma. It's just Freda Cromwell and some others being themselves. If Freda couldn't find a way to set herself in the middle of a problem, she'd keel over, stick her toes up, and take her last breath."

"I sure hope you avoid that woman. She comes into the store today, you tell her to get out and stay out."

Miss Amelia shook her head and lifted an eyebrow at her daughter. "Nope. Why, I'm thinking I'll pay a condolence call on Freda. Let her know how sorry I am about King Charles."

She looked around at her family's shocked faces. "Well, I am sorry for him dying. I always felt bad for old King Charles, living with Freda. I swear, blind or not, that dog would roll his eyes every time he saw me, like he was hoping to be rescued."

"You're going to give her a heart attack, she sees you on her front porch," I warned, only half kidding.

"Think I'll take her a pecan pie."

We all laughed.

"Bet you anything gluttony trumps fear of being poisoned," she added.

I shook my head and made my way out to my truck, then around by the river road to my greenhouse. I could just as well talk to Hunter out there as in the house.

Sometimes the noise people make gets to me. I'm no hermit, but the one thing about trees is they don't say dumb things. I've got no Freda Cromwell tree in my test garden complaining and accusing me of paying more attention to the other trees and crying crocodile tears and telling lies that would get her attention. If I ever had a tree like that, I'd rip it out by its roots and choke the little thing until it turned up its toes . . .

Chapter Twenty-one

It felt good to walk between stainless steel tables lined with new cultivars in pots of all sizes. The smell of earth and water and the heat of the greenhouse were what I knew best. For the last five years, since getting my master's in biological and agricultural engineering at Texas A&M, I'd had the same dream. For too many years, growing up on the farm, I'd seen the heartbreak of trees that didn't bud, of trees riddled with scab fungus or powdery mildew, vein spot, *articularia* leaf mold, and on and on. I'd seen years when the meat inside the pecans turned brown and rotted. Years when pink mold destroyed the crop. The pecan trees were prone to one thing after another, from too much water to none at all, to aphids and other insects burrowing into the bark.

Too many ranchers went far into debt and never recouped their losses. Some lost their farms. If I could stop even part

of that heartbreak, all my years of study and hard work
would be well worth it.

I reached out to turn a pot and then to brush dirt from
the shining tables to the floor. I didn't hear Martin Sanchez
until he was standing behind me.

"Good to see you." Martin removed his hat and dipped
his head.

I returned the greeting.

A short man with a thick head of steely white hair, Martin had a smile that was always wide and warming. As long
as I could remember, the Sanchez family had lived in the
plain old house that had been the original Blanchard home
on the ranch—the place where Jessie and I both grew up.

Martin quickly reported on the new cultivars we'd
recently transplanted to the test grove to harden off. "Doing
well," he said. "I've cut back on water."

I nodded. I felt this particular tree, one from California
that I'd crossed with the native Pawnee, was showing signs
of particular strengths, like a few of the others in my test
grove. Not just drought resistance, but resistance to some
of the fungus diseases, too.

Martin lingered awhile then said he had to get back out
to the groves. He was meeting Justin—a spraying program
getting under way.

"But, Lindy . . ." He stopped on his way out through the
gleaming tables. "Could you come by the house today?
Juanita said if I saw you, I should ask—whenever you can.
Jessie told her something. Well, I'll let her explain. I was
only half listening . . ."

I nodded. It would be a pleasure to stop and see Juanita.
My mouth watered at the thought of Juanita's hot chocolate,
and maybe a pan de yema, a sweet roll native to Oaxaca,

Mexico, where the family was from. If Juanita heard I was coming, she'd have it ready for me. Juanita never failed.

It was close to eleven o'clock when Hunter called and my work for the day was suddenly over.

"You coming back to town? We gotta talk. I'm starving. How about The Squirrel in forty-five minutes? Can you make it?"

"I want to stop and see Juanita first."

"Okay, make it an hour. I heard from Tupelo and we've got to go over some things pretty quick."

The front porch of the Sanchezes' house was a hanging garden. Pots of blue periwinkles and violet Laura Bush petunias hung from the ceiling. Terra-cotta pots stood along the porch floor. Everything looked freshly washed and alive. Juanita, in a large straw hat to protect her head from the strong sun, stood watering in a round bed of bright yellow daylilies and startling Mexican hat ratibida.

For a minute I suffered my familiar garden envy, having no time myself for flowers and bushes, but always meaning to do something around the ranch house, or some of the barns. Or maybe stick flowerboxes on the front windows of my greenhouse.

"Ah, Lindy!" Juanita, her pretty face stretched into a wide smile, greeted me. She threw down the hose she held in order to put her arms out and hug me as tightly as she could.

"Come in. Come in," the pretty woman insisted. "I made pan de yema. Martin told me you might be stopping by. And a pot of chocolate. Just like when you were a little girl."

Unable to resist, I followed Juanita up the high front steps and into the living room, where a round mahogany table covered with a massive lace tablecloth took up most of the central space.

Juanita fussed for the first ten minutes, setting out her sweet rolls on a pretty Mexican plate, then delicate cups for the hot chocolate. She didn't sit until I had sunk my teeth into the roll set on my plate and taken a sip of the sweet and thick Oaxacan hot chocolate that could make me swoon.

"You like it?" Juanita asked as always, then beamed at my quick nod, my mouth too full for words.

When the chocolate was half gone and the roll demolished, I tipped my head and grinned at Juanita. "Martin said you wanted to see me but I'm thinking you just knew I was in need of some of your hot chocolate," I teased.

Juanita shrugged and grinned. "Always that. Ever since you were little—coming to my front door: 'Can I have hot chocolate, Miss Juanita?' "

We laughed and then Juanita's face grew serious. "Jessie asked me to talk to you. She heard something at the library yesterday. If you want to stop by and see her . . . Anyway, she said a few of the older people were gathered in the vestibule—neither coming nor going. You know how people use the library as a meeting place." She waved a hand at the thoughtlessness of people who should only be there to take out books. "Anyway, she overheard one of the women say she was worried about something happening at the church. Jessie tried to hear but there were kindergarteners in for their first library card and she couldn't concentrate. Maybe it was nothing but the usual grumbling parishioners, but she thought—because of what happened to the parson—that you should, maybe look into it." She spread her hands. "Jessie didn't know whether to call you or just butt out. That's why she thought maybe if I saw you . . ."

I expressed my appreciation at anything being brought to my attention that might help Miss Amelia.

"I know. Can you imagine? I heard what that awful Freda Cromwell was saying about her old dog dying. That's a shame. The woman doesn't think before she opens her mouth."

I got up to go. "Miss Amelia was stopping by Freda's house this morning, to pay a condolence call, and bring her a pecan pie."

Juanita rolled her large, dark eyes and put a hand to her mouth, covering a laugh. "Good for Miss Amelia. Can you imagine the problem that woman will have? Trying to turn down a free pecan pie?"

I was out of there—after another fierce hug—and on my way into Riverville, out the red dirt ranch road to the highway. I rolled the truck window up and turned on the air-conditioning. The day was heating up. Probably over a hundred by afternoon.

I ran a hand through my hair and dug sunglasses out of my purse on the seat beside me. There was a lot to think about.

But right then, despite myself, I had to smile. All I could concentrate on was Hunter Austen, waiting in town to buy me lunch and look at me in that new way he'd been looking lately.

Chapter Twenty-two

At The Squirrel, I had to stop again and again for friends and neighbors reaching out to grab my arm and express their outrage that Miss Amelia was under attack, the way she was, by the sheriff and Freda Cromwell.

"Crazy, him thinking your meemaw'd do a thing like that. What I'm hearing," Elder Jameson, the florist in town, shook his head. "Everybody's getting together and going over there to the Nut House and buying every jar of her Texas caviar we can get our hands on. Just to show her how much we believe in her. You tell yer grandma that, okay? We're coming."

I assured one after the other that Miss Amelia would be grateful for their support and pushed my way through the tables to the booth where Hunter sat, tall and neat in his well-pressed blue uniform with the gold badge on his chest. Even the stultifying heat didn't seem to faze Hunter.

He was a man on the job. Face serious. Posture serious. He gave a serious head nod as I slid in across from him.

"Geez," I said, looking around at the people watching us. "Guess they won't be getting out a lynch party. Everybody here seems to be in Meemaw's corner."

Hunter smiled and handed me the computer-generated menu with a snarling squirrel at the top and a balloon above his head proclaiming: NUTS!

Cecil Darling's humor often went over the heads of his patrons though they came back anyway, figuring it was just English humor and they'd never understand. Rivervillians felt sorry for him. Poor man, never going to be a Texan like them.

"I'd say fish and chips," Hunter suggested, voice low.

"Is that chips as in French fries or potato chips?"

"Better not to ask. Cecil's in a tizzy today. Somebody suggested he had to bribe the judges to get his honorable mention and that set him off."

"I just ate," I leaned in to tell Hunter. "I stopped at Juanita's."

Hunter, having hung around Rancho en el Colorado since he was a child and a few cattle still roamed the fields, knew the scents and joys of Juanita Sanchez's house, too.

When Cecil came over to our booth, pad and pencil in hand, nose in the air, ready to respond to insults hurled his way, Hunter ordered mystery fish and chips and I asked for a glass of sweet tea, which brought raised eyebrows and a sniff.

When our order was taken and Cecil out of earshot, Hunter leaned across the table. "Got quite a bit on Shorty." He consulted a notebook he'd pulled from a back pocket. "His name's really Allen Temple. It's true; he's out of prison and living back in Tupelo. Seems it's also true, what Selma told you about Shorty getting religion. And not only religion, he got himself a new wife. Guess he met her through some prison program. She donated her time, teaching inmates how to use the Internet."

"Any recent trouble with him?"

Hunter shook his head. "Not since a complaint, like Selma said, about him harassing Parson Jenkins. Set Shorty back. Did extra time. Then nothing. The officer in Tupelo told me he thinks we're barking up the wrong tree, going after Shorty." Hunter looked up to gauge what I was thinking.

"We can't let it go. We don't have much else and Selma was scared. I think she really believes Shorty came to town and poisoned the parson to prove out some Bible verse."

"And that could be. What I can do is ask the officer in Tupelo to call on Shorty. Give me his opinion of the man."

I waited until Cecil delivered my glass of tea and Hunter's thick white plate filled with fried fish and fried potatoes before saying anything more.

When Cecil was busy with another customer, I looked hard at Hunter. "I'm going to Tupelo. We're not finding anything else that even remotely connects anybody to wanting to see the parson dead. I need to talk to that man. My grandmother's life and reputation are on the line here."

"You're not going near anybody who could be a killer." The voice was trying to be stern, but he knew me too well.

"I'll take Miss Amelia."

"Now there's a bodyguard for you."

"Hunter. I don't know where else to turn. Nobody wanted the parson dead. Nobody saw anything. I'm stymied. At least this guy had a reason to hurt Parson Jenkins. He blamed the parson for spiriting his wife out of Tupelo.

Any man sitting in a prison, with lots of time on his hands to stew over past wrongs, is a suspect, you ask me."

"Well, you're not going alone. That's a ten-hour trip. I'll take you, and I'll question the man so that anything he says is on the record."

"Just as long as we don't let a suspect get past us just because it's a little inconvenient." My comment came out as snide and judgmental. I didn't mean it that way.

"That's not what I was saying . . ." His voice went tight and official.

"I know." I reached over and patted his hand. "I'm just so . . . mad, I guess."

He gave me a bewildered look, as if he had no idea how to keep up with me.

"So? Are we going?" I asked.

Hunter made a face. "Guess so. Be at least an overnight. Then we'll have to see if the man will talk to us. I'll have no official standing in Tupelo."

"You could get help from the Tupelo police if we needed it, couldn't you?"

"Suppose so."

"Okay. In the morning?"

"Lindy. Think about it. People hear you and me went off on a trip together, there'll be talk."

I sank down into myself. "For Pete's sakes. Who cares? We'll each get our own room at a motel. Nobody's business what we do anyway."

"Just that I don't want to harm your . . ."

"What? Reputation? Think about it, Hunter. I was away at college for six years. You think I led a lily-white life all that time?"

He hesitated, avoiding my eyes. "I never thought about it, to tell you the truth."

"You never wondered if I was with some guy there?"

He slowly shook his head. "I had a girlfriend."

"Ooh, I remember. Joslyn Pickett. Wasn't that the one?"

His face was red. I could tell I was making him uncomfortable but didn't care. He nodded.

"Joslyn Pickett. Didn't they call her the town pump?"

"You cut that out, Lindy."

"I'm just saying. We're adults now. I want to help my grandmother. I'll see if she'll go with us, but if she can't, I'm going to Tupelo anyway. With you or without you. I'll find that Shorty Temple and I'll ask him how good he is at grinding spotted water hemlock and feeding it to old enemies."

"Keep your voice down." He glowered at me. "I said I'd go."

With that settled, I got up.

"I'll see if I can round up a chaperone." I bent toward him, mocking. "If I can't, you'd just better learn to hold on to your virtue, because we're going to Tupelo."

I was still fuming when I got over to the Nut House, and fuming more when I saw Ethelred Tomroy ensconced in the rocking chair by the counter, rocking up a storm.

"Come here." Ethelred crooked a finger at me as I tried to get past her, out to the kitchen, where Miss Amelia was probably baking more pies or mixing another batch of Heavenly Texas Pecan Caviar.

"Take a look at this." Ethelred held up a new brochure. This one had a huge ocean liner on the cover with the words "Salamander Cruises" bannered across it. "I'm thinking of taking one of these boats."

Miss Ethelred's face was deadly serious. "You think I'd like Jamaica or the Bahamas? Or say, what about this one? Greek Isles."

I was too astounded to answer. I stood still, looking down at Ethelred's brochure as if I really were thinking over Miss Ethelred's question.

Ethelred, when she looked at me, made her eyes into slits, and wrinkled her lips into a pursed "O." "Got plenty of money soon. No use putting it in the bank for those bankers to steal. You never know how long you got in this world. You know that, Lindy? You're young. You don't think about such things. But I'm getting on. Almost seventy," she lied then watched to see if I was buying it.

"Don't think you've got a thing to worry about, Miss Ethelred."

"You mean 'cause 'only the good die young'?" Ethelred threw her head back and gave a mighty laugh.

Margaret Sanford, known throughout the town for her piety, sidled up to where the two of us were talking. "Couldn't help overhearing, Ethelred," she said, then looked around to see who else might be listening. "You been blessed, have you? Shame not everybody can be. You ask me, that's an anti-Christian way to act toward folks." She let her voice go up a few notches.

Ethelred's face clouded over. She started to sputter but was stopped by Mrs. Sanford, now into full, red-faced, anger.

"Sure hope you rich people are ready to put your money where your mouth is and do things to help the people of this county. Tell you, Ethelred, too rich for a lot of us. We been talking about pulling out of Rushing to Calvary, finding a more Christian church."

I stood back and listened.

"Shame on you, Margaret. 'Course I'm tithing more. Everybody is, what I'm told. That's how we got the addition. Just what they promised, if we believed enough to stick with 'em."

Margaret leaned down and stuck her face close to Ethelred's. "Only for you people with money to hand over. I'm on social security. What am I supposed to do?" She nodded hard and fast.

Ethelred reached out to take Margaret's bent hand in hers. "You don't understand what I'm saying here. I'm getting out, Margaret. I'm taking my money back. Seems I got a thyroid problem. That's what the doctor says. They're taking tests tomorrow."

Margaret put both hands to her face. "My Lord! I'm sorry I was mean about—"

"That's why I'm taking a cruise. You never know how long you got left. It just hit me. I never did much of anything in this life. Time I did. Here, take a look at this." She stuck the cruise brochure into Margaret Sanford's hand. "I'm going and I'm not counting pennies. This one time I'm throwing caution to the winds, as they say."

But Margaret Sanford's face was stricken. "Oh dear, Ethelred. I'm truly sorry for taking it out on you. When will you know what's going on with the thyroid?"

Ethelred paused, knowing what they both feared most at their age. "Hope tomorrow. That's why I'm getting fat, the doctor says. 'Cause it's my thyroid."

Margaret's face went through a series of changes, from being perplexed to something else. "Hope you got somebody going with you," she said. "You're gonna need somebody there. Can't always fight people off the way you do when it's this serious. Why, I heard thyroid could sure be more than worry over getting a little fat. Lots of cancers found there. You best get it done fast as you can."

A startled frown crumpled Ethelred's face. "Doctor didn't say nothing about cancer. Just getting fat."

"Well, bless yer heart, he wouldn't now, would he? As I say, if you need a ride, just give me a call."

"Amelia's taking me," Ethelred, still frowning, grumbled. She nodded as Miss Amelia came through the kitchen doors with a large baking sheet filled with pies for the front cooler.

"Glad you'll have a good friend there." Margaret looked over at Miss Amelia, smiling a sanctimonious smile.

"Good for you, Amelia," Margaret Sanford called out to Meemaw. "All the troubles you got about poisoning people and not too upset to take on one more problem."

"Didn't poison a single person . . . yet." Miss Amelia smiled that stiff smile I knew so well.

"You want a pie?" Miss Amelia thrust her pan of pies at Margaret Sanford.

The woman turned and hurried away.

Chapter Twenty-three

I swear I could gain five pounds just by walking into the Nut House kitchen and inhaling. I followed Miss Amelia back into the huge room with granite counters and floor-to-ceiling coolers and wall ranges, and into air that was as thick and sweet as a sugar factory. Trays of cooling Classy Tassies were set along one of the long counters. Trays of melt-in-your-mouth Outhouse Moons took up another table. Treenie Menendez was packing pecan sandies into the one-pound boxes. She greeted me, hurrying over to give me a hug as she asked how I was holding up under all the family travail.

"Bien, gracias." I looked down into liquid warm eyes. *"Y usted?"*

"Tenga cuidado de su abuela." Treenie, face angry now, was telling me to look after my grandmother and I agreed.

Knowing the two of us probably needed a private place to

talk, Treenie grabbed up a huge wicker basket filled with bags of nuts and headed out to the store to fill counters that were getting low, rotate the stock, and then take day-old packages away to the mission in town, where the churches took turns feeding the homeless and the lonely and the elderly.

Nothing from Miss Amelia's kitchen ever went to waste. She often said she'd rather give it all away than throw her baked goods in a Dumpster.

I leaned against a table next to where Miss Amelia was folding pie boxes.

Meemaw glanced over at me, frowned, and asked, "Are you an ornament, young lady? You see very well I'm working my head off here. Start folding and boxing."

She pushed a stack of boxes at me.

Since I'd worked in one capacity or another in the kitchen since I was little, I fell easily into the routine of folding the cardboard oblongs into pie boxes, then slipping a pie into the box, closing it, sealing the box with a Blanchard crest sticker, and setting it on the rolling cart to take over to the refrigerator or out to the cooler in the store.

We fell into our old routine easily as I caught Miss Amelia up on what was happening and where Hunter and I were going.

"The two of you—alone?" Miss Amelia stepped back and frowned for a minute.

"Meemaw, I'm a big girl. I can take care of myself."

"Humph." She flipped box tops up, creased them, then set her pies down faster and harder. "It's not you I'm worried about. I don't think you should be pushing poor Hunter any farther than you've been pushing him."

"Meemaw, this is for you. This man could have been getting even with the pastor for religious reasons."

"No such thing as a religious reason to kill. That's man-directed stuff. That's power-hungry stuff."

"Still, that's why we're going."

"How long's the drive?"

"About ten and a half hours."

"Ten and a half hours! Alone all that time. I repeat, poor Hunter. You don't know about men, Lindy. A woman shouldn't push a man too far. Trouble comes out of—"

"Is this our sex talk, Meemaw?" I interrupted. "Don't you think it's a little late?"

"Lindy Blanchard!" Miss Amelia reared back on the heels of her sneakers and fixed me with a shocked look. "I wasn't talking about any such thing."

"You were, too. Anyway, I came over here to ask you to go with us. That way you can be our chaperone and talk to Shorty Temple yourself."

Miss Amelia made a sound that seemed to be a bunch of words backed up and stoppered in her throat. "I can't," she finally said.

"Why not? Treenie can run the store."

"You know darned well, young lady."

"Ethelred again. Right?"

Miss Amelia hesitated, as if not willing to share something with me. Finally, after storing more pies, she said, "She's got nobody else and I'm worried."

"I know you've known her a long time, but she's not exactly your best friend."

"Doesn't matter. That's what I'm going to do."

"You applying for sainthood? All that time in the car with Ethelred? Can't be much—the tests for thyroid trouble, if she's planning a cruise."

She shrugged. "Planning and doing are two different things."

After a long sigh, she added, "That Margaret Sanford's got a big mouth. I was at the doctor's when Ethelred learned about having the tests. He mentioned cancer right there and then but Ethelred's ignored the whole thing. She thinks she's going because of the pounds she's been putting on. No such thing."

I swallowed hard, thinking how I'd scoffed at Ethelred throughout my life. Ethelred really sick was a very different human being than the usual Ethelred—pain in the neck. "When will she know for sure?"

"That's what the tests are for. Could mean surgery. Maybe chemotherapy."

"Oh, no . . . Then these big new cars she's been talking about . . . and this cruise . . ."

"All just hoping, Lindy. Something you don't want to take away from anybody."

"And this money she's talking about?"

Miss Amelia shrugged. "Well, that. Swears she found the mother lode. There's some investment club at the church. They asked me to join but I'd rather see to my money myself, thank you."

She looked over toward the door and lowered her voice to a whisper. "But you don't have to worry about Ethelred going to the poorhouse if her investments don't pan out. Her daddy left her very well off. And she's been sitting on that nest egg like one of those pterodactyls. Just hope she didn't invest it all with that group, is what I'm thinking. And now, with this thing she won't admit to . . . well, Ethelred's planning the life she never let herself live, and I say, you go for it."

We hurried out into the store when the bell above the door rang and a busload of tourists, along with Deacon Hawley Harvey, walked in.

"Here for my special pecan pie." The man swaggered down an aisle, watching to see who looked his way. "Wouldn't miss it, Miss Amelia."

"Well, Hawley." Miss Amelia walked up the aisle toward him, putting out her hand to shake his. "Glad to see you're a man of courage."

"No such thing." He shook his head hard. "I know good people when I see 'em. Well, the whole thing's been so awful . . . you understand. But you're a fine upright Christian woman. None the like of. Sure hope you're doing pies for the ground-breaking ceremony next Sunday. Wouldn't be the same Riverville event without 'em."

"Tell somebody to ask," she said, giving him a skeptical look. "Not everybody in town thinks I'm above a little murder. Could be your event committee doesn't want 'em."

"Don't talk like that, Miss Amelia. Of course we want your pies." He leaned in close to smirk. "And your money, too, if you'd still like to invest with all the others."

She only smiled at the man. "Now, you just shop around to your heart's content, Hawley. Lindy and I'll go box up a very special pie out in the kitchen." She canted her head for me to follow.

Getting by Ethelred, rocking at a great pace as she reread her brochure, wasn't easy. Ethelred waved the brochure in my face, more frantic since her talk with Margaret Sanford. "You think the Bahamas, Lindy? I'm thinking the Bahamas. No native people there, are there? I don't want to end up in somebody's soup pot."

"Nope." I patted the woman's hand. "No cannibals in the Bahamas, Miss Ethelred. Leastwise, not yet."

Back in the kitchen, Miss Amelia had something on her mind and needed to share it. She pulled a boxed-up pecan pie from one of the coolers and tied it with string. "What was going on with Margaret Sanford? Sounds like jealousy, doesn't it? I haven't been paying much attention. Never do to gossip. Still, I'm just wondering . . ."

"That's why I don't bother going to church. So many little tempests in tiny teapots." I leaned back and folded my arms.

"Well, not so little to those people. You can't judge the importance of things until you know the confines of a life."

"Right, Meemaw. Chastised again. Still, you think it's anything?"

"I called Pastor Albertson. So much swirling around the church. Then one day he was there, the next he was gone. All we were told was that he retired. I got a card from him at Christmas. His news was sad. His wife, Sally, died. I sent him a condolence card and put his address in my regular daily book. He was surprised to hear from me."

"What'd he say?"

"First, I told him about Pastor Jenkins dying. He was deeply shocked. Said he hadn't heard a word, been on a fishing trip. I asked him if he knew any reason somebody would want to kill the poor man and he said he couldn't think of a thing."

"Nothing? Why'd he leave so fast? You ask him that?"

"Tried but he had to go. Said he'll call me back. Didn't have time to talk right them."

"So not to depend on that angle. Still, maybe he'll come up with something."

"He sounded real concerned. He'll help out all right, if he's got anything."

Before she would let me go, she had a few more questions about my trip to Tupelo with Hunter. There was an admonition to call her every couple of hours.

"Even overnight?" I teased.

"Especially overnight, young lady. I don't want you losing your virtue trying to help me out."

"Meemaw." I launched myself away from the counter, planning a fast getaway. "Remember Humpty Dumpty? 'All the king's horses and all the king's men . . .'"

"Why . . . I can't believe . . ."

I left my sputtering grandmother behind as I hurried over to see Jessie at the library.

Jessie was shelving books in the children's section. Her pretty, small face surrounded by a halo of black curls lit with a broad smile when she saw me coming down the aisle toward her.

We hugged as we always did—sometimes a tight hug when either one of us was miserable about something. We'd been friends long enough to have shared trouble like the loss of my father and Jessie's disappointment in my uncle Amos when he broke her heart. The kind of stuff that brings friends together.

"Let's go outside," Jessie said, giving me a meaningful look. Too many people in the library and we shouldn't be talking in there anyway.

Jessie stopped at the front desk to tell Miss Jenny Hopkins that she was taking a break. We went off to sit in one of my favorite spots in Riverville, a little garden that ran along one side of the low brick library surrounded by tall live oaks. We sat atop a low wall that curved around the flowerbeds, using the first minutes to catch up on how Miss Amelia was doing and how I was doing, how Jessie was doing.

"I stopped by your house this morning. Your mom said you wanted to see me," I said.

"I could've called but I never know who's around and I

don't want to cause anybody trouble. I don't gossip. Lord's sakes, I've been hurt enough by gossip myself."

I knew what she was talking about. Especially all that Uncle Amos trouble. After he had an affair with Finula Prentiss, she declared she was pregnant. Jessie's world blew up and some people weren't kind. Uncle Amos left town though no baby ever appeared. Later the family learned he'd gone to a rehab facility in Houston. The gossips had a field day with Jessie's heartbreak.

"Maybe this is nothing, but I was putting up posters inside the windows and couldn't help overhearing a couple of ladies talking in the vestibule. Something's got them stirred up. What I understood was that they belonged to your grandmother's church. The ladies were whispering but what I got was that there's something going on with the board. At first I thought it was that business of finding a new pastor. But that didn't seem to be it. Or at least not all they were worried about. One of the ladies said she was asking for "hers" back, and she wasn't taking any more stalling. I'm not sure I got it right, but since it was about the church, I thought I'd better tell you. Something about the tone of voice they were using. Pretty determined about something or other."

I frowned. "Asking for what back?"

"No clue. That's all I heard. I wouldn't have said a word except I figured anything to do with the church could be important to Miss Amelia right now. I think almost everybody in town is looking for answers and wanting to help her."

I called Meemaw from the truck on the way back to my apartment. "Jessie wanted to see me about something she overheard," I said.

I'd caught Miss Amelia on her way out. She sounded

tired. "What a day, Lindy. Ethelred's going to sit there in that rocker 'til hell freezes over, I guess. Appointed herself my guardian. Anybody opens their mouth to mention that poor pastor, she jumps right in and causes a ruckus. I'm almost glad I'm taking her to Columbus in the morning. Anything to get her out of the Nut House.

"So what'd Jessie overhear?" she went on after a long yawn.

"Stuff about the church. Women whispering by the library doors about getting something of their own back or getting something back—I don't remember exactly what Jessie said."

"Hmm. Could be anything, Lindy. Most times they're accusing each other of stealing recipes. Important as state secrets, those recipes. At least to the women who worked on them so long. Maybe something their mother left 'em. Still, I'll start talking to folks that come into the store. Only takes a couple of days and I'll see just about everybody from the church. Except maybe Freda Cromwell. Still won't come in, though she's taken to sitting in one of the rockers on the porch since I took her that pie. Poor thing. So lonely without King Charles snarling beside her."

"You won't see me in the morning. We're leaving early."

"Yes," Miss Amelia said absently, as if she'd forgotten she was sending me off into moral turpitude. "Hope I hear back from Pastor Albertson. I'm beginning to wonder if I didn't take him by surprise, calling like that."

Happy to be let off without another warning about separate rooms and keeping my knees together, I hung up and headed back home to pack.

Chapter Twenty-four

Grandma had done her job. For the first three hours of the trip to Tupelo, Mississippi, I sat up straight in the front seat of Hunter's Ford Escape with my knees tight together and my hands clutched in my lap.

Finally I saw what I was doing and got mad at myself and then mad at Miss Amelia. I relaxed, slid down in the seat, and made conversation that didn't begin with "Well . . . if you think so . . ."

"Lunch in Beaumont?" I asked, feeling my stomach growl and remembering I had forgotten to eat breakfast.

"Yeah, let's just get past Houston. Sure thing on Beaumont. Get some barbecue."

"We're doing this Dutch. Understood?"

He looked over at me, smiled, then nodded. "Sure thing. I'm not spending good money feeding you. You eat too much."

"I'm just making the rules clear. You don't need to be disagreeable about it."

"And you don't need to act like I'm going to bite you. Nothing to fear from me, Lindy. I still see you as that short kid with gaps where teeth should be." He chuckled. "Not that I don't remember the time you showed me your underwear . . ."

I sputtered and made a face at him.

His voice turned from teasing to serious. "I'm not saying I haven't thought about you and me." His look, when he turned those laser eyes at me, was deadly serious. "But now's not the time. You agree? I'll be back in night school this fall on top of working my regular shifts. You're tied up in your trees."

I was going to protest until I realized how right he was. There was something between us, always had been. Probably always would be. But not now. Not yet.

Without knowing why, I touched his arm, bare in his crisp beige short-sleeved shirt. No uniform today.

My touch was light. I thought I saw a hint of major regret in Hunter's eyes. I knew there was in mine, but for now we would have to live on "someday."

We drove in silence through the flat open land of Southeast Texas, with its estuaries and curving river coming in from the south. Together we pointed at a road sign advertising Bubba's Rib Shack. Ribs and fries and pickles with fried bread on the side. I could almost taste it.

Lunch was good. Sauce ran down my arm. Meat fell off the bones. Hot enough to leave my mouth tingling. A pickle that snapped. Fried bread that didn't drip grease but was hot and brown with just enough salt to satisfy every taste bud in my mouth. There was nothing like great home cooking that was never just food, but food that set off memories—the Texas State Fair with my daddy and mama; afternoons in Meemaw's kitchen with smells like something floating down from heaven filling me with anticipation; barbecue sauce dripping on my prom gown.

When we were ready to back out of the dirt parking lot into the weight of thick sun, Hunter claimed he needed a nap and threw the keys at me, which made me happy because I didn't like being at the mercy of somebody else's driving. I drove the rest of the way, passing the welcome to Louisiana sign later that afternoon. "Hey." I reached over after a while and punched Hunter's shoulder.

He sat up, bleary-eyed.

"Are we stopping in New Orleans or driving through?"

"I don't know. Didn't give it any thought."

"If you want to drive straight on through to Tupelo, that's fine. We'll take turns driving. If you're planning on stopping the night, then this is as good a place as any."

He nodded after deep thought. "Get us some beignets."

"Could go to Preservation Hall."

"Buy you a bourbon on Bourbon Street."

"Maybe we could stop at a nursery, see what kind of trees they're selling. Sometimes I miss something new on the market that could be just what I'm looking for."

"This isn't supposed to be fun, Lindy." He gave me a serious look.

"I'm talking about work, not fun. But I'll tell you what. I promise not to smile the whole time so we know it's not fun. That work for you?"

"Deal. Not going to make much difference anyway, whether we stop here or farther on."

"So where do you want to stay?"

"Let's look for a motel. Clean and cheap."

"No bedbugs."

"Something not much more than fifty bucks a night."

"Is that the no bedbug range?"

He laughed as I drove off the I-10 toward New Orleans.

The motel we decided on cost each of us fifty-nine dollars including a continental breakfast. Our rooms were next to each other but had no connecting door. We were in those rooms and back out—like two kids, excited about hitting Bourbon Street and talking about going to the casino, just to walk through. And so eager to find Preservation Hall.

My dad had taken me to Preservation Hall to hear what he called "real jazz" when I was fourteen.

Hunter and I found the nondescript place and then, for going on forty-five minutes, we stood in the low-ceilinged, bare-walled room on the creaking wooden floor and listened to three elderly men and one chunky young guy grind out some of the most heartbreaking jazz we ever hoped to hear.

We bought beignets on Bourbon Street and ate them as we walked up and down through the French Quarter, pointing out the wrought-iron railings on the buildings, stopping to watch a silver mime. Then over to Jackson Square to sit on a bench in the late-day sunshine, listening as a large black woman played the best clarinet either one of us had ever heard.

In the midst of a crawfish étouffée-to-die-for dinner at a backstreet café, my cell rang.

"I'm fine, Meemaw," I said then rolled my eyes at Hunter.

"Glad to hear it," Miss Amelia said in my ear. "Not calling about that, though I'm pleased to hear you're fine." She hesitated a minute. "I've been thinking, Lindy. Maybe this is all about something we don't even know to worry about. Maybe somebody hoping to make our church look bad for their own twisted reason. Maybe I'm reaching far afield here, but I've been racking my brains and coming up empty."

"That's a sad state of affairs."

"Now, Lindy. Let's keep our minds on what has to be done."

"Which is?"

"I called Pastor Albertson again. He told me before he was going to think on it a while, and I figured that was long enough. He's out in La Jolla, California, now. I got the impression not too many people from here in Riverville are in touch with him. It was kind of funny, the way he left. One Sunday up there preaching and the next just gone."

"So? What'd he say?"

"Couldn't talk. He's going to call me back later. Don't know why he keeps putting me off, but I sure hope he calls back. I told him it was really important. If he could come up with anything."

She hesitated. "You two in Tupelo yet? Make sure and visit Elvis Presley's house while you're there. Your mama will be mad if you go through and don't stop to pay your respects. Elvis always meant a lot to Emma."

"I don't think so. This isn't a fun trip, you know." I grinned at Hunter, just stuffing a bit of crawfish in his mouth.

"Where are you now?" Meemaw asked.

"We've having dinner in New Orleans."

"New Orleans? That as far as you got?"

"We'll get an early start in the morning."

"You have your rooms yet?"

"Yes, Meemaw. We got our 'rooms.' "

"That's good. You sleep well, you hear? And give my best to Hunter. You tell him I think of him like he was my own son and trust him . . ."

"I'm not saying that, Meemaw. You are embarrassing yourself."

"Well . . . Good night then."

Just the sweet face of Miss Amelia hovering in the air above our heads dampened the evening enough to send us back to our motel, to our separate rooms, and into a fine sleep that got us up early and back on the road.

It was good to see the green hills of Tupelo, and the trees, and the slow unfolding of the town ahead. Hunter went straight to Front Street and the Tupelo police. I sat in the car while he conferred with the police chief inside. The two of them came out together.

Hunter leaned in the window and introduced the chief, a tall, thin man with a large black mustache and a deadly serious face. "Chief Belmont's coming with us. Since I don't have any authority here in Mississippi, he thinks maybe we shouldn't be going out to Shorty Temple's place alone . . ."

The chief leaned in the window. "Might be better if you went on in the station here and waited 'til we get back," he said, giving me one of those patronizing smiles that boiled my blood.

"Thanks for your hospitality, Chief. Think I'll just tag along."

"Could be trouble, ma'am."

What I wanted to say was that I would just fold my hoop skirt up around my head and hide, but I only smiled. "Seen trouble before, Chief."

He wasn't happy about getting into the backseat, pushing a suitcase and carrying bag aside, while I held on to my seat in the front.

The chief pointed the way off Front Street. "We're heading

toward Elvis Presley Lake," he directed. "Not to the lake, just in that general direction."

He turned his long face toward me, pasting on a smile. "You been to the Elvis Presley house yet?"

I said my meemaw told me not to miss it and he seemed happier with me, as if having relatives meant I wasn't some stray cat he could get saddled with eventually.

At the end of a dirt road a few miles out of town, the chief pointed to a low, white house, checked the address he'd written on a pad of paper, and indicated that Hunter park the car on the road.

"We'll walk on up to the house. I don't know Shorty, but I heard tell he got in a lot of trouble some years back. Tell the truth, I didn't even know he was out of prison. Probably should've known. Thing is, the man's caused no trouble at all since coming back here."

The front yard was nothing but dirt, stomped on, flattened, bare dirt. An ancient pickup, looking like it was painted with pure rust, was parked up beside the house, under a falling-in carport.

Chief Belmont knocked hard at a screened door with a flap of loose screen shivering at being moved. It took a while but eventually the inside door opened and a small woman in a long, washed-out dress, with brown hair hanging to her shoulders and a worried face stood there, just looking us over—one after the other.

"Shorty Temple live here?" the chief demanded.

She nodded.

"He home?"

She nodded again.

"Could we come in and talk to him?"

She said nothing, only stepped back to make room for a

very tall, very skinny, very stooped man to step up to the door. I got the irony of calling him Shorty. He was one of the tallest, skinniest men I'd ever seen. Like a long, colored-in shadow.

"Officer." Shorty nodded to the chief, then slowly moved his eyes, cold blue and lost in a map of wrinkles, over Hunter and me.

He pushed the door open and stepped out onto the small wooden porch, forcing us backward, down the steps into the dusty yard.

The chief took over as the four of us stood in heat that was ramping up over one hundred. "You hear about Parson Jenkins over in Riverville?"

Shorty said nothing, only looked from face to face.

"Used to be your brother-in-law. Imagine you'd recognize the name."

Finally Shorty shook his head. "What about him?"

"Dead."

Shorty made a sorrowful face. "Sorry to hear it. Good man."

Chief nodded slowly in return. "Thing is, Shorty, Hunter here is a deputy with the Riverville, Texas, sheriff's department. He's come all this way to talk to you about the pastor."

"Where's that? Riverville?" Shorty squinted down at Hunter, who was taller than most men ever reach.

"About halfway between Houston and San Antonio." Hunter tried hard to look official.

"Don't think I know it." The man scratched behind his left ear and looked off into the distance. He turned some pretty fierce eyes on me. "Who're you?"

I gave my name and held out my hand, which the man ignored.

"Anyway, I'll let Deputy Austen finish telling you why

we're here." The chief swept his hand out toward Hunter, whose face was growing red from the sun.

"I don't know about the rest of you, but I'm not standing here melting," Hunter said and moved back, into the elongated shade of a tall black gum tree. The only tree in the sorry yard.

"What I'm here for, Shorty, is because the parson was murdered," Hunter explained when we were all shaded and somewhat cooler.

The man took a step back, as if almost bowled over. "Murdered? Why would anybody do that to Millroy? When I said he was a good man, I meant it. I got no problem with him. To tell the truth, I'm happy that Selma had people like Millroy and Dora to take her in. I wasn't a fit husband for 'er. Not a fit man until I found the Lord in prison."

Hunter nodded. "Good to hear. But about Millroy—we don't know why anybody wanted to kill him. That's what we're here for."

"You don't think I'd do something like that, do you? Maybe, back when I was drinkin'. I was crazy back then. How'd he die?"

"He was shot," Hunter lied, then watched Shorty's face closely. "You pretty good with a gun?"

"Fer the Lord's sakes." Shorty shook his head again and again. I could swear he had tears in his eyes. "I won't even have a gun in my house, knowing how a human being can be drug in by evil. Must've been a robbery or something, eh? That Riverville a rough place? I hear Texas got plenty of criminals."

"No robbery. Done on purpose."

"Awful for Dora. I'll be on my knees soon as I get back in that house. Me and Georgia will be prayin' all day for the poor man. I thank you for bringing me the news. But it's got nothing to do with me. I hope you can tell Dora and Selma that Shorty's sorry for their trouble." He turned as if to go back into the house.

Hunter stopped him, calling out, "So you got religion in prison. Seems kind of convenient, hiding behind God."

The man turned back slowly, his craggy face wreathed in sorrow. "Found my Lord and Savior, Jesus Christ. Yes, I did. I know what I done before. Never gonna happen to me again."

"That mean you're not trying to get even with Selma? That's not what we heard."

"Hurt Selma? Not anymore. Why, I'd go down on my knees in front of her this minute and tell her how sorry I am for what I did—if she'd let me. What I learned is that the biggest favor I can do Selma is to stay far away from her. What the chaplain in prison taught me was that trying to apologize in person was a thing I wanted for myself and that 'myself' wasn't the important one here."

"So you had nothing against the pastor?"

Shorty took a long time shaking his head. "You really think I did something to Millroy? Don't even own a gun."

"He wasn't shot, Shorty," Hunter answered. "I didn't tell the truth about that. He was poisoned."

"Poisoned! What the heck you come talking to me about it for? That's women who poison people. Not men."

"Well . . ." The chief stepped in. "Not exactly true, Shorty. More men than women use one kind of poison or another. Maybe in the olden days a woman could do in her husband with a dose of ant poison and get away with it. Not now."

"You aware of a scripture that says something about a man only proving he was truly righteous by taking poison and living?" Hunter asked.

He nodded. "Know it. Mark. 'Bout true believers: *'They will throw out demons in my name, they will speak with new tongues, they will take snakes in their hands, they will drink poison and not be hurt, they will lay hands on the sick and make them well.'* Snake handlers quote this when they're takin' up rattlers."

"Seems like the kind of thing a man with a little too much religion might use to kill off an enemy. You know, quoting scripture while doing evil. Like if the parson drank poison and lived, he was truly a good man after all."

"Not me. I know better than to be fooled by false gods and false words. Alcohol's the evil I let into me, but I haven't had a drink since the first day I come out of prison. Living the best life I can now. Georgia used to drink, too. Lost her husband. Kids hate her. We're all we've got—just the two of us. I wouldn't do anything to mess my life up any more than I already done. Especially not to a good man like Millroy."

I knew the truth when I heard it. I looked at Hunter, who gave the same message back to me. I thought of one more thing and broke in for the first time.

"Would you write a letter saying what you just said about Selma? How sorry you are?"

"'Course. You give me an address."

I shook my head. "No. We'll take it to her. Why don't we just wait out here in the car. A couple of lines will be enough. Tell her you're sorry for hurting her and say you're not drinking and you're getting your life together. Wish her well and promise you'll never bother her. It'll mean a lot to her. Maybe set her free in some way. That all right with you?"

Shorty nodded. He promised to be right back out and went into the house while the chief, Hunter, and I sought out the air-conditioned car.

The tall man was back in fifteen minutes carrying a single sheet of paper in his hands. He shoved it in the window at me, nodded, and sauntered back to his house.

I read the paper out loud:

Selma. As God is my witness I am sorry for ever hurting you and I swear I would die a hundred times before I ever hurt you again. Your old husband, Shorty Temple.

PS—I heard about Millroy. You tell Dora he was a good man.

Chapter Twenty-five

Mama called just after we dropped off the chief. When she heard we were in Tupelo, her voice went up into a teenager's trill.

"Tupelo! Why, for heaven's sakes. Don't miss Elvis's house. It's on Elvis Presley Drive. Signs everywhere. You know he was there in 1936, the year the big tornado hit Tupelo? More than two hundred people dead. Can you imagine, Lindy? Elvis was spared. And we all know why, don't we? You miss it, you'll be sorry your whole life long."

"Mama, we found that man Selma was married to."

"'Course. What was I thinking about? Just the name 'Tupelo' took me back. What'd the man say? What did the police there say about him? I know Miss Amelia will be on pins and needles, waiting to hear what you found out."

"We don't think he had anything to do with the parson's death, Mama. The man's very sorry for what he did to Selma. Got a new wife. Very religious."

"Hmmp. Lots of people get religion in prison. I wouldn't be too quick to fall—"

"Mama," I interrupted. "Tell you what. I'll ask Hunter to drive by Elvis's house just so I can say I saw it and then we're heading home."

"There's something else, Lindy. We're both so busy we don't often get a chance to talk, but it's this Jeffrey Coulter. You know your meemaw can't stand him, and I don't like the way Bethany's falling all over him."

"You have a talk with her yet?"

"I tried last night. She thinks we're being unfair. He's got her bamboozled. I'm talking to Justin today. I want that man out of my house as soon as we can get him to go."

"I thought Meemaw said something to Justin about Jeffrey not being what he thought he was."

"I heard that. Didn't seem to do much good. I never knew Justin to go against your grandmother's feelings like this. I just wish I knew what was going on."

"You try asking him?"

"Justin? You ever try asking him anything? That boy's as tight-lipped as a statue. Think I was the CIA, I ask him what's up with a single thing he's doing."

"I'll talk to him when I get back there. He's got to see it's not working, having Jeffrey underfoot. Especially now, with so much trouble hanging over our heads."

"Thanks, Lindy. You and Justin are close. Tell him we don't need somebody always sneering, like we're a big joke to him. And having him laying in bed all morning and coming down, expecting somebody to be feeding him. Can you imagine? Bethany was complaining because 'poor Jeffrey' got nothing for breakfast this morning. I told her to give him directions to the refrigerator or The Squirrel. Now she's not talking to me."

"Mama, I promise. I'll talk to Justin as soon as I get back."

"Well, I thank you again, Lindy. You drive carefully, ya hear? And tell Hunter what a fine boy I think he is. More like a son . . ."

"Yes, Mama. I'll pass on the word."

Although he groaned, Hunter found Elvis Presley Drive and slowed as we drove by the white shotgun house where Elvis was born. The house was set up on blocks, and a swing dangled from hooks on the front porch. There were other buildings. Signs pointed to the church he attended as a boy, a chapel, a museum. A kind of Elvis Presley complex.

"You want to go in?" I was excited, now that I was there. "Maybe just walk through the house."

"Don't know if you can do that. It's the whole thing, I'll bet. And we really should be heading back."

I slumped. "At least I can tell Mama I saw it. She was here when she was a teenager. Can't see my meemaw bringing her. Maybe the senator was more indulgent. She even put up a huge Elvis poster in my room, insisting every young girl needed one."

We settled down for the ride home. Hunter drove for the first two hours. I took over after that. There wasn't much enthusiasm about stopping in New Orleans this time.

"Want to just keep driving?" I asked.

"Think that's best. We got what we came after."

He took the wheel after a quick potty and peanuts stop.

"To tell the truth, I hate to tell Miss Amelia," I said when we were back on the road. "I should call her."

"You told your mama. Miss Amelia knows by now."

"True."

"Anyway," Hunter said. "I was hoping right along with her. Thought maybe we'd have Shorty locked up and waiting extradition to Texas by the time we started home."

I felt depression slowly settling in. "Poor Meemaw. What do we do next? You have any ideas?"

He shook his head, glanced down at the speedometer, and slowed. "One thing's still bothering me, though. I hate to bring it up. Probably it doesn't have anything to do with anything, but it's about why Miss Amelia dished up more of her Texas caviar for the parson. It's the only solid thing I know of that doesn't fit anywhere and it's driving me crazy."

I thought a minute. "I asked her."

"What'd she say?"

"Something about wanting him to taste the real thing."

He looked over at me, making a face. "What wasn't real about the stuff he judged?"

I shrugged. "Don't ask me. Meemaw's funny about her recipes. Maybe, since she didn't win, she was afraid that judging batch wasn't up to what it should've been."

"Like it could've gone bad or something?"

"That's what she was afraid of."

"What's in that stuff?"

"If I remember, it's black-eyed peas and jalapeños and peppers. Lot of vinegar, I know. Garlic. Cumin. Nothing to spoil, if you ask me. And anyway, something going bad wasn't what killed the parson. Somebody deliberately laced Miss Amelia's caviar with ground-up spotted water hemlock."

"I know. Just can't quite figure why she was giving him her caviar when she wasn't supposed to. Weren't the winning dishes the only ones served? Kind of pushy, making him taste more of her caviar. Doesn't seem like your grandmother."

I leaned forward and looked hard at him. "You're not

back to thinking Miss Amelia had anything to do with it, are you?"

"'Course not. Just feels wrong. There's something else. Her losing like that, then serving more of the losing dish to the man. Something smells really wrong there."

"Why don't you go ask her yourself?"

"Don't get huffy. I'm trying to figure out what happened just as hard as you are."

There was quiet in the car for miles after that, until we stopped to eat, and afterward, I took over the driving again. The trip was going fast.

I was just back on US 45 when my cell rang. Mama again. Maybe checking to make sure I got to Elvis's house.

"Lindy?" Mama's voice trembled. "Something awful's happened. I don't even know how . . ."

"Slow down, Mama. What's the matter?" I looked over at Hunter, who sat up, listening hard.

"Just awful, Lindy. You gotta come straight back here. I mean . . . we need you."

"Mama, of course I'm coming straight home. Now get ahold of yourself and tell me what's going on."

"Oh, Lindy. It's Treenie Menendez."

"What happened to Treenie?"

"Just awful. She's in the hospital. Treenie could die."

"What! Mama. Tell me. What's going on?"

"She found a jar she thought was some kind of spice left out on a shelf in the store. No label on it. She stuck her finger inside to taste it and was choking and gagging in fifteen minutes. Because of what happened to the pastor, the doctors started treating her for that spotted hemlock right away. She might make it, but they don't know. Miss Amelia is distraught. Absolutely distraught. She won't leave the hospital though Sheriff Higsby's got a guard on Treenie's room and won't let Miss Amelia go in to see her."

"Oh, no. You mean he thinks it's something Meemaw did? I can't believe this is happening."

"I need you here, Lindy. Miss Amelia's been crying and asking for you."

"Fast as I can, Mama. Fast as I can."

Chapter Twenty-six

We didn't get back until almost morning—those last few miles being torture, slipping into slow motion so I thought we'd never get there.

Hunter hurried down the hall to talk to the deputy guarding Treenie's room while I went looking for Meemaw. She was asleep in a waiting room chair. She sat up, startled, when I put my hand on her arm and whispered her name. I'd never seen my grandmother this disheveled and wild-eyed. I squeezed her hand hard, holding on but not knowing what to say to her.

Miss Amelia closed her eyes and leaned back, her head against the wall. "Poor Treenie. Can't believe this is happening."

"Why would she go ahead and taste something when she didn't know what it was?" I was mystified.

"That's what cooks do. We know what things taste like. It was just a small bottle left out on a shelf in the store. I mighta done the same thing. I've done things like it many times. When a label falls off a spice bottle. When the words get worn off . . ."

"Who would have put the jar on a shelf in the Nut House? Wouldn't someone have seen them do it?"

Meemaw shook her head and waved both hands as if pushing reality away. "Heaven's sakes, Lindy. I don't always know what's going on in that store. When those tourist buses come through, the place is jam-packed for half an hour or so. Plenty of times we got people roaming up and down the aisles, looking at stuff, touching stuff, putting things back on counters and on shelves then taking them down again. I don't have eyes in the back of my head, you know."

Miss Amelia reared back to fix me with an impatient look. "And don't you go asking me, like the sheriff did, if any strangers were in. We've always got strangers in the store."

"I don't think whoever's doing this is a stranger," I shot back, then went on to tell her what we'd learned in Tupelo, that Shorty Temple was an upright citizen, changed by his time in prison.

She nodded, then pushed steely gray hair back from her eyes, patting it in place. "I heard and I'm just as glad. Been awful if Selma thought she had any part in this."

"So let me ask it differently." I felt I had to get ahold of something in this big mess. Just one thing, a path I could go down and say, *"There, that's who's doing this to my grandmother."*

I asked, "Anybody from town come in recently who doesn't usually come in? Any group maybe?"

"Morton Grover and Suzy Queen were in this morning with some of the girls from the saloon. Just to say how much they support me. They nearly bought me outta pies. And . . . let me see now . . . some of the people from church. I think it was Hawley Harvey's idea, to come over and show people like Freda Cromwell they are all in my corner. Thought that was a nice gesture from Hawley."

She hesitated a minute, then put a hand to her mouth. "Oh dear. Oh dear. After this, nobody's going to believe I didn't poison Reverend Jenkins. And nobody's gonna want to buy anything I make. You think the sheriff's going to arrest me?"

"Sounds more like somebody's after you. No use blaming you just 'cause the sheriff doesn't know who else to blame."

I looked at her face. Set and determined. I truly believed Meemaw didn't have a whole lot to worry about—at least I fervently hoped not.

She held my hand extra tight, hard enough to break my heart.

"I've got to think. Just got to think," she said, looking around the waiting room where two people sat reading old magazines. "Somebody's doing this 'cause they want me put away in a prison. For heaven's sakes! Who'd have thought I'd ever done something so bad to anybody . . ."

She shook her head.

"Not just put you away in prison. If they put that jar or bottle or whatever on one of your shelves, who'd be most likely to taste it?"

Her eyes got big. "Why, Lindy, I think you're right. So poor Treenie's in there suffering and maybe dying because someone's after me."

She moaned. "I hate to think I'm the cause of more misery."

"Not your fault and you know it. Let's think hard on this. We know it had nothing to do with Selma and that ex-husband of hers."

"My head's spinning . . ."

"You go with Ethelred to the hospital in Columbus?"

She nodded. "Yesterday."

"She get results yet?"

Miss Amelia nodded. "Not the worst news. Still, since Margaret Sanford planted the idea, Ethelred's sure she's gonna die. She's gonna have to get that thyroid out and then have some treatments. But you can't tell her it's not a death sentence. Still wants to blow all her money on a big car or a cruise so the state doesn't grab it when she dies. Hope she can get it out of that investment club at the church. Don't know. From what I've been hearing, that addition's cutting into profits the investors were promised, and people who invested are starting to rumble about wanting their money back. I said all along—don't mix religion and money. People should've learned that a long time ago: no money changers in the temple."

"I'm really sorry to hear about Ethelred. As much as the woman annoys me, I don't want to see her sick."

"Me either. Whatever's going to happen, I already promised I'd be with her through the whole thing."

"Oh, Meemaw. You've got a handful of your own troubles right now."

She thought a minute, then gave a small, rueful laugh. "You're right. I could be sitting in a jail rather than in a hospital with Ethelred."

"Can I ask you something else?" I asked, wanting to get away from thoughts of jails and prisons. "Tell me the truth now. You gave the parson more of your caviar after he showed he didn't like it by not voting you a prize. Why?

There's more to the story than you've been telling. This is Lindy, remember?"

There was a long, thoughtful pause. I was determined to wait her out. When she looked back at me, I saw a little bit of sadness, and a lot of embarrassment written on her face. She bit at her bottom lip. "If I tell you, will you keep it a secret?"

I shook my head. "Not on your life. I'm telling Hunter and the sheriff and anybody else who needs to know. We've got to move on with this, Meemaw. I don't know who's after you and I don't know why, but it's obvious that the first target might have been the parson but the next target is you. You're the one somebody's trying to blame for what happened. I need to know everything. And I mean everything."

Meemaw gave a long sigh before looking around the waiting room. She got up and motioned for me to follow her out into the hall, where no one could hear us. Out there, she leaned in close.

"This can't get around. It would just kill . . . well, you just can't . . ."

"Kill who?"

"It was all about Ethelred."

"Ethelred? What's she got to do with any of this, beyond taking up that rocking chair in the store like she's watching you?"

Miss Amelia, looking disappointed, shook her head at me. "I just felt so sorry . . ."

"Sorry? For what?"

"Let me finish talking." She lowered her voice as a nurse walked by. "It was something I cooked up with the pastor, because he was going to be a judge in that last event. I knew about Ethelred's medical problems. I was thinking it might be worse than it turned out to be, what with her symptoms and all. The woman was scared and looking peaked. Something told me I couldn't go on being selfish and keep her from winning. I knew I had to do something for the poor soul, make her happy in some way. It's said you can beat a lot of things in life if you've got a happy outlook. Well, Ethelred's never been one to be very cheerful." She gave me a long look. "It was something I had to do, and winning that award was the only thing that would put a smile on Ethelred's face."

"And the pastor went along with you?"

She nodded. "Had a hard time at first. He didn't like the thought of cheating. That's what he called it. But I told him it was just this once and for the highest of causes. He was the only one I told about Ethelred facing serious health issues."

"So he agreed to throw the contest." I was astounded. I knew my grandmother was good at persuasion, but persuading an upright man like Millroy Jenkins to throw a contest . . . well, the idea made my jaw drop.

"Stop it, young lady. It wasn't throwing anything. What you've still got to learn is that there are times in life when you aren't the most important person on the planet. Ethelred needed happiness right then, and me and the parson were the only two people around to give it to her."

"Meemaw." I shook my head at her. "That was . . ." I was going to say "awful" but figured I'd save the effort, since she was convinced her reasons for throwing the contest Ethelred's way were high moral ones. Instead I took another direction. "Did the parson ever talk it over with anybody besides God?"

"I don't know. Millroy was a very upright man. I could see he wasn't happy about doing what I was asking. Still, there are times . . . even for a pastor . . . when doing good work means breaking some of the rules. Anyway, he agreed and that was that. I don't know if anybody but God was in on it." She shrugged. "Maybe Dora."

"So the pastor voted for Ethelred. But how'd he get the other two judges to vote for her?"

Miss Amelia colored just a little. "I didn't make that first dish of caviar taste too good."

"Oh, Meemaw."

She shrugged. "Had to do it. Piles of garlic and the teeniest bit of alum. Makes the mouth pucker a little. Then my pride kicked in and I told the pastor I was giving him some of the real stuff later, at the dinner, to prove I still knew what I was doing. That was something just between the two of us. Almost a kind of inside joke, you might call it."

I wanted to groan. "I'll tell Hunter."

"Do you have to?"

I didn't even answer. She knew better than to think her little secret was safe with me at that point.

I glanced down the hall to where Hunter stood talking to a doctor, just outside a room I figured had to be Treenie's.

"Would they let me go in and see how she's doing?" I nodded toward the deputy.

"I don't think so. Wouldn't even let me in."

"What'd they say about the poison?"

"They're treating it as if it was spotted hemlock, same as Millroy's poisoning. At least until the toxicology report comes back. Wanted to get it right on this one." She sighed. "Sheriff's upset. But I don't think it's so much with me. I think he still believes I had nothing to do with any of it. But who knows for how long? First the poison's in my caviar. Then it's in my store. What's next? Caught with the stuff in my hand? Good thing is, the man doesn't take me for a fool—putting it into my own dish and having it in my own store."

"I'm glad to hear that."

"Still, if we don't find out what's behind this, well, of course he's got to take another look at me."

"It's not 'what's behind this,'" I said. "It's 'who's' behind it."

We sat still, thinking hard. I ran things around in my head. There had to be something else. Something we were missing or didn't even know to wonder about yet.

"You hear back from the Reverend Albertson?" I took in the circles under her eyes and the new sag to her usually straight shoulders. I didn't know how much more she could take. Now a good friend put in danger . . .

Slowly, she shook her head. "Been too upset about Treenie to even think about anything else. All he had was the store phone number to call back at. If you go there and you want to open up—'cause I'm staying here—would you check the answering machine for me?"

I'd already planned to go to the store, but not to open. I needed a shower and a change of clothes. First I needed to talk to Hunter, tell him what I'd found out. I led Miss Amelia back into the waiting room, where I assured her I would certainly check the answering machine. As she began in earnest to describe which products had to go into which refrigerators and which had to be baked off, I waved both hands at her and fled as she called after me. "And if Justin wants to help out in the store, don't let him bring that Jeffrey Coulter with him. You hear me, Lindy? There's something about that boy . . ."

Hunter was back from checking on Treenie, smiling. "She's going to be okay. Just talked to the doctor. Close, but she didn't get enough to kill her."

"Meemaw's got news for you, too, Hunter. Think there's more than one or two little intrigues going on here."

I got the look I expected to get from my grandmother. Shock and annoyance. Then eye-narrowing outrage.

"You tell Hunter all about it, Meemaw. I'm going home to shower and change clothes and maybe even lay down for a couple of hours. I don't want anybody calling me or knocking at my door. I'm going to sleep. Then I'm going to eat . . ."

Now she had new concerns to worry about. "Don't forget Pastor Albertson. If he called, you've got to call him back. And you were going to talk to Justin. Remember? About that Jeffrey. Oh, and tell Bethany to take that Outhouse Moon dough out of the refrigerator and let it stand awhile . . ."

I turned my back and left, thinking maybe I'd go back to school. A Ph.D. would be a good thing to have. Or I'd move into my greenhouse. Lock the door. Never let anybody in. Become a hermit with trays of food left outside.

For most of the way back to the Nut House, just the idea of solitude calmed me down.

Chapter Twenty-seven

I stayed in the shower until I ran out of hot water, which could have put a strain on anybody cooking in Meemaw's kitchen below—had anybody been down there. I heard my cell ring a couple of times while I basked in steamy water, but there are moments in life when what a person needs most is to be away from ringing phones and frightened voices, and yet one more dire event. This was my moment.

It's not like those phone calls disappeared into some gentle ether. I dried my skin and shook my hair dry—much like a dog coming out of a river, and went to stare down at my cell before picking it up to see that both Justin and Hunter wanted me.

I still had a few minutes to myself and found clean white clam diggers and a yellow tee and a pair of sandals that actually looked almost new. When I checked the half of me I could see in the bathroom mirror, I thought I was passable. Could get through another day of whatever was coming my way and at the same time do the Blanchard family proud.

It was a toss-up, between Justin and Hunter, but I thought I'd better get Justin out of the way since Meemaw and Mama wanted me to talk to him anyway. Family was always supposed to come first, especially in emergency times like these.

"Lindy, yeah," Justin greeted me. "We gotta talk about some things."

"First off, who's with Meemaw at the hospital?"

"Mama should be there by now. Heard Treenie's going to be okay."

"Bethany open the store?"

"Yup."

"Thought I heard somebody down there. Hope she didn't bring Jeffrey in with her. I'm telling you, Justin, Meemaw and Mama don't like Jeffrey Coulter."

"I know." His voice dropped. "But what do you expect me to do? Chase him outta the house?"

"I'm not saying that but right now, geez, don't you think you could ask him to go? I mean, under the circumstances, wouldn't you think the guy would offer to clear out?"

"Guess he doesn't see things . . . well, like we see them. His daddy's real rich, Lindy. I mean New York City rich. Jeffrey's, well, he takes some getting used to."

"Nobody likes how he's coming on to Bethany. She's acting ditzy."

"She's always acting ditzy."

"No, don't blow it off. Find him another place. How about one of the other ranches? They're all your friends."

"You don't understand, Lindy . . ." His voice trailed off.

"Then explain it. I don't think you even like him much."

"Lindy . . ."

"Come on, Justin."

"He did me a big favor back in college."

"Uh-oh. He save your neck or something?"

"Kind of like that. I got caught with pot in my room. Probably some other friend left it there. I wasn't doing any of that stuff, I swear. Still, campus police got a tip and they came in and found it. I could've been thrown out of college. You know what that would have done to Mama?"

"So? What happened?"

"Jeffrey said it was his. He took the fall on it, but his daddy came up with some pretty big lawyers that got the school to slack off prosecution and expulsion."

"What if it was his to begin with?"

"Said it wasn't."

"Oh, Justin," I moaned. "Look, that was a long time ago. That man's got to go." I took a deep breath, thinking it was time to move on to another disaster—whatever Justin called me for.

"Okay, so why did you call?"

"Bethany's at the Nut House, like I said, and she's afraid to call you. She said she's getting all sorts of phone calls, people wondering when they could pick up pies they'd ordered. She said she's overwhelmed and there's nobody but you to help out. Think you could? Work the rest of the day?"

"Is she going to run off on me? Go someplace with Jeffrey?"

"No. That couple from Sheridan's coming in to sign their contract for the wedding. She says she can't do that and take care of the store, too."

"Crap! You know what? I'll call Jessie. She offered before to help out."

He was relieved to know he'd be getting Bethany off his back.

"You tell her she better not take off with Jeffrey. She does that and Meemaw will snatch her baldheaded."

Jessie, as usual, was not just dependable but eager to help out. I worked with her the first couple of hours after letting Bethany go. Between onslaughts of people, I filled her in on what had been happening.

"I'm going over to talk to Dora and Selma. Me and Hunter went to Tupelo."

"I sure heard about that." Jessie pulled at her Rancho en al Colorado T-shirt. "People are wondering what's going to come first, the wedding or a baby."

I groaned. "Tell 'em it was business. Strictly business."

She laughed, then got serious.

"You find out anything about Selma's ex-husband?"

"You knew about that, too?"

"My father heard from Justin."

"Yeah, well, we found out he's the one did damage to Selma's leg. Found out, too, he's the reason they left Tupelo. He was in prison and still threatening Selma."

"Sounds like a good candidate for murderer."

"Yeah. Turns out he got religion in prison. He's got a new wife. He truly is a changed man. Very worried about Selma. I've got a note he sent to her. He wishes her well and asks for forgiveness. I don't think he had anything at all to do with murdering the pastor."

"At least you're getting things out of the way—I mean, people who can't have done it. Like this new thing with Treenie."

I agreed. Shorty was the first one off that list. But the list didn't have many names left. And when I crossed off the last one—what then?

I checked the answering machine, in case Pastor Albertson had called. Nothing from him on there.

It was almost one o'clock by the time Bethany was back at the Nut House and I got over to the parsonage to call on Selma and Dora and deliver Shorty's note. Water spouts, shooting from the garden's sprinkling system, shot rainbows of water over the flowers, making foliage and colors shimmer in the sun. I walked deliberately through an arc of cold water, enjoying the feeling on my hot skin.

I was refreshed after eating a huge sandwich with a couple of the cinnabuns as dessert. Now I was ready to go.

Selma was at the far end of her garden, large straw hat clamped to her head so only half her face showed beneath it. She waved and peeled off her gardening gloves. Still very much the Southern woman, she gardened in a skirt and blouse, making me want to groan at how far some of these women still had to go.

"Why, Lindy! I didn't know you were coming over," she greeted me.

The transformation in Selma was all too obvious. She was holding her head high again, even smiling. The beaten-down woman who'd hung behind her sister seemed to have disappeared. She came up the walk fast, her limp barely noticeable.

"Hunter and I saw Shorty and . . ." I fumbled in the pocket of my slacks for the note.

"I know. I know. You'll never guess. Shorty called me. All apologies. He told me he would never do anything to hurt me, and didn't do a thing to Millroy. I believe him, Lindy. I really do believe him."

"That's what his note says." I handed it over. Selma unfolded the note and scanned it quickly.

"I'm sorry I sent you on a wild-goose chase, but I was so afraid. I mean, I heard he was out of prison. He could've gone on one of his old rampages, coming here and punishing Millroy for getting me away from him, the way he did."

I smiled back at the glowing woman. "Not a wild-goose chase. I got to see Elvis's house."

"Did you?" Selma beamed. "Isn't that just the most remarkable place? Why, I've been through it more times than I'd like to admit."

"Is Dora home?" I figured Selma had missed the irony of Elvis taking the place of finding a killer.

"She sure is. Come on, let's go up to the house. I got sweet tea in the fridge."

"And, Selma. We still don't know who dug up that hemlock by the river."

She wrinkled her face. "We don't, do we."

As we walked, I kept talking about why I'd come though Selma pointed out new blossom after new blossom, seeming so relieved that Shorty would never bother her again that she was forgetting Millroy's death.

"I been meaning to ask you about those people who help out here in your garden. You said folks from the church come on in and do what needs doing."

She nodded, her hat wobbling so she had to hold it with her hand.

"Anybody in particular? I mean, anybody here a lot?"

"Oh, so many. Ladies from the Women's Garden Society. Your grandmother comes once a week. Even some of the men come over when they've got a minute or two to do a little weeding. I just love watching them stroll over from

the church, knowing they love the garden as much as I do.
And in return, I help them as much as I can. I do the flowers for all the dinners and luncheons. Whatever they need
over there."

"Nice," I said. "But no special help. Any one person . . ."

"Well, you know it was the board that put in the sprinkling system for me. I couldn't believe it, the day Millroy
came home and told me they'd put the garden right into
their budget. He said they thought it was an asset to the
church and to the parsonage. I even got a warm letter from
Tyler Perkins, thanking me, in the name of the board, for
all my work in beautifying the grounds."

"Tyler ever come over to help?"

"He's not much of a gardener. But Hawley comes, time
to time, to do a little edging and things like that. Paid for
some of that irrigation himself. Hawley's a fine man."

"But nobody you've ever seen going down to the river?"

We were at the front door. Selma stopped to think then
pushed the door open. The house was warm. Fans turned
lazily overhead. The blinds were shut against the sun. Cool
enough.

Selma shook her head at me and put a finger to her lips
before calling out to Dora that she had a guest coming in
with her.

Dora was at the kitchen table, a notepad in front of her,
pen in her hand. She didn't smile or look happy when she
looked up. Didn't even look sad.

"Dora." I nodded and got a brief nod back.

"How are you, Lindy?"

"I know this is still a bad time but I had to come over to
talk to you."

"My bereavement hasn't stopped Sheriff Higsby from
asking questions. Why should it stop you?" She set her pen

down and folded her hands on the table. "I heard about Treenie. Terrible thing. Whoever's doing this has got to be stopped. It's like . . . well, I don't know . . . a kind of Biblical plague starting up."

"Nothing like that, Dora. You're just grieving so bad maybe you see things darker than they really are. Treenie's going to be okay. I was at the hospital this morning."

Dora shot a telling look at her sister. "Well, I'm relieved to hear it. I heard tell the poison was right on the shelf at the Nut House."

I sighed. "In an unmarked bottle. Treenie stuck her finger in to taste it. You know how women do."

Dora nodded. "I'll say one thing, Lindy. I'm beginning to see how this doesn't have a thing in the world to do with Miss Amelia. Your grandmother is not stupid enough to keep poison on her store shelves. Most people I've been talking to feel the same way. Instead of making everybody suspicious, it's making all of us see somebody's trying to pull the wool over our eyes."

I felt enormously relieved, just hearing the words.

"So now that I've got my head together a little bit . . ." Dora's brief smile was sweet. "I want to help you in any way I can. I owe Millroy finding the truth, and me and Selma are dedicated to bringing whoever did this to justice."

"I'm truly happy to hear it, Dora. Miss Amelia's been suffering, as you may well expect."

"What I've been doing is going over the last weeks before Millroy died. In my head, you know. Thinking and thinking about how he'd been, if he'd been acting different, if something was on his mind."

"What'd you come up with?"

"Let me tell you." She pointed to a chair, inviting me to sit.

Selma joined us then hopped up to take down three tall glasses from the cupboard, go to the refrigerator, and pour sweet tea for everybody.

"Millroy was acting like he was sad about something. I mean, like he had a heavy weight on his shoulders. I even asked him one day if there was something he wanted to discuss. For a minute, I thought he was going to confide in me, but Millroy doesn't like to put burdens of the soul on other people—eh, I mean didn't—if he could handle things himself. Comes from his years being a pastor to a flock. A lot of secrets get told to a man of the cloth. One thing a pastor has to do is learn to shoulder people's problems and keep them to himself.

"Anyway, I could see he was worrying. The day before he was killed, we were having breakfast . . . you remember, don't you?" She'd turned to Selma, who only shrugged.

"That day Millroy sat right here in this kitchen and told us he'd been praying hard on something."

Selma nodded now. "Yes, I do remember. I thought it was about the color to paint the addition. Something like that."

Selma smiled at her sister. That these two would always care for each other was pretty obvious. It made me think for just a second how I often treated Bethany. But then . . . I started excusing myself . . . Bethany could be a big pain, especially over this Jeffrey thing . . .

"On his way out the door the morning before he died, Millroy kissed me good-bye, the way he always does, and said something about deciding to get ahold of Pastor Albertson. He was going to ask the previous pastor's advice. I told him I thought that was a very good idea."

"Advice about what?"

"Well, *that* I don't know. If Millroy wanted to share

with me, that was always fine. But like I said, a man of the cloth is sometimes sorely burdened."

"Did he call Pastor Albertson?"

"I couldn't tell you. You might want to talk to Tyler Perkins. As president of the board, you'd think he'd know if there was something going on."

I finished off my tea and got up to leave.

"I saw him going in the church a while ago," Selma said. "Might still catch him."

Chapter Twenty-eight

I was out of there and sprinting across the lawn between the two buildings. No word from Hunter yet. There was only one car in the parking lot, a red Cadillac. Somehow the white-steepled church and the shiny Cadillac didn't go together, but I figured, as the only pharmacist in River-ville, Tyler had to do pretty well for himself.

I went on inside because I figured a car in the parking lot meant the man was still there. The church was stifling hot. I guessed the board saved money on air-conditioning when there were no meetings or services going on.

I heard the low rumble of voices from the back, where the church offices were located. I made my way back there, to Tyler's office. He was seated at his desk, a phone clamped to his ear.

Tyler swiveled around to face me, then motioned me to a chair. He was saying something about an upcoming ceremony but cut it short to turn and give me a nervous, tight smile.

"Well, look who's here." He leaned back after he hung up. He put his arms behind his head. "What brings you, of all people, to church?"

The smirk on his face was irritating.

"I was over talking to Dora." I launched right into what I had to say.

"Poor soul. No clue where she's going from here. They came from Tupelo but I hear that's not her and Selma's home. Guess they'll figure it out. Church board's offered them the parsonage 'til we get us a new preacher."

I smiled, letting him know I thought that was a fine gesture.

"Dora mentioned that Pastor Jenkins had been worried about something lately. She said it was something to do with the church."

Tyler Perkins wrinkled his brow at me, thinking hard. "Can't imagine what that could've been. He didn't say a word to me. Seems, on the contrary, we're doin' fine. Maybe a little grumble here and there but nothing . . ."

"Grumble? Over what?"

"Nothing that concerns you, Lindy. You know we've got big plans for our little church. Ceremony for the new addition on Sunday—despite losing the pastor. Everything in place, Hawley Harvey says. Might as well get on with it. To tell you the truth, Lindy, we all been doing real well, with Hawley's careful guidance. Still, some of the folks don't think the money's comin' in fast enough. That's all I ever heard. You know how greedy folks can get."

I wanted to say I had no clue how greedy folks got, but didn't. "Could one of those people have upset the pastor? I mean, complaining about their money going for the addition? Something like that?"

"Guess you'll have to talk to Hawley Harvey. Think he'd be the one Millroy would talk to, if he was worried about something. Hawley's handling all the money—if that's what it was about. Doin' a fine job of it, too."

"Dora said the pastor intended to call the Reverend Albertson, talk to him about whatever was on his mind."

The deacon's arms came down and he shot forward in his chair. His face was red with anger. "Call Pastor Albertson? What on earth for? The man didn't exactly leave us on good terms, you know."

"No, I didn't know."

"We think he was trying to cause trouble for the new pastor. Always that way—the old one gets mad if he didn't want to go."

"You told me he retired."

"Well, yes. He did that. But there are times retirement comes with a little push."

"What happened?"

He coughed and looked away. "Nothing really. Didn't mean to bring it up. Just a little disagreement before he left. Still, I would have warned the pastor not to call the man. Reverend Albertson doesn't know a thing about what we been doing here since he left. Hope he didn't go ahead and call." His face was getting dark. The man looked very angry.

Unnerved by the unexpected anger, I calculated what would happen if I told him Miss Amelia was calling Pastor Albertson, too. I decided to throw caution to the winds and watch what would happen.

"My grandmother's got a call in to Pastor Albertson right now. She had the same feeling as Pastor Jenkins, I suspect."

"Well, you tell your grandmother for me . . . you tell her it was Tyler Perkins, himself, who said this. Church business is church business and it's not up to her or anybody else to stick their nose in and stir up trouble that don't need to be stirred. You got that? Think you can remember to tell your grandmother what I said and call her off from phoning Pastor Albertson?"

If a person can feel steam rising in her ears, I was that person at that moment. I'd been talked down to plenty of times in my life. Every woman has. But this was so blatant, and reached out to touch my seventy-seven-year-old grandmother. I wished I could put a hand across the miserable man's desk and bang him on the head. Instead, I stood and glared.

"Deacon, one man is dead. A woman's in the hospital for tasting the same poison that killed the pastor. Whatever's happening in Riverville has moved way beyond 'church business.'"

I stretched taller, as regal as I ever get, and glared down at Tyler Perkins.

He smirked though his red face matched his red hair. "Well, that's what we got a police force for, Lindy. No need for little girls like you going around and muddying the waters."

"I'm not a little girl." I bristled up like a wild boar then told myself to get out of there as fast as I could before I tore the place apart. From the doorway I allowed myself one last pointed question. "By the way, where'd you get that shiny new Cadillac? Drug business in town must be booming. The legal kind, I mean."

He cleared his throat and moved his head back and forth on his squat neck. "Yes, ma'am. Been doing well this year. The Lord is surely being good to members of Rushing to Calvary."

"Glad to hear it. But red . . ." I couldn't help turning the knife one more turn. "Isn't that the devil's color?"

Tyler was sputtering as I made my way back through the empty church, out to my ten-year-old Ford truck of a color nobody could name.

Chapter Twenty-nine

It wasn't so much that I didn't like Tyler Perkins as that I didn't like his type. I looked at the flashy red car again as I drove out of the parking lot, wondering just how religious Tyler really was, or how much his affiliation with the church had to do with socializing and schmoozing in the community. Word was that the Rushing to Calvary Church was growing fast. I wondered, if the church had been a tiny backwoods place, would Tyler Perkins spend so much of his time there?

But that was mean of me, I told myself, casting aspersions on a man's motives just because he drove a big red Cadillac that was somehow stirring ire in me I hadn't felt since I was a kid and Hunter got a red dirt bike while I got Justin's hand-me-down boy's two-wheeler.

I could hear Miss Amelia's voice in my ear now, as I had back then, telling me that jealousy was beneath me. I could hear her telling me to think higher thoughts. Unhappy that she could sneak into my head so easily, I immediately whispered to my meemaw to let me alone. With Meemaw out of the picture, I thought, who else but the town druggist would know how to grind hemlock roots and know just how much could kill a man?

I reminded myself to find a new drugstore in another town, then headed over to the hospital before it got too late. On the way there, I fielded worried phone calls. First from Mama wondering what was going on and saying she just left the hospital. Meemaw was staying there with Treenie.

Then a call from Bethany, warning that Jeffrey was on his way to town to see me. Something about me helping him secure a piece of property he was after. "He's on his way, Lindy. So get right over here. I'm still at the Nut House. People from everywhere buying pies and things. We're not going to have anything left if Meemaw doesn't get back soon. Anyway, I've got a date with Jeffrey tonight so hurry back soon as you can . . ."

"I'm on my way to the hospital," I said, meaning to stand firm.

"Oh, no. Jeffrey wants to see you—"

"Guess he'll have to wait."

"But we've got a date."

"You can't close until six. And I don't know what your friend's talking about: me helping him with a property. And I don't think I'm interested in having any dealings with Jeffrey Coulter. Personally, I think the man's a phony."

"That's terrible. Why I—"

"I'll be there when I can, Bethany. 'Til then I guess you just have to hold down the fort."

I got off the phone with a sputtering Bethany in full umbrage, claiming she had to get out of there and get home before her date. Her favorite pink outfit was in the dryer and . . .

The phone rang again. It was Miranda Chauncey. What a breath of fresh air it was, to hear Miranda's terse voice.

"Me and Melody's comin' to town. All this awful bull crap going on, figured we'd better be there to protect whoever needs protecting. I'm bringing my pistol with me. Figure that's better than walking in places with my shotgun. You know, don't you, Lindy? Rattlers come in all sizes. You got female rattlers as well as males. Otherwise wouldn't get no more rattlers. Couldn't get ahold of Miss Amelia, but you tell her, okay? I'll be sitting on the front porch of the Nut House watching and Melody will be helping inside the store."

"Oh, Miranda, that's so good of you but Bethany's at the store right now. Miss Amelia's at the hospital with Treenie."

There was a pause and then Miranda turned away from the phone, talking to her sister behind her.

"Seems Melody's sure she can help Bethany while I just sit out there with my gun letting people know they'd better not fool with Miss Amelia anymore."

I wanted to tell the twins not to come to town; our hands were full as it was. But then I thought about Bethany's face when the girls walked into the Nut House. Too precious not to take advantage of. Bethany would know she couldn't leave Melody alone there, taking care of customers. Meemaw always gave the girls a deep, deep discount on anything they bought, knowing their ranch wasn't producing the way it used to. If Melody started selling things for the prices they paid, we'd be out of business in a day or two.

And what was wrong with Miranda sitting on the front

porch with a gun nestled in her lap? It would be like Wild
Bill Hickok, Belle Starr, and Billy the Kid smiling at customers while cocking a pistol within their hearing.

I promised to be there later.

That was fine with Miranda. "You can be sure, Lindy, me
and Melody will take care of the place for you. Give your
grandmother our sincere wishes for things to clear up."

I promised I would do that, hung up, and called Bethany, so pleased with my news I couldn't wait to tell her.

Bethany wasn't as excited as I was. In fact, she said she
was going to chase the both of them right out of there.

"Best friends with Meemaw," I reminded her. "You do
that and you're dealing with her," I said as I hung up.

Laughing felt good.

I'd just parked in the hospital lot when the phone rang
yet again. Hunter.

"Hey, you at the hospital yet? Your grandmother's dead
on her feet. You gotta take her home to get some sleep. I
keep telling her Treenie's fine but she thinks she got to be
here to protect her. Like there's a bunch of killers on their
way in."

"Do you blame her? With what's going on?"

"Won't help with her in there with Treenie, sound asleep."

"Where are you?"

"Home. Had to take a shower. Did you get over to Selma
and Dora's the way you wanted to?"

I told him how relieved Selma was. Then told him about
Dora saying Millroy had been calling Pastor Albertson
before he died.

"Miss Amelia said she's been trying to get ahold of
him, too," Hunter said.

"I know. But no return call yet. Think we'd better get
after him."

"I got a call from Morton Grover," Hunter said.

"What's Morton want?"

"I don't know. He asked me to come over to the saloon to talk to him. You want to come after you get through at the hospital? Say about nine thirty. Have a couple of beers, relax, see what Morton wants? He asked me not to wear my uniform. Guess it kind of makes people nervous to have a cop sitting there."

I wanted to groan. One hour's worth of sleep hadn't done much for me. It was wearing off fast. And Hunter hadn't slept any more than I had.

Still . . . if it was something that could help us.

"Got some other things to tell you," he said by way of enticing me to join him.

"Me, too," I answered. "But do you really think a postage-stamp-sized table in a loud saloon is the best place to talk?"

"Who's gonna hear us?"

Chapter Thirty

Nothing was happening at the hospital. There was another deputy on duty outside Treenie's door. When I went in, Treenie and Meemaw were sound asleep: Treenie in her bed and Meemaw in a high-backed chair.

I tiptoed out, figuring Justin could pick her up when he came to town. I headed back to the Nut House. As I hurried up the steps to the still lit store, I was fooling with my keys, trying to isolate my apartment key from all the others. The noise coming from one of the big wicker chairs was of a deep throat clearing and then somebody saying, "That you, Lindy?"

Miranda Chauncey sat up in the deep shadow of the porch. I heard her gun clink against something and hurried to answer.

"It's me, Miranda. Store still open, I see."

"Yup, but the crowd slowed down some."

From the swing on the other side of the porch, someone else piped up.

"You woulda thought you'd be helping out here today, Lindy." Ethelred Tomroy got the rocker going at a fine pace.

"Hello to you, too, Ethelred. I already did. This morning."

"Have a nice time in Tupelo? You and Hunter Austen?"

"Yes, ma'am. A fine time. There checking out a suspect."

"Really? Heard you was at Elvis Presley's house. Always wanted to go there but I never had a gentleman to escort me. Not that I'd go without being married to the gentleman. But that's just me. Got very high morals. Always did."

I could feel words churning just behind my mouth. Maybe in the vicinity of my brain. Sometimes I resent being a nice Southern girl. I resent having to be polite just because a nasty person is old. I resent having to keep smiling when an old biddy stings me with her superiority.

I bit off words just beginning to leak out of my mouth and bade both ladies a good evening, but Ethelred wasn't going to let me off that easily.

"Hold on a minute," she said and struggled up from the moving chair. "I'm not doing well, Lindy. I really need to talk to Miss Amelia. Think she'll be back from that hospital soon? Treenie must be sleeping by now. Heard she was all right. Miss Amelia shouldn't be hanging around like that."

"What's wrong with you, Miss Tomroy? Not worried about being poisoned, are you?"

"Not that, Lindy. I got other troubles."

For the first time in my life I looked hard at the protruding eyes and long, craggy face, wild hair sticking out everywhere above it, and wanted to put my arms around her.

"You think Miss Amelia'll be here herself in the morning? I was thinking she'd be worn out, all of this hullabaloo going on. But I got something I need to talk over with her. I think she's the only one can help me make sense of something I don't understand."

"I'll pass on the word you need to see her. She's been through a lot. She might not open tomorrow. Could be home catching up on her sleep."

Ethelred nodded, every wiry hair doing a dance of its own. "I understand. It's just that . . . oh well . . . you can tell her I'm worried. Especially now, when I'm going in for some treatments. Nothing you need to know about. What I'm saying is I need to have my life straightened out. Know where I'm headed in the future. But somebody's saying I shouldn't be doing things I want to do right now."

"What things? Maybe I can help."

She shook her head hard. "Need Miss Amelia. She knows all about it."

"You're not talking to a fortune-teller, are you, Miss Ethelred?" I stood in the open doorway, holding the door only wide enough for me to get inside.

"Fortune-teller! Bah! I'm talking about the riches I'm coming into. But I'm not discussing it with you. You just pass on the word to Miss Amelia, will you?"

I promised, wished Miss Ethelred a good evening, and hurried inside the store, where I saw Bethany coming down an aisle, calling my name, and telling me to hold on a minute.

Which I didn't, only hurried up the stairs to my apartment and closed the door behind me. Answering machine was blinking. I wanted to ignore it. I had Bethany pounding on the door. People needing me to return calls. What I wanted to do was climb in my tiny bed and pull the sheet over my head, which wasn't a very adult thing to do so I sat down to decide which bell to answer—Bethany or the phone.

Bethany's teeth were clenched. "Jeffrey is downstairs

waiting to talk to you, and some pastor's calling about every half hour. Told him there was nobody here. I gave him your number. Hope you've got a lot of calls to answer."

I let her go on without stopping.

"I'm closing up now. You and Jeffrey can talk in the kitchen. If I don't get rid of Miss Melody soon, I'm going straight out of my mind. All she asks is when we jacked the prices up the way we did. I keep telling her we haven't raised a price since I don't remember when, but she says I'm wrong and we keep going around on it. I am totally worn out and here I have to get home and change into my pink outfit while Jeffrey's getting impatient waiting downstairs. Please go talk to him and I'll run to the ranch to get ready to go out."

"Got to return those calls. Me and Meemaw both have been waiting to talk to Pastor Albertson."

"Pastor Albertson? That him? Why didn't he say? Anyway. When you get done with the pastor, go down and talk to Jeffrey. If you're my sister at all, you won't turn on me now. What'll he think if you keep dodging him? Why, he's our guest, Lindy. You know about Southern hospitality."

I knew about Southern hospitality all right. And I knew about killing somebody with kindness. But still, I had other things to do rather than talk to Jeffrey Coulter about property, which had to be a ruse since I didn't know what he was talking about.

Bethany was gone and I locked the door behind her. The pastor didn't say much in his message, just to call him back, he had some things to talk about. Second message was the same—only faster. Third was a plea to call him "Please!"

Which I did.

Identified myself as Miss Amelia's granddaughter and

explained how Miss Amelia's friend was poisoned with the same poison that killed Pastor Jenkins and we were very worried what was going on and hoped he might be able to help us.

The man's voice was slow and resonant. I thought I wouldn't mind listening to this voice on a Sunday morning.

"Give my best to your grandmother and tell her I am so very sorry to hear about her troubles there. And I've been thinking hard on what she called to ask about and I think it's time I came back to town. I've been nursing a deep grief since Sally died. And besides that, nursing a bruised ego after the board dismissed me the way they did, but from what you're saying—awful things are happening there in Riverville. I think I'd better get back to see what I can do to help straighten it all out."

He went on, "I'm going to be flying into Houston tomorrow morning. I'll be renting a car and driving over to Riverville. Can't say for sure what time I'll be there, but I gotta . . . What I'm saying is, I'll need a safe place to stay."

He hesitated and then cleared his throat.

"Considering what happened to Millroy Jenkins, I gotta ask if I can stay someplace where nobody can get at me. Taking precautions, you see. Just want you to know Millroy called me the day before I heard he died. He didn't know much more about what was going on than I did, but we were going to figure things out together. Anyway, I'll call you when I get close to town. Maybe—wherever you think it's safe for me to stay—we could talk there."

I played it all back in my head to make sure I heard it exactly. *Taking precautions. Wherever you think it's safe for me to stay . . .*

Cloak-and-dagger stuff. The man was afraid of something, or somebody. All my own plans went flying out the window. I looked at the clock on the wall. Seven. Whew, what a long day. Now I had to get ahold of Miss Amelia. Tell her about the pastor's message. We'd have to come up with a place for him to stay—unless he stayed with us, which might not be the best thing if anyone was looking for him.

I called Meemaw. When I laid out what Pastor Albertson said, she was quiet a long time.

"How about the farm? Think that's safe for him?" she asked.

"I don't know, Meemaw. We're kind of at the heart of this whole thing right now. You and me. Whoever did this has to know we're looking for him."

Quiet again. "You think Martin would take him in? Jessie could watch him . . ."

"Meemaw. I don't want to put the Sanchez family in any danger. Let's think harder."

Which we did, until Meemaw exclaimed she had it.

"The girls!" she said. "We'll meet him at their place. Those two can take care of themselves and the pastor, too, if anybody can."

I almost laughed out loud. Great way to get Miranda off the porch.

"They're here at the Nut House right now. Maybe Melody's gone because Bethany closed up, but I'll bet anything Miranda will still be there, at least until dark."

Meemaw gave a hoot.

"Could you talk to Miranda on your way out then? Tell 'er they're going to have a guest coming in the morning. That'll set Melody to cleaning up a storm and Miranda to squawking and hollering about all the dust. Then we can meet out there whenever he shows up. This has got to mean something, Pastor Albertson flying back like this. I sure would like it if he knew what was going on and knew who killed Millroy and tried to kill somebody at the Nut House. I'll tell you, Lindy, I'm about worn out."

"Ethelred's on the porch, too, waiting to talk to you. Wouldn't tell me what it was."

There was a groan and then a sigh. "Could be about her treatments for the thyroid thing. Don't blame her for being scared of what's coming though the doctor said she's going to be fine."

"I don't think that's it. Something about wealth she's depending on and somebody is telling her not to do anything right now."

"Probably Ben telling her not to take all her daddy's money out of the trust he left her. She's hell-bent on buying a fancy car or taking a fancy trip. Don't know what's gotten into Ethelred. That's not the way she was raised."

"Ethelred's never gone anyplace nor owned much of anything. I can see where this thyroid operation she's facing and then the treatments would shake her up. Just think, she's never been married, Meemaw. Never had any kids. Closest thing is a bunch of nieces and nephews she doesn't see much. I think I'd be worried about dying, too. And never having lived."

"Okay. I'll see to her. If she's still outside waiting, tell her I'll call in the morning. You talk to Miranda and Melody. Set that part up. Could you pick me up here and take me out to the ranch afterward? My car's there at the store. I'll be needing clean clothes and such, for morning. Then I'd like to come back into town and stay with you at the apartment. That way we'll be together when the parson calls."

"I've got to meet Hunter at nine thirty, over at the saloon."

"What? You becoming a drinker? I don't know . . ."

"Meemaw. Grover called Hunter earlier today, asked

him to come over tonight. He's got something to tell Hunter, and Hunter thought I should be there."

"Well, I doubt I'll be staying up 'til you get in."

"You take my bed. I'll sleep on the sofa."

She made a noise. "That little thing? I'll take the sofa, thank you."

I flipped on the light downstairs to make my way back outside, talk with Miranda, then get over to the hospital to pick up Meemaw.

"Lindy," a voice called from the kitchen doorway.

Jeffrey Coulter stood in the shadows, leaning to one side as if he'd been standing there awhile.

I'd forgotten about him.

I gave a small "Yipe" and put a hand to my chest, wanting to ask what the devil he thought he was doing standing there, eavesdropping on me.

"The store's closed," I told him fast and hard.

"I'm not here for a pie, Lindy. Bethany knew I was staying. I only wanted to ask if I could bring someone out to your greenhouse tomorrow. Have a look around. The man's thinking of selling off some acreage close to Austin and buying around here. I happen to have my eye on his property for Father's mall. The one glitch is the man wants to go into pecan ranching—same as you. Wants to look around here for property but wants to know more what he's getting himself into first. I told him you were working on new kinds of trees and he expressed an interest in seeing your operation. Justin said it was fine with him but that I'd better check with you. He said you kept your greenhouse area locked up tight."

If ever I wanted to let loose a string of curses, this was

the time, but I heard Meemaw, back in my head again and clucking her tongue, reminding me to be "a lady." Whatever that was supposed to be.

I tried to stick on a big, Southern-charm smile, but it fell off before reaching my cheeks. Still, I came up with a so-sorry voice, one of those Southern voices that must have greeted a few Yankees trying to join the Daughters of the Confederacy. For good luck, I crossed my fingers behind my back. "Geez, Jeffrey," I said. "I can't let anybody in there right now. Kind of a quarantine, I guess you'd call it. Had a little trouble with a few of the trees and we're not sure where it came from—this particular virus. Just gotta keep the building off-limits to visitors awhile. Tell your friend I'm sorry as can be. Maybe another time. Another year or so."

Jeffrey knew he was being snowed. He turned, stomped off across the wooden floorboards, and slammed the front door behind him. I couldn't help but feel a strong giggle starting down around my belly and working its way up. With everything going on, with putting up with Tyler Perkins, with Pastor Albertson coming in, with poison and more trouble than I could shake a stick at, this one little victory felt so damned good.

The porch was empty. We'd have to call the Chaunceys.

I locked the Nut House door securely behind me and hurried out to my truck, thinking what I always thought when things were going to hell in a hand basket.

"After all . . . tomorrow is another day," I sighed, using my best heroic, Southern woman voice.

"Yup. Tomorrow's another day," I said again then thought how much further downhill another day might take me.

Chapter Thirty-one

Miss Amelia was sitting at the foot of a sleeping Treenie's bed. Aldonza, Treenie's grown daughter, sat near Miss Amelia, tatting lace as the two talked in quiet voices.

The news on Treenie was good. She would make a complete recovery, both women told me.

"Doctor said she didn't take enough to kill her." Aldonza smiled a happy smile that changed her whole plain face. "I told her before, don't go putting things in your mouth you don't know what it is. But you know my mama. Hurry, hurry, hurry. Stick a fingertip in a jar, stick your tongue out. Tell me, Lindy, who does that, eh?"

I put a hand on one of Aldonza's blunt hands and smiled down at her.

"You know there's talk in town about a cult moving in from Dallas." She looked up at me. "There are people who want to take over the town, is what I hear. Some are saying that's who killed the parson. He found out about it and tried to stop them. That's what cults do, you know? They poison people to clear the way . . ."

I made a face at her. "Oh, Aldonza. They're not really saying things like that, are they?"

Eyes wide, she nodded. "It's happened in other places."

"Where?"

She looked perplexed. "I don't know for sure, but that's what people are saying."

"I wouldn't credit it too much," I said. "More like somebody we all know. Maybe somebody involved in something illegal. Anyway, the sheriff's on top of it . . ."

She made a derisive sound. "Sure, by blaming your grandmother. Nobody's falling for it. That's how these cults work. They get to the people in power first. Back in Mexico . . ."

Meemaw got up heavily from the bed. I turned to help her as Aldonza's wild theory died off in her throat.

"I'd better get going now." Miss Amelia bent to kiss Aldonza lightly on the cheek. "I'll be back tomorrow."

"No, no, no." Aldonza put up a hand. "You stay home and rest. The doctor said Mama might get out tomorrow anyway."

She turned back to me. "Nobody's blaming your grandmother for anything, Lindy. There's evil in this town, but it has nothing to do with Miss Amelia."

"Evil often wears a familiar face, Aldonza," I said as I followed Miss Amelia into the hall. "Just not my grandmother's face."

On the way out to the ranch, Meemaw made me call the Chaunceys, who were just getting home. Miranda didn't get it at first, then she effusively said to bring him. They'd keep the man safe. If she could shoot out the eyes of a rattler at a hundred feet, she sure could shoot a murderer before he got up on the porch.

"Ya know, Lindy, me and Melody been out here on the ranch alone since Daddy died. That was, let me see now, maybe fifty years ago. We've been through the worst and the best Texas can throw at a person and we're still standing. Run this ranch alone—no help except with picking and packing. We'll take care of your pastor for ya. Just call when he's on his way."

Meemaw was pleased. "I'd rather trust Miranda with that gun of hers, than any man I ever knew."

At home, I helped her pack an overnight bag, explain to Mama why she was going back into town, and though Mama sputtered and got very close to being mad, we were out of there in fifteen minutes, on the way back to the Nut House.

First thing, back at my place, Meemaw was yawning and looking completely done in.

"You get to bed," I told her. "I'll be back later."

"Humph. Of all places, the Barking Coyote. For goodness' sakes, Lindy. I hope you're not planning on consuming any alcohol."

"Meemaw." I pretended to shock. "Would I—"

She shook a finger at me. "Not a place for a proper lady—"

"Meemaw," I stopped her. "Wasn't it just a few months back we went there together?"

"That was different. Amos was dead and we were trying to find out what was going on."

"And didn't you and Jefferson Tomlin do a mean line dance together?"

Her face slowly reddened. Her eyes snapped fire. "That's public relations, Lindy. Goodwill for the store, was all it was. You should know a little about being gracious . . ."

I was gone, certain that, no matter how tired she was, she would be waiting up for me to get home.

Chapter Thirty-two

The saloon was going strong when I drove in at the half-lit sign of a coyote baying at the moon and down the wash to park behind the saloon, pulling in between two pick-ups with serious gun racks mounted on the back. The funky old wooden building stood away from the arroyo, settled low as if it had floated there after a particularly tough frog strangler.

Dolly Parton met me at the door, belting out "Baby I'm Burning" on the jukebox. There was the clink of glasses, that yeasty smell of old beer, maybe a bit of something sweet going on under the beer stink, and then—when people saw who'd just entered—from table to table they called out:

"Hunter's in back, Lindy."

"Been waiting a long time for ya, girl."

"Good thing he's a patient man."

They thought that was a funny one.

And then:

"Hunter, Lindy's here!" Table called to table, like they were treetop sentinels.

So much for anonymity and a private place to talk. By the time I stopped to greet everybody, Hunter came up front to lead me beyond the long bar, to a table as big around as a basketball. He had a sweating beer waiting for me and I'll have to admit—grandmother or no grandmother—that beer looked and then tasted great.

Hunter leaned toward me. We clinked bottles. "It's for sure," he said, voice raised against Dolly Parton and women laughing and men singing along with the jukebox. "The poison in that bottle at the Nut House was spotted water hemlock. Seems like our killer's got a taste for local products."

"Anything else?" I took a long swig and relaxed before the beer hit my stomach.

"Sheriff Higsby's got it in his head it's some nutcase here in town. More like a serial poisoner than anybody really after the pastor. Right now he's kind of focusing on Freda Cromwell. You know Freda and her outrage over just about everything."

"Tell you the truth, I don't care who he thinks it is, as long as he stays away from Meemaw."

He nodded.

"You talk to Morton yet?" I asked.

"He's coming over as soon as he can take a break."

I looked around the smoke-filled room. "See Finula?"

He nodded over to a small table in the darkest part of the room. Squinting hard, I made out Finula Prentiss at a table with three cowboys. When she looked my way, she waved and I waved back.

I told Hunter about Pastor Albertson coming to town but told him he had to keep it a dark secret.

He nodded. "Let's see what the man's got to say. I'm going out with you. You knew I'd insist on that."

I nodded. "That's why I'm telling you. Just the three of us—and the Chaunceys. I just can't figure what he'd be afraid of, can you?"

"Maybe having to eat anything while he's here? Maybe afraid somebody'll see him as a threat?"

"I saw Tyler Perkins this afternoon, too. He had a few things to say about Pastor Albertson. Turns out it wasn't all cozy, the way he and Hawley Harvey said it was. Not just retiring. Something was going on. That's got to be what the pastor's coming to talk about."

Morton Grover made his way through the crowd, two fresh bottles of beer in his hands held high above his head. He plunked the bottles down and smiled at us before bringing a chair over from another table.

"Thanks." Hunter held the new beer up in salute. "Good thing I'm off duty."

I looked at the sweating beer in front of me and thought maybe I'd skip this one. As a usual nondrinker, and as tired as my brain felt, I was already light-headed and inclined to want to sit back in my chair and sing along with Dolly.

"You hear about that cult?" Was Morton's first question. My hopes for anything new dropped. Back into the town's conspiracy theory.

Hunter didn't stop him.

"Somebody bought the old Keystone Ranch and is fixing it up. What I hear, it's an older couple from over near Beaumont. Thing is, they're not too friendly and they've been bringing a bunch of strange kids out there with 'em. I can see where people are putting two and two together.

"That ranch house was pretty run down." Morton

glanced over his shoulder like a spy. "Those groves haven't been tended in years. Not much value to the pecans. Makes everybody wonder . . ."

"Sheriff went out there," Hunter said. "First time there was nobody around. Second time the man was there. He had some teenage boys with him. They were working on one of the barns. Sheriff said the house looks really nice— even got a swimming pool at the back."

"So? What's he doing here? Finula was saying it's some kind of cult."

Hunter shook his head slowly. "Turns out they're problem kids he hired to help him renovate the place. Gives them a job for the summer and a couple of months away from some pretty bad homes. New program a church in San Antonio started. Nothing suspicious. But tell that to people in Riverville, looking under their beds at night, expecting a mad poisoner to jump out at them."

"So, no cult?" Morton looked disappointed. "Thought I was bringing you something you ain't heard of before."

"No cult, Morton. But I sure do appreciate you bringing me any information you hear in here. One thing I can tell you, you want to spread the word around, what we're thinking is, because the poison came from roots dug up over near the parsonage, this is no stranger to town. To do that digging and figure they wouldn't get caught, whoever did it had to know where to find the hemlock and how to get down to the river without anybody seeing 'em. Then they had to know how toxic it was."

"And to be so blatant about it . . . had to know how the Ag Fair worked and about the Winners' Supper," I put in.

"But how'd he know about Miss Amelia's extra dish?"

"All the women brought an extra dish of their entry, in case they won and had to serve it at the supper," I said.

"So that means they knew a lot about how the judging worked. But what about knowing which one was Miss Amelia's? How'd they know that?"

"Our coolers have the Blanchard crest on them."

He looked disappointed for a moment. He thought a long while. "Then tell me, Lindy. How'd he know Miss Amelia wasn't going to win and her dish wouldn't be out on the table with all the others? You think the parson wasn't the real target and the poison was supposed to get to everybody at the supper?"

"I don't get what you mean." I was pretty foggy by this time.

"Sure you do. Miss Amelia almost always wins everything she enters. If she didn't get first place, you knew, sure as anything, she'd get at least second or third. So how'd they know she wasn't going to win anything this time? If it was me, I'd be betting the other way."

Since it wasn't up to me or Hunter to tell on Miss Amelia, we looked at each other and just kept looking puzzled.

When Finula Prentiss sashayed up to the table to pull Hunter by the hand, drawing him out to the dance floor, where she pasted herself against him, moving like a snake in heat, I started on that second beer after all.

I think Morton Grover saw what was happening and put his hand out to me. I told him I was too tired to dance. Anyway Hunter cut it short with Finula, coming back before the song ended.

"Sorry, Lindy. I—"

I waved it all away. "Finula just being Finula."

Music I really loved came blaring out across the big, dark and noisy room. Tim McGraw singing, *"I don't know why I act the way I do . . ."*

All I wanted was to shut my eyes and listen, but Hunter

was having none of that. He put his hand out and escorted me to the crowded dance floor, where he pulled me so close we only took up room for about a half a couple.

It was after twelve when we left. This time Hunter paid without me giving him a hard time about it. I was so tired I just wanted to get home and fall in bed—or on my sofa—whichever I ended up getting. I kept my fingers crossed that when I got in, Meemaw would be sound asleep.

Turned out she was and, to tell on her, snoring to beat the band.

Chapter Thirty-three

Me, Miss Amelia, and Hunter were on our way out to the Chauncey ranch by noon, soon after Pastor Albertson called Miss Amelia to say he'd landed safely in Houston, was standing in line at the car rental counter, and would see us in an hour and a half or so. He knew of the Chaunceys and where they lived and congratulated us on our choice of safe havens.

The ranch was almost ten miles out of town, along a flat, two-lane highway with bare land stretching out on either side. The road was usually deserted, but I noticed a white car following along behind us. Strange. Lots of white cars in Texas, but I remembered the one in town, following me and Meemaw the other morning. Also, unusual for Texas drivers, the guy made no move to pass me at a hundred-ten miles an hour. He hung back so I couldn't get a look at his front license plate. I figured it was my

well-deserved paranoia kicking in and concentrated, instead, on finding the opening in the fence that announced
the twins' ranch.

I turned in where the sign read, KEEP OUT THIS MEANS
YOU ATTACK COYOTES ON GUARD, all written in big red letters. I saw in my rearview mirror that the white car kept
right on going.

After the turn, it was a matter of following a dusty two-
track, winding through dry hills and bone-dry arroyos,
back to the old house built by the girls' father, weathered
now to a fine patina, much like the twins themselves.

I pulled up and parked in front of the lonely place with a
grove of graceful pecan trees beyond, and a small lake that
had formed years before, a backwater of the Colorado.

The house, built low to the ground with a wide front
porch and an old shingled roof that jutted down to just
above head height, was set at the top of a small rise looking out over other rises—empty, low hills stretching as far
as the eye could see. The front porch was a museum of old
stuff I remembered from the time my daddy, Jake, had
brought me out here with him. There was a collection of
pecan packing boxes standing off to one side, a cushion-
less glider as old as a glider can get without being a pile of
junk, and then there were clay pots with small trees sticking out of them, and then another row of pots filled with
flowers. Because of the way my mind was bent, I recognized a bright yellow flower as the four-nerve daisy or, as I
knew it, the *Tetraneuris scaposa*. Then the pink evening
primrose or *Oenothera speciosa*, and even a few large pots
of greenthread (*Thelesperma filifolium*). The porch might
be a jumble of old things, but the flowers made for bright
spots of well-tended space.

The girls came out the door together, pushing each other to be first to greet us.

"Man's not here yet." Melody, the winner, stopped to adjust the jeweled belt at her waist and straighten the collar on her turquoise-colored shirt. Melody was dressed for company.

"You sure he's coming?" Miranda, right behind her, wore the same clothes she wore every day from the down-at-the-heels old boots to the khakis to a shirt with a lot of missing fringe down the sleeves. "Cleaned out a whole room for 'im. Put sheets on the bed. He'd better show up after all of that."

Miss Amelia hugged both girls and thanked them for their efforts, while assuring them she'd heard from him and he was on his way.

Hunter and I got handshakes by way of a greeting, then followed as the girls led us into a low-ceilinged room as cluttered as the porch, but somehow all the homier for it.

"Gave him my daddy's old room." Miranda chuckled and pulled at her ancient pants. "Like shuffling through our whole life, going in there. Chauncey history lesson."

Melody clucked at her. "Nothing in there but Christmas ornaments and stuff."

Miranda scoffed. "And Daddy's guns and his stacks of agriculture magazines and his pipes and, fer heaven's sakes, I even found an old license to shoot bobcat."

"That's why you were in there half the night. All I asked you to do was cart the stuff out, not catalog it."

"Where was I supposed to go with all of it?" Miranda demanded as Miss Amelia stepped in and thanked them both again for taking the trouble.

I took a look around the living room and wondered

what they considered throwaway stuff and what they thought might actually be necessary in a living room. Stacks of papers and magazines graced every old table. On one table a stack of shotgun shells teetered. A collection of old radios took up half of one wall—floor to waist high, while bags of dog food leaned against another. But no dog in sight.

The girls herded us to a table that had to be cleared of books and cans of green beans before we could sit down. Melody brought a flowered teapot in from the kitchen and proudly set it in the middle of a giant lace doily she'd spread out. Miranda went to a huge sideboard with piles of dishes stored behind glass doors. She brought over cups and spoons. When she couldn't find four saucers to match the cups, Melody got upset and found them herself while Miranda grumbled and ambled back to the kitchen for a bottle of milk she set at the middle of the table, sending a mad look at Melody, daring her to object.

We sat like guests at the Mad Hatter's tea party, pouring and stirring and clinking. I couldn't look over at Hunter, making room for his gun at his side, long body hunched over his delicate teacup.

"How's your mama, Lindy? Doing fine?" Melody asked.

I nodded. "Miss Emma's fine, thank you for asking."

"And Justin? The ranch going okay?" She addressed Miss Amelia.

She nodded.

"Bethany doing well with that event tent you folks put up?" This was for me.

"It's coming along. Sometimes things are slow and she gets worried, but I'd say—all in all—she's building the business."

"That's very good to hear." Melody turned back to Miss Amelia. "The Nut House doing well?"

Miss Amelia, looking around to see how far we were going to go with this refined stuff, said, "Considering some folks think I'm a mad poisoner, I'd say business is doing just fine."

"Humph." Miranda fidgeted in her chair. "That's a pile of bull, you ask me. You never in your life hurt a single soul, Miss Amelia. One of the most loved women in town. Anybody who thinks you did a thing like that is more than half out of their head. We heard Freda Cromwell was even blaming you when her dog died. Just goes to show how crazy people can make themselves."

"Why, thank you, Miranda. That's awful nice of you to say. I appreciate it."

"Okay, now let's cut the crap and get to the reason the Reverend Albertson's staying with us." Miranda set her cup down and slapped her hands on her knees. "Why's he coming here and not your place? Mind going over that for me?"

"He's worried, Miranda. With Pastor Jenkins's death, well, he's thinking he might know something that would help us here. He didn't say what that was."

"Just let anybody try anything out here and they're coming up against a thirty-eight and maybe a shotgun. He'll be safe enough. I got ears on me like an owl. Hear a car turning in down at the highway. If I miss that, there's that cloud of dust I can see from a mile away. Try sneaking in around those hills and the rattlers will take care of 'im."

Miss Amelia was about to launch into the fact that the reverend was worried about something going on here in Riverville when Miranda, head in the air, put a finger up, stopping her. "See? Already heard the pastor's motor. He's getting close."

"Might as well act like we're civilized," Melody huffed and stood. "First time we ever had a pastor staying with us. Let's get out there and greet the man."

Melody had her hand on the door latch when we heard the first gunshot ring out.

Chapter Thirty-four

The man lay on the ground in front of a blue car. The back of his summer suit jacket was soaked with blood. He had one hand on the bumper, trying to stand, then looking up at us, fear in his eyes, as we ran to him.

Hunter, yelling at us to keep down, crouched behind the car with his gun out as he grabbed his radio to call for help. "Shooter at the Chauncey ranch. One man down. Need an ambulance and any cars in the area."

He waved all of us back, though Miranda, her own gun miraculously in her hand, crouched down beside him.

Miss Amelia whipped off the cotton sweater she'd tied around her neck in case of a temperature dip to below ninety-five, and got to the downed and groaning reverend, stuffing the sweater up under the man's shirt to stanch the blood staining his suit coat and now running down the front of his shirt. I ran to his other side, helping to get him on the porch, lay him down behind the packing crates, and run back in the house for towels. Melody was ahead of me, sticking a stack in my hands.

Miss Amelia quickly added more pressure to the wound in Reverend Albertson's back, and then to one up at his shoulder.

The white-haired man, face drained of any color, eyes blinking to stay open, looked into Miss Amelia's face and tried to smile. "Not the welcome I expected," he said, his voice weak.

"See what you meant about not wanting people to know you were here."

He took a deep breath that caused him a lot of pain. He tried to nod but that hurt, too.

"Just rest," Miss Amelia told him. "We'll talk after we get you patched up."

"A lot of blood?" he managed to gasp out.

"I've seen worse," Miss Amelia answered.

The ambulance and patrol cars arrived with sirens blazing. The pastor was treated there on the porch then loaded on to a gurney, the suitcase from his car stuck underneath, and he was off to the Riverville Hospital.

Hunter was tied up with the officers that arrived. With guns drawn, they fanned out in the direction of the line of fire, where Hunter pointed.

Minutes later, Melody came running from the house behind us, demanding to know if anybody had seen Miranda.

In the confusion, I couldn't honestly admit to seeing her. I thought she was on the porch with us.

"Darned fool's gone. I told her one day she was going to get herself killed. Now she's out there with a killer."

"Oh my God. And a bunch of armed and nervous cops." I couldn't believe our problems had just multiplied.

Hunter got back on his phone. The sheriff, on his way

out to the ranch, called Deputy Sam Cranston, who was monitoring all phone and radio messages at the station, to contact anybody he could raise in the search party and warn them that an elderly lady with a dead-eye and a quick trigger finger was out there, too, and not to shoot her.

Miss Amelia, torn between wanting to get to the hospital and wanting to make sure Miranda was all right, sat nervously in a hard-backed chair Melody had dragged from the house. Melody brought out a bucket of water to throw on the blood left on the porch, but Hunter stopped her. Everything was part of a crime scene, and until the techs had been there and gone, nothing was to be touched.

I sat on the steps next to Hunter as he scanned the horizon, watching for anybody coming back from the hills.

"I'm gonna need statements." He turned to me. "Got to get this all down. Guess the pastor was right to worry."

"Who could have known there was this kind of danger? Why—"

I was stopped by the faraway sound of gunfire.

"Lord." He dropped his head into his hands. "Just don't let it be Miranda."

Melody moaned and shoved both fists in her mouth. All I could think of was the armed eighty-eight-year-old Miranda Chauncey, who was out there on her own ranch facing down the gun barrels of eight on-edge cops, and one murdering coward.

Hunter ran down to one of the patrol cars pulled up every which way in front of the house. He was on the radio, getting information from Sam Cranston and relaying it to us.

"Nobody's hit," he turned back to say. "That was Miranda getting herself another rattler while she was out there. They're all on the way back now. Seems Miranda did find something, though. Shell casings. Should have left them where she found them but they're in her pocket. Won't matter. Lab will be able to tell us what kind of gun was used then narrow it down to the specific gun."

When the sheriff got there, we all answered questions and finally were allowed to leave. Soon enough the whole town would know Parson Albertson was shot. The part I didn't like to think about was that Miss Amelia had been in the middle of things again. Soon somebody was going to begin asking how unlucky one old lady could get.

Chapter Thirty-five

There was nothing we could do at the hospital. The pastor was in surgery. He had a bullet in his left shoulder. One went straight through the side of his neck. The doctor who came out said to go home, the pastor was fine, and would be sedated until at least the next day.

Sheriff Higsby had already made arrangements for a guard at the parson's door. A deputy from another town stood there with his hands behind his back, taking the job very seriously. I couldn't help but feel that was a little like shutting the barn door after the horse was gone, but then I told myself that wasn't true at all. Whoever was afraid of what the parson knew would be after him again. We had to figure out who that person was and keep that barn door guarded.

I was eager to get Hunter and Miss Amelia alone. We needed to talk. There were things right outside our grasp, I could feel it. Something we had to latch on to.

A reporter from the *Riverville Courier* stopped us on the way out to the parking lot, but he knew as much of the details as we did at that point. He wrote down Miss Amelia's comments on how terrible this all was and how we were wishing the pastor a full recovery, but that only opened her to questions everybody in town must have been asking by then.

"Why is all of this happening around you, Miss Amelia?" the young female reporter asked.

I could see the anguish on Meemaw's face and couldn't do a thing to help her.

"I'll tell you, dear." She pulled in a deep, shivering breath. "I sure hope we find out who is doing all of this and why it's happening around me, and find out pretty soon. Never wanted to hurt a soul in my life before. Now, well, to tell you the truth, I'm after this killer's blood."

I wanted to groan. Miss Amelia was never one to mince words but just a tweak here or there to that statement and it would come out sounding like a confession. I took her arm and led her over to the truck before she thought of something else to add.

We'd agreed that going for lunch at The Squirrel would only increase the stir swirling through town. We decided Rancho en el Colorado was the best place for all of us. Hunter had a report to get in and a meeting with the sheriff but after that he said he'd be out to talk. We settled on three o'clock. In the meantime, at home I tried to get Miss Amelia to lie down and rest. When that didn't work, I made us sandwiches and sweet tea and took everything out to a table under one of the oldest pecan trees on the ranch, branches spreading all around us.

Hot, hot day but cool dampness under that tree that had seen so much of Blanchard history. I could hear Martin and his men out working on ditches in the groves. The voices came slow through the trees. What I wanted most to do was settle back in my chair, drink my sweet tea, listen to the buzz of bees, and do nothing but fan my face, complain about the heat, and speculate whether a storm would blow up. I wanted to be Maggie in *Cat on a Hot Tin Roof*. Shelby in *Steel Magnolias*. No, not that one. I think Julia Roberts dies, and that's not what I'm after on this fine afternoon with people getting poisoned and shot all around me.

Bethany sauntered out from the house, fanning herself. "Hot day. Don't know how I'm supposed to dress for a client when all I do is sweat out everything I own." She took the glass of tea I offered but waved away a sandwich. After falling into one of the cushioned seats, she complained that she hadn't seen Jeffrey all day and they were supposed to go into town. She was further upset, she added, because now our mama was expecting her to come in and help at the Nut House and she had all these other details to take care of for an upcoming wedding in the event tent.

"Booked another wedding today." She examined her fingernails. "I'm thinking of having the doves sprayed pink this time."

"Might kill 'em," I muttered toward her, not in the mood for pink doves or pink tulle or towering centerpieces.

"Oh, Lindy, you always say things like that. I know you're only kidding but I have to take this seriously. We're not the only event tent in town, you—"

"You hear what happened today?" I sat forward, just a little incredulous.

"You mean about the pastor? Yes, I heard something. He get shot at the Chaunceys'? I sure hope Miranda had nothing to do with it . . ." She sniffed and took a long drink of tea.

Before I could fill my clueless sister in, Hunter walked out from the house and almost fell into one of the metal lawn chairs. He had enough strength to inhale two sandwiches then lean back and eye us, one by one.

"So first off," he said, looking around the table again, "we've got to figure out who knew the pastor was going to the Chaunceys'. Or even that he was coming to town in the first place."

Miss Amelia sat up, feet together, hands in her lap. She thought awhile then dismissed an idea and went on to a new thought, then on to another. Finally she said, "Seems like it would have had to be me letting the cat out of the bag. I'm the one called the Chaunceys."

"From where? Anybody overhear you making arrangements?"

"Not that I know of. Let me see, where was I when I called?" She thought awhile. "Why, from your apartment, Lindy. Nobody could have heard anything."

"What about the Chaunceys themselves?" Hunter pressed on. "They seemed kind of excited about having the parson come to stay with them. You think one of them would have said something to somebody?"

Miss Amelia shook her head. "They knew it had to be kept a big secret. Think you could've put a gun to the head of either one of the twins and they wouldn't have said anything."

"That kind of leaves you, Lindy." He turned to me as I was expecting since I'd been racking my brains as to who might have overheard me telling Hunter.

"Told you at the Barking Coyote. But I remember checking before I said anything to make sure nobody was close enough to hear what I said."

Bethany looked up quickly. "You went to the Barking Coyote, Lindy? I thought we weren't supposed to go there, something about being standard bearers for the family. Isn't that right, Meemaw?"

Miss Amelia gave her youngest granddaughter a long, hard look. "Lindy was there with Hunter, Bethany. They're working on who poisoned Parson Jenkins. They weren't there to have fun."

I squirmed, remembering our dance, but added nothing to Meemaw's defense.

"What about that white Malibu that was behind us on the way out to the Chaunceys'?" Miss Amelia asked.

I thought very hard. "And one other time, there was a white car sticking right behind me there in town. But I can't swear it was a Malibu."

Bethany sat up, her head turning back and forth, from me to Miss Amelia.

"What about a white Malibu?" she demanded, frowning hard, then sticking a finger into her mouth and biting at the nail.

"A car like that was behind us on the way out to the girls' ranch this morning," Hunter told her. "Probably nothing. Just don't want to miss anything important—"

"Jeffrey rented a white Malibu that day we went to Columbus. You remember." She turned to face me.

I shrugged, remembering no such thing. Hunter was quiet. Finally he turned to Bethany. "You know where he rented it? I thought he was using a ranch vehicle. That's what I saw him driving."

She shrugged. "That's what Justin gave him."

"A white Malibu wasn't much better," Bethany said, but in a subdued voice. "I think he rented it over at Avery's Car Rental."

"Does he have it now?"

"I haven't seen him today. He could."

Hunter stood. "Think I'd better check with Avery."

I put a hand out to stop him. Something had been crawling around in my head. A very small memory.

"Jeffrey was there," I said.

"Where?" Miss Amelia sat forward.

"At the Nut House. When I picked up the parson's message that he was flying in this morning."

"What do you mean he was there?" Miss Amelia sat up straight.

"He was standing in the doorway when I turned around. He wanted to bring some friend out to my greenhouse, show him around. I told him I had a virus out there and it was under quarantine."

"You never had a virus. Your trees are the best anywhere. If there was anything wrong, you wouldn't have entered them in the fair," Meemaw sputtered.

"I know." I half rolled my eyes at her.

"So? You were lying." At first she looked disappointed. Then she got it.

Now she really sputtered, trying to come up with an excuse to cover her gaffe. "And a good thing, too. Can't take any chances with those trees of yours." She gave a quick glance Bethany's way, but Bethany wasn't paying attention.

"You think Jeffrey could have something to do with what's been going on here in Riverville?" she asked in an almost breathless voice. "With somebody shooting at the parson this morning. Why, that low-down . . ."

"Watch your mouth, young lady," Miss Amelia chided.

Bethany sat up straight. She leaned forward, elbows on the table. "What can I do to help you get him?" she asked in a husky, familiar, Blanchard voice.

Hunter looked her straight in the eye. "If you're willing," he said, "I've got a few ideas. First let's go out to the barn and talk to Justin. Then I've gotta get to Avery's Car Rental."

That left me and Meemaw to try to make sense of what was going on.

"Jeffrey Coulter's a stranger," Miss Amelia kept muttering under her breath.

I thought I got what she was talking about. No stranger poisoned Parson Jenkins at the Winners' Supper. Jeffrey Coulter wouldn't have known about the spotted water hemlock. Jeffrey Coulter wouldn't have known how the winners' dishes were handled. He wouldn't even have known Meemaw carried her entries in a ranch cooler.

Unless someone told him. Some neighbor right there in Riverville who'd know all they had to know.

Chapter Thirty-six

Miss Amelia sat for a good fifteen minutes without saying a word. I knew better than to interrupt deep thought and tried to think a few deep thoughts of my own. Nothing much came except a slight titter of glee—I knew Jeffrey was a jerk. Hooray for my instincts.

But more than a jerk, I brought myself up fast. If he was the one who shot at Pastor Albertson—what was it all about? I didn't think a stranger came to town in the guise of an old college chum and then randomly killed a couple of pastors.

There had to be a link between all those men. Some common thread. Maybe just a phone call—Millroy to Pastor Albertson. All I could think was that we had to talk to Pastor Albertson since he was the only one alive who could help.

Just as I was getting into some deep thought of my own, Miss Amelia stood and headed toward the door. I got up fast, almost chasing her.

"Where're we going?"

"Ethelred's."

I wanted to groan. I'd been to Ethelred's before and didn't relish the memory of mothballs and dust and old furniture that should have ropes draped across it.

"Mind if I ask why?"

She shook her head. "I don't know myself. I've just got to talk to her. There's something going on there. Remember Jessie said she overheard people at the library talking about asking for 'hers back,' and wanting to look into it. I think maybe Ethelred can help with all of this and doesn't even know it."

Ethelred's little brown house stood under a clutch of dying live oaks. I remembered the distinct underscent of mold when I'd been there last and reminded myself I was allergic to molds of all kinds, as well as perfumes and shaving lotions. She hadn't been expecting us so her long face fell farther than ever when she answered the door and stood there looking dumbstruck.

"Well, what brings you two over to see me? I was just getting ready to drive to the Nut House, see if I could help you out any." She opened the door and held it wide for us to walk in to stand in her crowded vestibule filled with a huge chifferobe, an umbrella stand, a side table draped with a silk banner from the Second World War, and a boot rack with no boots.

"I need to talk to you, Ethelred," Meemaw said, not wasting time. "But first I need to know how you're doing. They schedule the surgery?"

She shrugged. "Couple of weeks. The doctor keeps telling me I'm gonna be fine. He doesn't see anything beyond getting the dang thyroid out—then he thinks medication will do it." She pushed at the ratted roll of gray hair circling her head today and seemed pleased with herself.

"I'll be fit as a fiddle come time to go to the Bahamas," she added.

"You sign up yet?"

"No, like I told you, gotta get that money in the bank first."

"That's what I was wondering about, Ethelred."

We hadn't been asked into the parlor to take a seat, so I settled my body to stand and wait to hear what was on Miss Amelia's mind.

"You said you invested with the church, right?"

"Sure did."

"Now, from what I heard, people been making money hand over fist with that investment club they got going."

"I told you to get in on it. You wouldn't listen and now it's too late. I went over to the church the other day and Hawley Harvey said Tyler's distributing the funds the morning after the ground breaking. From what he says, he's kind of got the money mixed up with the addition money right now, but it'll all be taken care of after the ceremony."

"I don't understand how you all made so much money in less than a year."

"Well, that's why you've got to have trust in the men leading the fund. What I hear is a friend of Hawley's found this overseas investment that's paying twenty percent on every dime we put in. Invested all the church's money, too. That's where we got the million and a half to start the addition. With how the church is going to grow . . ."

She spread her hands wide to show how big the small church was going to get.

"We'll have an auditorium that'll seat ten thousand people."

Miss Amelia narrowed her eyes. "How many members do we have now, Ethelred? Eight hundred?"

"About that."

"Then where's this ninety-two hundred more coming from to fill that auditorium?"

"Wish you would've come to some of those first meetings, 'Melia. You'd understand better if you heard Hawley explain it."

"And what happens if you don't get your money back?"

Ethelred snapped her thin lips shut. "I was just over there to the drugstore talking to Tyler. He told me again and again, everybody's gonna be so happy when they see what the church board has done for them. You don't mean to doubt Tyler's word, do you, 'Melia?"

"You got anything to prove you've put money into the club, Ethelred?"

"Sure do. Not that I needed 'em. Got certificates written in gold letters. Can't call *me* a Doubting Thomas—that's what Hawley and Tyler, both, call people who just couldn't get it through their heads this was the chance of a lifetime. I remember, Hawley said the Lord was bringing this to us with His own hands. Then he asked who the heck we thought we were, turning our faces away from Him?"

She closed her eyes and sank into piety. "You tell me, Amelia, who are we to turn away the gifts of the Lord?"

Meemaw made a kind of sour face then forced a smile and patted Ethelred on the back. "That's what you believe, Ethelred, more power to you. I, for one, would rather think the Lord gave me a brain and a world of opportunity so as I could make my own way without expecting Him to dump a load of cash in my lap."

"Well, that's you, Amelia. What you still gotta learn is to have faith. You've always been some kind of skeptic. I'd say a little of your dead husband, Darnell Hastings, rubbed off on you."

Miss Amelia smiled so wide I knew it was a sham, and I knew what was coming. "Why, bless yer heart, Ethelred. I can only hope some of that good man rubbed off on me. I can only hope to be that smart."

On our way out the door, Meemaw thanked Ethelred for her help and told her not to go to the Nut House. She needed to rest up for that operation ahead of her. I was hoping we'd make a clean getaway but Miss Amelia had one more question for Ethelred.

She called from the front seat. "Who'd you say you talked to most about your investments? Did you say Tyler or Hawley?"

"Mostly Hawley. He's the one telling us all to wait until the day after the ground-breaking ceremony. Be this Sunday, case you both want to come. I'm telling you, 'Melia. The excitement is sure growing. I'm not the only one in town looking at cruises and cars. Riverville's gonna empty out for a while when people get what's coming to them."

Back out on the main road, I asked Miss Amelia if she got what she'd come for and she said she thought so.

"Where next?"

"The drugstore. Think I'll have a little talk with Tyler Perkins."

"Good luck with that one." I remembered the bruising my ego took just being in a room with that supercilious man for half an hour.

Perkins Pharmacy was right at the center of town, where the bell tower stood and the streets radiated out like spokes on a wheel. There were only a few customers. Tyler was in the back, behind the drug counter, weighing and tipping potions into bottles. I knew he saw us waiting for his attention. And I also knew he'd keep us waiting just to impress us with how busy he was.

I shouldn't have counted out Miss Amelia's impatience. "Like to talk to you, Tyler." She leaned over the counter and turned her head toward him.

Tyler didn't look up. He frowned. "Have to wait a minute, Miss Amelia, got some prescriptions to fill 'fore I can stop to talk."

"Only take a minute," she called back sweetly.

I went from simmer to full boil faster than a microwave oven. Not Miss Amelia, who waited a full minute before leaning in again.

"Tyler, if you want me calling my business down to you there, I'll be glad to do it. I was over talking to Ethelred. You know she hasn't been doing so well lately and we got to talking about that money she's got invested with the church board and—"

He was standing in front of us.

She lowered her voice.

"Ethelred says she's getting all her money back, plus twenty percent, as soon as the ground-breaking ceremony's over Sunday."

"Well, the next morning. That's true. Gotta have time to write out the checks." He smiled one of those smiles that look like somebody drew it on with a Magic Marker. "Hawley asked everybody to keep it quiet, though. Jealousy and all of that. Wish she wouldn't have gone around talking—"

"She didn't go around anywhere, Tyler. We're friends. I'm a little worried. There's no trouble about the money the parishioners are owed, is there? I mean, that addition. From what I hear, it's a million and a half just to begin construction."

"True. We've got it all worked out. The parishioners opened their hearts and wallets and now they're getting their just rewards. Mayor's coming. Everybody knows it's going to be big for Riverville, when people from all over start coming for services."

"You musta got some of your own money out already, by the looks of that big red Cadillac out at the curb."

"I'm president of the board, Miss Amelia. Think I owe it to people to show 'em what a little faith in the Lord will bring you."

Miss Amelia nodded. "Yes, faith in the Lord, Tyler. That's all it takes."

She turned as if to walk away then turned back again.

"But you don't have a parson yet. How you planning on bringing all these new folks in without a man preaching to them?"

"A detail, Miss Amelia. Have a new one within the month. Hawley's been looking all across the country. Gotta be careful this time. Need a real progressive man. A great speaker. One who'll hold on to the crowds that'll be coming."

"You're not saying there was something wrong with Pastor Jenkins, are you? He was a good man."

Tyler's face drew in tight. "Not saying any such thing. He was a very good man. Maybe not the vibrant speaker we thought we were getting, but still a good man."

"You hear Pastor Albertson's back in town?"

"Heard what happened out at the Chaunceys' place. Terrible thing. Miranda think he was a rattler?" He smirked as if he'd made a joke.

"No, someone deliberately took a couple of shots at him. Sheriff Higsby's on it. Think they know who did it."

"Well, good for the sheriff. Care to say who he suspects?"

"Can't. Not yet. Still looking for him."

He nodded a couple of times then looked back to where he'd been filling prescriptions. "Gotta get back to work, ladies. Suppose I'll see the both of you at the ground breaking. You won't want to miss it."

"Oh, I wouldn't miss it to save my life, Tyler. Why, if I'm not mistaken, the whole Blanchard family's going to be there." Meemaw pretended to walk off again, then turned back, leaving me going in circles. "Oh, Tyler, Hunter Austen asked to find out if he could take all your mortar and pestles in for testing."

"What do you mean 'testing'?" he demanded, no pretense of friendliness now.

"Why, for spotted water hemlock, of course. Somebody had to grind the stuff to put into my caviar. He says he wants to eliminate everybody he can. So I'll tell him it's all right for him to pick them up?"

"You tell him no such thing, Miss Amelia. I use my mortar and pestles every day. What's he think I'll use for grinding some of these medications I'm dispensing?" He turned back. "And you tell Hunter Austen I'd appreciate it if he comes in and does his asking himself. I don't think it's professional or even seemly for him to send women in to do his dirty work."

Chapter Thirty-seven

Next was Riverville Memorial Hospital. On the way over I asked Meemaw about that mortar and pestle business and she smiled a devilish smile at me.

"Thought I'd see what he'd say. He got mad, but Tyler's one of those people who always get mad if you ask them anything. I don't know if he's hiding something or not, but I'll bet he wouldn't take a chance using his drugstore equipment to grind up poison."

Hunter was there ahead of us, standing outside the parson's door. His turn on guard duty.

Parson Albertson was awake and smiling at us from his bed. He motioned us to the two chairs set at his bedside. His face was still pale. The blue gown he wore was drawn over wads of bandages on his shoulder.

"Morning, ladies," he said, inclining his head toward us though the gesture brought a grimace of pain to his face.

We asked how he was doing and how he'd passed the

night and if he needed anything before getting down to business.

Miss Amelia, back straight, leaned in from her chair to talk to him as Hunter stepped into the room and asked if he could see me outside. Miss Amelia motioned for me to go—she'd talk to the pastor.

What Hunter wanted was to catch me up to date on what he'd been doing.

First off, I had to know why he was on guard duty when he should be out hunting for a shooter.

"Be just until Sam can come on over. Accident out on the 10 he had to get to."

He hurried on, looking first one way and then the other down the hall. "Talked to Avery over at the car rental. White Malibu rented to Jeffrey Coulter all right. Still out. Got the license number and Sam found the car parked right here in the hospital lot, where the doctors park. That's really why I'm here, in case Jeffrey's coming back to get the pastor."

"I still don't understand." I had to be honest with Hunter. "Somehow I can't see Jeffrey Coulter mixed up in any of this."

"Yeah, well, I didn't either until we found a rifle in the back of the car. Being tested now. We got that shell casing Miranda found. And, Lindy, I talked to Justin a while ago. Said he was on the shooting team with Jeffrey at college. Said he was a crack shot.

"Another thing." Hunter looked me straight in the eye. "Bethany called 'cause I asked her to check his room at your house. Cleaned out, she said. He's gone."

"Bethany's really helping?"

He nodded. "Her and Justin are both calling Jeffrey's phone every half hour. If he answers, they're going to pretend they don't know anything and see if he'll say where he is. My guess is he's on his way back to New York City."

"How? If the car is here at the hospital."

Hunter hesitated. "I don't think he's working alone, Lindy. Somebody's helping him."

"That's what Miss Amelia says, too. Any ideas?"

"Not yet. Well, a couple, but no proof. Thinking of maybe asking a few locals to bring their shovels in for testing. Somebody had to dig up that hemlock. Be like soil and grasses on a car. Could tell where they were digging."

"Miss Amelia told Tyler Perkins you wanted to test his mortar and pestles at the drugstore."

He laughed. "Bet that went over big."

"Let's just say, Tyler wasn't smiling when we left."

Hunter went back to guarding the door and I went back to see how Miss Amelia was doing with the parson. A sheaf of papers was spread out over the parson's bed. He was holding a paper out to her but waited until I sat back down and Miss Amelia explained what he was showing her.

"Some papers the pastor brought with him from California, Lindy," she said, then looked back at the man with sad circles under his eyes. His white hair was standing up at the back from lying against the pillow.

"The thing is," he said in my direction, "Pastor Jenkins called me before he died. Said he was worrying about something here with the church and wanted my advice. To tell you the truth, with Sally dying and all, I hadn't been thinking about much of anything else from my past, so I didn't get it straight at first. Then it all came back to me. An ugly business with Hawley Harvey and Tyler Perkins, but some other church members, too."

He drew in a deep breath and laid a hand gently at his

shoulder. "What I was worried about was the rate the church board was trying to expand the building. I mean, we were never exactly flush with money, and all of a sudden the board's talking about a big addition to accommodate all the new folks coming in. I never saw that influx of parishioners and I was starting to worry about our financial responsibility to keeping the church going the way it was. What I did was call a meeting with Tyler Perkins, since he was board president. And all Tyler told me was not to worry, that money from investments was pouring in. When I asked what investments, Tyler just laughed and told me things were progressing and I'd be brought in on it very soon."

We were interrupted by a nurse who came in to stick a thermometer in the pastor's mouth, ask how he was feeling, and check the bag of fluid going down a clear tube and into his arm. When she was gone with a cheerful "Have a nice day" to all of us, the parson took up where he'd left off.

"Well, maybe you don't remember exactly how I ran my church, Miss Amelia. But it wasn't with the deacons keeping me in the dark about something as important as finances. Next thing I did, I called Hawley and got the same runaround. I said I was going to take it to the people of the church—all the people. Next thing I knew the board voted me out of there and I was asked to leave as soon as I could vacate the parsonage."

"So that's what it was about." Miss Amelia sat back, thinking. "We weren't told much, just that you wanted to retire."

He hooted then winced. "As if I was given a choice."

"I wondered what happened. Didn't seem like you to up and leave the way you did. Sally was a friend and I didn't even get a phone call."

"Well, now you know. None of it was my idea. We were

told to clear out and not contact a soul or they weren't paying off the rest of my contract."

"So what'd you tell Pastor Jenkins?"

"Well, at first I just didn't want to get involved with that
old business again. Sally hasn't been dead long, you see. I
felt I didn't owe anything to you people back here or even to
Pastor Jenkins, who took my place. Then I started thinking
it over and called him back. His wife said he was dead. Well,
I heard that—then heard what happened to him, that he was
murdered, why, I started putting two and two together and
figured maybe, because he was asking questions the same
way I'd been asking, maybe I'd better start looking into
things. What I did was call a man I'd been wanting to call
before I left Riverville. He's with a church in Atlanta. I'd
heard some gossip and thought I'd give him a try.

"Called and he filled me in on things going on there you
wouldn't believe. Sent me all these newspaper clippings . . ."

He picked out one newspaper clipping and held it out
to me.

It was from the *Atlanta Constitution*. Dated the year
before.

The pastor went on talking while I read, saying almost
the same thing I was reading. A church in Atlanta had
been scammed by a huge Ponzi scheme run by a couple of
church deacons, getting people to invest in what they
called: Private Investment Trading Platforms. Investors,
who were swayed by scripture and calling on the Lord's
name, were swindled out of five million dollars.

I looked at Miss Amelia and then at the parson. "Is this
what the whole thing's about?"

The pastor shrugged. "Can find out pretty fast by having your sheriff call in the Securities and Exchange Com-
mission to go over the church books. Should be able to tell

if any investments have really been made, or if the money's being recycled a little at a time with most of it being funneled back to the man pushing the investment club in the first place."

"That would be who?" I asked, needing a name to latch on to.

"I'd say Hawley Harvey. He's the one making most of the promises."

"But Tyler's got the red Cadillac."

Pastor Albertson shrugged. "Could be the way Hawley keeps him from asking too many questions."

"I don't get how this thing works. How does Hawley pay off anyone if he's not investing the money?"

"Same way that Bernie Madoff, up in New York City, did. Take money that comes from new investors and pay off the people who first invested—or give them enough to keep them quiet. When it gets too hot, they're out of there. Gone with the money."

"Or maybe they promise investors they'll get all their money back after the church addition is in progress . . ." Miss Amelia added, then groaned. "Poor Ethelred."

"Do you know this Jeffrey Coulter the sheriff thinks is the one who took shots at you?" I asked.

He shook his head. "Never heard of him. But if you read some of these other articles, and the sheets of Ponzi schemes I pulled off the Internet, you'll see a lot of the cheaters had partners, or other people in it with them, and not always people in the area. Sometimes, I guess, it took money to build the scheme to begin with."

"Money like giving Tyler enough to buy his big car and keep him quiet about the rest of the investors." Miss Amelia's voice showed her disgust. "Money like Jeffrey's rich daddy could give him. And you know what? I just remembered something I wanted to tell you. Marti Floyd, the man who handled scheduling the church's visit over to the Ag Fair barns? You remember, Lindy. I called him and he said it was Hawley Harvey who scheduled that visit. And it was Hawley Harvey who was early. So he was in the barn at the right time."

"I remember something, too . . ." I was riffling through pictures in my head. "Jeffrey and Hawley were talking at a great rate at Parson Jenkins's funeral. I didn't think anything of it at the time. Just Hawley talking up anybody who'd stand still to listen. But I wondered all along why Jeffrey wanted to go to a funeral for a man he didn't even know."

"Hawley Harvey." Meemaw tasted the man's name in her mouth. "Been in town about ten years. I always wondered about that investment company of his. Never seemed to be doing as well as he claimed. Something Darnell used to say would run through my head once in a while: 'If it quacks like a duck, and it walks like a duck, you got a duck on your hands.' I always thought Hawley Harvey was kind of an odd bird. Trying too hard at everything."

The parson smiled. "Guess he thought he finally found something he could sink his beak into."

"Did you know that the people doing this, murdering Parson Jenkins and shooting at you, tried to put the blame on my grandmother here?"

"I didn't until just now." He looked over at her. "Think maybe you should call the sheriff? I think there's enough to stop that Jeffrey, and maybe at least bring in Hawley Harvey."

"Have to do something before the ground breaking or I'll bet anything Hawley'll be gone right along with Jeffrey Coulter and all that money before anybody sees a dime." Meemaw was thinking hard again.

"We'll get him on the fraud all right," Hunter said. "But what about the parson's murder?"

Parson Albertson raised his eyebrows. "That's right. There's no proof . . ."

"Unless I do something," Miss Amelia said.

I could see she was hatching a plan and sat back to wait and see what kind of duck she came up with this time.

Chapter Thirty-eight

Meemaw wouldn't tell me a thing. I gave up and followed orders, which began with waiting down in the lobby
of the hospital while she talked to Hunter.

When she came out of the elevator, tapping gracefully
across the white tiles toward me, I could see something
had lifted from her heart. Her face was back to being its
cheerful, customer-greeting face. Her eyebrows rose when
she saw me. Something was going on and I knew I'd be
better off going along with it.

"Where to?" I asked, falling into step with her as we
crossed the parking lot to my truck.

"I want to go over to Hawley's office."

"Hunter coming? The sheriff going to meet us over
there? You going to confiscate a shovel?"

"Hunter's not coming. Last thing we want to do is put
out signals we're bringing trouble."

"Not involve the police?" I slammed my door and started the truck, the motor taking its usual three turns to catch.

"No, ma'am. I know my customers. Last thing we want to do is give Hawley any sign we're on to him."

"Then what are we going to his office for?"

"You'll see soon enough, Lindy. I want you in there with me but I don't want you saying a single word."

I had my role down pat. Miss Amelia's muscle. Or her stooge. I didn't say anything all the way over to the Alamo Building and Hawley Harvey's financial services office, but I hoped she wasn't about to blow the whole thing.

Hawley came out to greet us himself after his receptionist announced we were waiting in the lobby.

"Well, well, well . . ." He stuck his small hand out to take first Miss Amelia's and then mine and shake them hard. "Good to see the both of you. Bet you're all excited about Sunday. Going to be the biggest thing ever to hit Riverville, I tell you . . ."

He kept talking as he escorted us back to his office, which seemed a little bare for a busy investment banker. Not a single picture on the walls. A desk, two chairs, and not much else.

He saw me looking around the empty room and waved a hand. "Fall cleaning. Got to stay on top of things. Now, what can I do for you two ladies? As you might imagine, I'm running around like a chicken with my head cut off. So many plans for the ground breaking . . ."

He raised his eyebrows at first one then the other of us. "Thinking of investing in the church fund, Miss Amelia? Can't get you into this one, but I got a lot of other fine investments I can arrange. Some paying as high as twenty percent on every dollar invested. I've got a bunch of brochures, but what I'd advise is this one account I keep going only for very special friends . . ."

He stopped to smile. Miss Amelia took her chance to break in.

"To tell the truth, Hawley, I'm worried about Ethelred. You know she's got an operation coming up soon."

His pliable face went from happy to sad—like one of those bald-headed pictures you turn upside down. "Heard. Hope everything goes well."

"Me, too. But what she's worrying about now is the money she's got invested with you."

He frowned and waited.

"She's dead set on taking a cruise to the Bahamas and wants to get it all planned before she goes in for that operation. You know, something to look forward to."

Again he only waited.

"She was hoping she could get her money out of the investment club today, instead of Monday."

Hawley sat back in his chair and pulled at his bottom lip. "You know everybody's getting their checks soon as the addition's started and the builder gets what he needs."

"Well, yes, that's what I heard, but I thought—"

"Can't make exceptions, Miss Amelia. Why don't you go back and tell Miss Ethelred she'll get her money right along with everybody else. Best I can do for you. You understand, it wouldn't do for me to play favorites."

Miss Amelia stood reluctantly. "I can see what you're saying, Hawley. But I have your word she'll have that check in her hands by Monday?"

He nodded as hard as a man can nod. "And you can tell her for me, she's going to be greatly pleased by the numbers she sees on that check. Did better than expected."

"Well, thank you for your time, Hawley."

I almost couldn't believe the wide smile she gave the man.

"Oh, I was just wondering. Selma doing the flowers for the ceremony?"

He nodded. "Kind of her. That garden's going so good. Guess you could say I'm kind of a horticulturist myself. Know a thing or two about flowers. Worth all the effort we put into that garden. Why'd you ask?"

"You hear that's where the killer dug up the spotted water hemlock? Selma found a big plot of it down by the river, roots half dug away."

Hawley Harvey said nothing for a long minute. "You don't say. The board thinks it's somebody at the pastor's last church had a grudge. Nobody here would do a thing like that."

"Seems they did," Meemaw said quickly. "And to try and put the blame on me, why, I don't think I can ever forgive a person who would do a low-down thing like that."

Hawley Harvey's face went through a whole display of emotions. When he settled on suspicion, I was hoping against hope he'd forget himself and blurt out something.

He didn't. "Sounds kind of like a threat, Miss Amelia. I sure hope you don't think I'd have anything to do with murdering people. Why, you know I've always held you in the highest esteem. One of the Blanchard family. Even if it is just by marriage, still one of the most respected families in the county."

Miss Amelia smiled a cold smile. "I saw you talking to Justin's friend at the parson's funeral, that Jeffrey Coulter? You know him?"

Hawley made a face and shook his head. "Talked to a lot of people. Always do. That's my business, talking."

"Just thought I'd ask," she said from the doorway, an icy smile lifting her lips. "Oh, and I understand the sheriff's picking up shovels from anybody who gardened over there at the parsonage."

"Shovels? What for?" He thought a minute. "Tell the sheriff I don't own a shovel."

I could tell he thought he'd outsmarted Miss Amelia, and maybe the sheriff, too. Couldn't prove he'd used the shovel, even if they found traces of hemlock on it. Could have been anybody.

"Well, I suppose just about every citizen here in Riverville could say the same thing, am I right, Hawley?" Miss Amelia asked.

"Suppose so."

"Then we'll see you Sunday at the ground breaking. I'll be making something special for the buffet table. Hope you like it. Had you in mind when I came up with the recipe."

He didn't go into his effusive thanks and looking forward to it and all the things he would normally have said. I thought I saw him grab at his stomach as we walked out. He sat down hard and fell into deep thought.

If nothing else, Meemaw had given Hawley Harvey a few things to worry about.

Out in the truck, I couldn't help but worry Miss Amelia had given Hawley a kind of heads-up, let him know we were on to him. What else would the man do but take off as soon as he could, if that's what the plan was?

When I told Meemaw my fears, she gave me a self-satisfied smile. "Hunter's over talking to Tyler Perkins now. The man might be a smug son of a gun, but he's not a crook. That checkbook's going to be lost and the funds in the bank frozen. We're figuring Jeffrey and Hawley were planning on taking the money and running as soon as the ground breaking was over but now they have to wait."

"They'll run anyway, as soon as they realize the sheriff's on to them."

"Not without the money. And until they go, they haven't committed fraud."

"Anything on Jeffrey? He's probably long gone, I'd imagine."

"Ha. Without the money? He's the seed man. Set Hawley up to begin with. I know people, Lindy. That boy's hanging close until his share of the money's in his hands."

"What about the parson's murder? I thought you didn't want Hawley getting away with it. If he's arrested for the Ponzi scheme, he'll never confess . . ."

She gave me a look dripping with tolerance. "Don't you worry. I've got that covered. You just go along with everybody else Sunday at the celebration. No matter what happens, Lindy, you follow my lead."

Chapter Thirty-nine

Sunday morning dawned with a few white clouds high in the sky and nothing but sunshine on the horizon. The church grounds buzzed with activity. People milled around in groups or singly, searching out someone they'd agreed to meet. Cloth-covered tables were lined along the outer church walls, each holding a large urn filled with lovely flowers. Wrapped dishes of food waited for the first shovel of earth to be dug, and then the speeches, and all the congratulations that would follow.

Greeting us as we walked up from the parking lot was a huge easel holding a drawing of what the addition would look like. A monstrous building that would dwarf the old board-sided church. The drawing showed where the auditorium would be. First there were huge front doors, dwarfing the old entrance. A long stage dominated one end of the auditorium. There were offices behind the stage, dressing rooms, a conference room, enormous lavatories. It could have been a design for a concert hall.

There was a schematic graphic of all the lighting that would be hidden around the walls and ceiling. Enough to illuminate the scene for a TV show, if that was in the future.

People stopped on their way around the building to ooh and aaah over the plans, never having seen so complete a workup before this afternoon. And then, all of us dressed in our very finest, we made our way around to wait for the great moment with friends and townspeople, many not even members of the Rushing to Calvary Church, but there because of the excitement about the day and the future of Riverville.

Sid Johnson, from the *Riverville Courier*, made his way in and among the people, stopping to ask questions and writing down one-word responses or well-pondered answers. From time to time he pulled out his small digital camera and snapped pictures of people who'd given him particularly pointed remarks to print.

Shirley Craig, Riverville's mayor, stood with a glass of sweet tea in her hands, talking to Tyler Perkins and Hawley Harvey, both men dressed to the nines in new white summer suits. Other members of the church board, dressed as splendidly, gathered with parishioners, all talking and laughing and praising the weather. The temperature for this very special day in Riverville, Texas, was down to the low nineties. The breeze was only strong enough to keep the ladies' noses dry.

Shovels, which had been coated with gold paint, stood waiting while the builder, Russell Howe, moved things around, crawling up on the bulldozer he'd had brought in for the occasion, then down to talk to one of his men.

Ethelred Tomroy stationed herself at the head of the long food tables, shooing flies as they landed. She straightened napkins and paper plates as a tiny breeze ruffled them, then lifted lids on the drink urns, checking to see they stayed filled. Ethelred waved to us then fell into deep conversation with Miss Amelia.

After we'd made the expected rounds, all of us split up. Mama made for Ben Fordyce, our attorney, standing with Deputy Sam Cranston and Sheriff Higsby. Justin sauntered over to stand with other ranch owners. Bethany—not one to let grass grow under her feet—headed for Tyler Perkins's good-looking son, Rick. Meemaw and I moved over the grass to talk to different groups of people, going from one to the other, wishing everybody a good day, remarking on the weather. Just passing time until the ceremony began.

I can't say that any of us were there to celebrate. It didn't really seem like a glorious day, not down inside me. I would just as soon have stayed home and skipped the whole thing, but that was just me wishing I could retire to my greenhouse and my gated grove of new saplings and not come out until I'd found my perfect tree and Meemaw was back to being hostess and chief cook at the Nut House—all cleared of suspicion, and Jeffrey Coulter was in jail, and Riverville was back to being the sleepy Texas town it had always been.

I moved over to check the covered dishes the churchwomen had prepared as treats for the big day. They looked much like the entries at the Ag Fair. I recognized Cecil's spotted dick—done up in little paper cups. There was Suzy Queen's Blessed Pecan Dip and so many others I knew by sight. I looked around for something Miss Amelia brought. I'd seen her put a dish in the ranch cooler and watched Justin set it in the back of his truck, but it hadn't made it to the table yet. I thought how you just had to admire her courage—facing criticism from people like Freda Cromwell and fear of poisoning by others who, I'd heard, were whispering it wasn't that Miss Amelia meant to poison anybody. Just that she was losing it. As if she happened to keep a bottle of ground spotted water hemlock around just in case she forgot to put the cinnamon in her cinnabuns.

But then, as I worked my way toward the mayor and the two church leaders, I reminded myself that just such a bottle had been found at the Nut House, with Treenie Menendez hospitalized for sticking her finger into it.

The mayor, a very pretty woman with long blond hair and bright round blue eyes, smiled ear to ear when she saw me. Shirley Craig and I had gone to Riverville High together. We hugged and held each other to stand back and admire how well we were looking—and all that stuff women do. I got through her business of "Aren't you just so excited about what's happening here in Riverville?" And on to "Don't we owe a great debt to Hawley and Tyler for persevering in all of this?"

I knew to say a simple "yes" to everything Shirley said. But it had always been that way, ever since she'd been a cheerleader and was always asking, "Isn't this just the best team ever?" with all those white teeth shining and those blue eyes shooting out sparks of happiness.

As I got close to Hawley Harvey, he rocked back and forth on shiny new high-heeled boots. A new, and bigger than ever, cowboy hat was clamped firmly to his head. He ignored me, turning to talk to someone behind him. The man was obviously in his element, glad-handing left and right and laughing up a storm at people's congratulations and wonder at the size of the addition.

"We got plans," he said again and again. "Big plans."

I'd never seen a happier man, becoming nervous only when Meemaw walked over, big as day, and asked in a loud voice, "You really going ahead with this, Hawley?"

The talking and laughter around them died down. Hawley was nonplussed for only a minute before he nervously started laughing, looking around at people watching them, and putting his hands out to hold Meemaw by the shoulders. "Why, yes we are, Miss Amelia. Yes we are. Despite the awful things been done to try and stop us, we are triumphant today. Doin' the Lord's work gives us that cloak of righteousness, ya know. A giant cloak of righteousness."

Hawley switched right back into his roundhouse grin and pumped a fist in the air, which brought cheers from people standing nearby. "This is the Lord's day, Miss Amelia. We have faced down the devil of doubt and here we are."

Meemaw looked down at the short man with his big hat and shook her head. She turned to walk away but Hawley, evidently sensing some kind of victory, held her in place. "I know you've been having a bad time of it lately, Miss Amelia. But it'll pass. Let me tell you, you won't always be going through things like this. Yer getting on in years but that doesn't mean you don't have a good long time ahead of you to enjoy those grandkids of yours." He turned to the people ringing them. "Right, folks? Let's give Miss Amelia a loud round of applause for all she's done here in Riverville."

With that, he let go of her arm. She stumbled back a step or two then got her balance and shook her head at Hawley. But he was already on to other triumphs, off toward the roped area where he and Tyler were going to dig the first shovelfuls of dirt to signify a new start, new growth, and the future of their beloved church.

When I turned to head toward the ground-breaking area, I looked at the happy faces around me and thought about all their work and their sacrifices, and their belief in goodness—putting money into a church-led investment club and expecting the rewards of their faith. It wasn't just that my blood chilled for a minute, I was struck with an irrational thought: I could split Hawley Harvey's head open with that gold-plated shovel and show people there were only dollar signs inside.

But that's just me, I guess. A nonrepentant, angry woman who expected people to be who they pretended to be.

Hawley dug a shovelful of dirt first and dumped it over to one side. The crowd clapped appreciatively. Tyler went second and then the builder revved his bulldozer but only as a symbol of what was to come. The building would begin on Monday morning. All I could hope for was that the poor man was going to get his money.

Hunter came up behind me and tapped me lightly on the arm. I looked back and made a face at him.

"Got Jeffrey Coulter," he leaned down to say, then he was off without a word, taking a place over to the side where he could keep an eye on the crowd.

When I checked behind me, I saw that Sheriff Higsby was near the line of tables. Around behind me Deputy Cranston stood with his hands crossed in front of him. I recognized a couple of other deputies and a few I didn't know, probably brought in from other towns for crowd control.

If nothing else, I thought, those golden shovels were well protected.

Hawley held up his hands, stopping the loud applause. He gave a short speech about hard work and diligence and belief, which Tyler echoed in his speech that followed. "And now for the celebratory feast the ladies have provided." Hawley rubbed his ample stomach. "I'm gonna be first in line folks. Better get yer runnin' shoes on."

To laughter, Hawley sprinted off toward the table where Ethelred and a couple of other church ladies stood waiting to scoop out treats the parishioners of Rushing to Calvary, like me, knew all too well.

Ethelred welcomed Hawley to the table, pointing out the bounty of foods and following him down the line of tables, scooping beans and rice on his plate and pushing one dish after another until the man's plate was piled high.

I saw her leaning down close to whisper in his ear at one point. At first Hawley looked up at her, confused and ready to shake his head. Ethelred smiled—an unusual occurrence—at least that big a smile, and motioned, with one finger, for him to follow her to the end of the table. There, with a glance around behind her to see who was watching, she bent down, lifted the edge of the tablecloth, and pulled a small cooler out. She opened the cooler and took out an oblong platter, covered with plastic wrap. Hawley bent to look at what she had, then up into Ethelred's face as she kept shaking her head, assuring him of something.

The man reached out and, with tentative fingers, plucked first one then another cracker with topping and set it on his plate. It seemed that wasn't good enough for Ethelred. She obviously wanted him to taste her special treat, nodding and smiling and encouraging him.

Finally, with an indulgent smile, Hawley lifted the first of the crackers and popped it into his mouth. He crunched down hard and seemed to be about to congratulate Ethelred on her wondrous treat, when his eyes opened wide and he spit out what was left of the cracker in his mouth.

He looked up at Ethelred as he clutched at his throat. Everybody heard the choked words he screamed at her, "Miss Amelia? Caviar?"

He danced in circles, spitting and coughing and choking.

"Poison," he seemed to be trying to get out but with his lips puckered so tight the word barely formed.

Hawley grabbed on to Hunter's arm and pointed to his throat. Since I'd moved in close, along with the rest of my family and every cop there, I heard him choke out the word "Ambulance!"

"Now, settle down here," Sheriff Higsby, who ambled over, warned the man. "I can't understand what your problem is if you keep choking like that."

Hawley, face red, eyes running, bent over and lost most of his cracker in the grass.

Sheriff Higsby patted him on the back, sympathetic and concerned that he go sit himself down and rest awhile as town police and the sheriff's deputies ringed the man, keeping the people away from the deacon.

The sheriff took the agitated man's arm and pushed him into a folding chair. Hawley leaned out, trying to see around the bulky sheriff. His eyes pled from one side to the other, begging someone to listen to him but anyone who might have helped was blocked by Blanchards and police.

"You stay there 'til you get ahold of yourself, Hawley," the sheriff cautioned in a loud voice, trying to hold him in the chair. Hawley Harvey popped up and tried to run, to get to the people rubbernecking around the wall we'd formed.

When the sheriff caught at his arm, he veered off and ran smack into Miss Amelia and me. We stood there with Justin and Bethany behind us, and then Mama and Ben Fordyce. Ethelred was somewhere in the middle of the tightening line of police.

"You need help, Hawley?" Miss Amelia leaned close to the terrified man.

He tried calling out around us. "She's . . . getting . . . even. Help!"

"Getting even for what, Hawley?" Miss Amelia, her face wreathed with sympathy, asked.

He shook his head again and again then turned around, shaky voice calling out his wife's name, "Eula? Eula? They're trying to kill me?"

Everybody looked around but there was no Eula to be found.

"You want help, Hawley? Before it's too late?" Meemaw asked.

He nodded again.

"Then tell these folks what I'm getting even with you for."

"Poisoning . . . pastor."

Miss Amelia rocked back on her heels. "You mean that was you? You're the one dug up that spotted water hemlock, ground it up, and put it in my caviar?"

He nodded fast then gestured toward his throat.

"You're the one stealing from these good people around you here?"

Only his eyes moved from one side to the other. He hesitated.

Miss Amelia said, "Antidote, Hawley. Keep thinking 'antidote.'"

She made as if to walk away.

He croaked out, "I'm . . . stealing. Help . . ."

"And you're leaving right after the ceremony, is that right? With all the good folks' money and that Jeffrey Coulter, who helped you cook this up when he first came to Riverville a few years ago? Am I right on this?"

"Please . . ."

"Tell me."

"Yes . . ." He sank to his knees, looking like a man inches away from the grim reaper.

Miss Amelia turned around to Hunter and demanded, "You get that?"

Hunter held up a tape recorder.

She turned to me. I held up the phone I'd been recording on.

A few of us cheered in earnest as poor Hawley crept over to pull on Miss Amelia's skirt hem. He raised his hands in supplication. She smiled down at him.

"Don't worry, Hawley." She patted his cheek. "It's only alum. Puckers your mouth awhile is all. You'll live. At least until the state of Texas gets ahold of you."

Epilogue

In late October there was another ground breaking at the Rushing to Calvary Independent Church. This one was more subdued, and cooler, with the temperature in the low eighties. The new minister, Pastor Joel Highborn, a Texan out of Houston, officiated, thanking all the generous folks for their contributions to what was a much smaller, more practical, addition to the church.

"This one won't be making us feel like tiny people when we walk in," Ethelred was the first to note. She added that it was her way of giving thanks that the thyroid had no cancer attached and all she had to do was take pills for the rest of her life, which was bad but not considering the alternative.

Ethelred had the best reason in the world to be first to comment on the new plans. She'd led the charge to raise funds, improve their church, and have a place where the ladies could have bake sales and raise even more money for good works.

The thing was, even though everybody in the investment club was offered all their money back from the suitcases found at Hawley Harvey's house and in his stripped-down office (where Eula, ever the devoted wife, was caught trying to haul one of the suitcases out to her car), every single soul decided to tithe ten to twenty percent of their funds to build a more modest addition on to the little white church. Along with millions of dollars in suitcases, the sheriff had found Jeffrey Coulter, who'd been hanging around town, waiting to flee with Hawley Harvey.

It was all everybody in town talked about for a month or so, how Jeffrey Coulter's father, the New York financier, was behind the whole scheme and how the scandal that started in Riverville, Texas, swept all the way to New York City, which seemed to give the whole business a juicy edge to certain folks in Riverville. Folks like Freda Cromwell, who didn't exactly apologize to Miss Amelia for the things she'd said about her, but did say she hoped it would never happen again in her lifetime.

Mayor Shirley Craig showed up at the scaled-back ground breaking to praise the people of the church for their steadfast goodness in the face of a terrible scourge. Even the governor of Texas helicoptered in for a photo op, then out so fast a lot of people were just beginning to whisper he was there when he wasn't.

The blueprint stuck up on the easel this time showed one big open space, two small lavatories, and a kitchen area at the back. No grandiose lighting designs. No stage with elaborate curtains and elevators so a preacher could come up out of the floor amid a swirl of phony smoke—which always seemed to be like coming up from hell to me—but I guess Hawley didn't think it out that far since it was all a trick anyway.

Miss Amelia and I left the church grounds early to set up at the Nut House for the crowd that was coming for tea and tarts afterward. Miss Amelia had been adamant about doing the whole thing herself, saying she had surprises in mind to celebrate the glorious day, and called on all of us Blanchards to help out though Justin and Bethany grumbled about not being happy with some of the folks in town and the way they'd believed the worst about Miss Amelia. But Meemaw, ever herself, told them to get over it.

"Why, I'd believe an old lady could make Texas caviar and throw a little hemlock into her mix for good measure, if I didn't know the little old lady in question," she said and brushed away any residual anger any of us were feeling.

Back at the store, Justin, and Hunter, who'd offered to help but mostly hung around me, pushed displays out of the way to open the center of the floor for tables that would hold platter after platter of wonderful things Miss Amelia and Treenie Menendez had whipped up, with the scents coming up into my apartment driving me crazy all week long.

Pastor Albertson was back in town to speak at the ceremony and to give his seal of approval to the new pastor, who was young and earnest and blinked a lot though nobody was calling him Blinky behind his back. Though that would come as people learned to love him. Pastor Albertson was one of the first to walk through the door of the Nut House, greeting everybody with a blessing on the store and all who labored therein.

When Miss Amelia lined us up and handed us platters of food to pass, we gasped and then snickered at what each was called.

When I got a platter of Toxic Tassies, I thought I'd heard wrong, but Miss Amelia swiftly nodded and frowned, stopping my laughter dead. She set a little engraved card with the treat's name on it directly at the center of my platter. She gave a firm nod and went on to the platter Mama held.

Mama's platter of luscious-looking small cookies got a Nightshade Nuggets sign.

By the time she got to Bethany's Spotted Hemmies, we were all laughing so hard our platters shook.

Hunter got Strychly Stacks, Meemaw's version of old-fashioned stack cake cut into narrow slices. This one made everybody groan and brought Mama to ask, nervously, if this was in good taste. "Considering . . ."

Meemaw's face scrunched into disapproval.

"Young lady, I'm doing what Texans always do, making fun of the evil that came amongst us and was vanquished." She raised a stiff finger heavenward. "In the spirit of the Alamo, where our men fought to the death; in the spirit of the cotton pickers of 1896. For Andrew Jackson and Mance Lipscomb. And for that warrior, Audie Murphy—I'm doing what I have to do. I'm not disrespecting anybody. I'm laughing at what was done to me."

She handed Justin a huge platter of cinnamon buns named Cyanide Cinnies.

But she'd saved the best for last. Her own platter held colorful mounds of black-eyed peas and cut-up tomatoes and jalapeños and peppers on small, crisp toasts. "Socrates' Favorite Texas Caviar," her card read. She planted it directly at the center of the plate then proudly held her platter out as the people of Riverville came in, led by a triumphant Ethelred Tomroy.

Recipes from Miss Amelia's Nut House Kitchen

Although Miss Amelia doesn't see anything funny about being poisoned, or being blamed for poisoning anyone, she does have a sense of humor and introduced these specialties at the Nut House for one day only.

TOXIC TASSIES

Lovely little cups of goodness for any tea party.

DOUGH

1 (3-oz.) package cream cheese, softened
½ cup butter
1 cup sifted flour

FILLING

¾ cup brown sugar
1 tbsp. soft butter

1 egg
dash salt
1 tbsp. Garrison Brothers Texas Straight Bourbon
⅔ cup broken pecans for dough cups

Blend the cream cheese, butter, and sifted flour. Chill and shape into 2 dozen 1-inch balls. Press into ungreased 1¾-inch muffin cups—bottom and sides.

Beat together the brown sugar, butter, egg, salt, and bourbon.

Divide half of the pecans among the dough cups. Pour filling mix into each cup. Top with the remaining pecans.

Bake at 325 degrees for 25 minutes or until set.

Cool and remove from the muffin cups.

NIGHTSHADE NUGGETS

A nice touch of orange and pecan in an easy-to-make cookie.

1 cup shortening
½ cup white sugar
½ cup brown sugar
1 egg, well beaten
2 tbsp. Garrison Brothers Texas Straight Bourbon
1 tbsp. grated orange rind
2¾ cups flour
¼ tsp. soda
¼ tsp. salt
½ cup pecans, finely chopped

Cream together the shortening, sugars, egg, bourbon, and orange rind. Sift the flour with soda and salt. Add to the creamed mix. Stir in the pecans. Shape into a roll about 1½ inches around. Chill. Cut into thin slices, place on a greased cookie sheet, bake at 350 degrees for 10 minutes. Yields about 5 dozen cookies.

SPOTTED HEMMIES

Great icebreakers for parties. Have your guests guess what the heck's in the dish anyway! A Thanksgiving favorite at the Rancho en al Colorado.

1 large orange, chopped
1 medium apple, chopped
½ medium-sized white onion, diced
2 whole cups cranberries
¼ cup Garrison Brothers Texas Straight Bourbon
¼ cup water
1 (16-oz.) can jellied cranberry sauce
½ cup sugar
½ tsp. cinnamon
½ tsp. nutmeg
½ tsp. allspice
crackers
chopped pecans
bacon bits

Put the orange, apple, onion, cranberries, bourbon, water, cranberry sauce, sugar, and spices into a pan and bring to a boil.

Reduce heat and simmer until mixture thickens—30 to 35 minutes, stirring occasionally.

Served chilled on crackers with chopped pecans and bacon bits sprinkled on top.

STRYCHLY STACKS

In the South, when people were a lot poorer, they used to bring layers of this kind of cake to weddings, to help make the wedding cake. The more friends you had, the taller the cake. Be fun to start the tradition by sending the recipe along with the invitation and see if they get it right.

LAYERS

½ cup sugar
½ cup shortening
⅓ cup molasses
½ cup buttermilk
1 egg
3½ cups flour
1½ tsp. ginger
2 tsp. baking powder
½ tsp. soda
½ tsp. salt

Combine the sugar and shortening in a mixing bowl. Cream together the molasses, buttermilk, and egg, and add to the sugar mixture. Sift the flour, ginger, baking powder, soda, and salt and add to the mixture. Mix well and roll out as pastry. Cut to fit a 9-inch cake pan or a heavy skillet. Bake the layers at 350 degrees for 10 to 12 minutes.

When cool, stack the layers with sweetened, highly spiced cooked apples made with cinnamon and sugar to taste, and added pecans.

GLAZE

½ cup powdered sugar
1 tbsp. maple syrup
1 tbsp. Garrison Brothers Texas Straight Bourbon
1 cap vanilla

Stir until all the lumps are gone. Pour the glaze over the top of the cake.

Best when made ahead and left to stand—the flavors will meander through the cake and give it a punch.

CYANIDE MINI CINNIES

Good for a hungry crowd. Just watch for sticky fingers. Miss Amelia and Treenie make these by the hundreds. This recipe makes about 40 mini cinnies.

DOUGH

2 cups milk
½ cup canola oil
½ cup sugar
2½ tsp. active dry yeast

4½ cups flour
½ tsp. (heaping) baking powder
½ tsp. (scant) baking soda
2½ tsp. salt

GLAZE

2 sticks butter
1 cup finely chopped pecans
½ cup light Karo Syrup
2 tbsp. Garrison Brothers Texas Straight Bourbon
¾ cup sugar
2 tbsp. cinnamon

To prepare the dough, heat the milk, canola oil, and sugar in a large saucepan until warm but not boiling. Remove from heat and set aside to cool a bit until lukewarm. Sprinkle the yeast over the top of the liquid, and add 4 cups of the flour. Stir to combine, then cover the pan with a dishtowel and let rise for 1 hour.

Stir in the additional ½ cup flour, baking powder, baking soda, and salt. Set aside.

To prepare the glaze, in a separate pan, melt 1 stick of butter and add the chopped pecans, Karo Syrup, and bourbon. Stir to combine, then remove from heat and set aside.

Melt the additional stick of butter. Set aside.

To prepare the rolls, preheat the oven to 375 degrees. Roll out the dough into a 30-by-8-inch rectangle. Pour on 1 stick of melted butter, then sprinkle sugar and cinnamon evenly over the surface. Starting at the far end, roll the dough into a long roll, rolling toward you. With a sharp knife, cut into thin slices, about ½-inch thick.

Spoon ½ to 1 teaspoon of the pecan-butter-syrup mixture into mini muffin tins. Set a sliced roll into each muffin tin, pressing slightly.

Bake for 15 to 18 minutes, or until golden brown. Remove the pans from the oven and allow the rolls to cool for at least 20 minutes. Invert carefully on a platter or cookie sheet. Dig out any pecan mix left in the tin and drip on the rolls.

SOCRATES' FAVORITE TEXAS CAVIAR

We all know what happened to poor Socrates and the hemlock. Miss Amelia thinks a good dose of her caviar would have saved the man and a lot more thinking would've gotten done.

2 (16-oz.) cans black-eyed peas, drained
1 (15-oz.) can diced tomatoes, drained
2 fresh medium jalapeños, stemmed, seeded,
and minced
1 small onion, diced
½ yellow bell pepper, stemmed, seeded, and diced
¼ cup chopped fresh cilantro
6 tbsp. red wine vinegar
6 tbsp. olive oil
½ tsp. salt
½ tsp. pepper
½ tsp. garlic powder
1½ tsp. cumin

2 cups finely chopped pecans
¼ cup Garrison Brothers Texas Straight Bourbon

Mix all the ingredients, cover, and refrigerate for up to 2 days. Before serving, adjust seasonings to taste. Serve with taco chips, crackers, or toast rounds. *Do NOT leave the bowl just lying around if you've got murderous relatives.*

All of these recipes feed as many as they can. Some of you might make the cookies big, some not so big. It all depends on what kind of eaters you're feeding. Personally, I like to double everything.